The Watchman

Also by Rob Parker

The Ben Bracken Series
*A Wanted Man*
*Morte Point*
*The Penny Black*
*Till Morning is Nigh*

Novel
*Crook's Hollow*

BEN BRACKEN BOOK FIVE

# THE WATCHMAN

Rob Parker

*To Sean,*
*Thank you for everything, brother.*
*All my very best,*

LUME BOOKS

**LUME BOOKS**

Published in 2021 by Lume Books
30 Great Guildford Street,
Borough, SE1 0HS

ISBN 978-1-83901-288-4

Typeset using Atomik ePublisher from Easypress Technologies

www.lumebooks.co.uk

# About the Author

Rob Parker is a married father of three, who lives in a village near Manchester, UK. Author of the Ben Bracken series *A Wanted Man, Morte Point, The Penny Black* and *Till Morning is Nigh, The Watchman*, and the standalone post-Brexit country-noir *Crook's Hollow*, he enjoys a rural life on an old pig farm (now minus pigs), writing horrible things between school runs.

He writes full time, as well as organising and attending various author events across the UK, while boxing regularly for charity. Passionate about inspiring a love of the written word in young people, Rob spends a lot of time in schools across the North West, encouraging literacy, story-telling, creative-writing and how good old fashioned hard work tends to help good things happen.

To my three beautiful children,
Avalyn, Sylvia and Robin.

And Becky. Always.

'*Corruption is authority plus monopoly minus transparency.*'
Anonymous

'*This nation will remain the land of the free only so long as it is the home of the brave.*'
Elmer Davis

# PROLOGUE

## SINCLAIR

It had just gone 10.00 pm when the grand planes landed south of the Brunei river, on a dirt airstrip surrounded by trees that seemed impossibly tall. There was no fanfare, nor any grand welcoming committee for the three Blackburn Beverleys as they descended from the soft clouds above, packed to the rivets with two companies of soldiers from the British army's 1st Battalion.

As soon as the planes were still, those soldiers disembarked with caution. They weren't expecting any resistance at the airfield, not yet, as the militia was yet to arrive and forcibly swallow it – like they had the other two airports in Brunei. Sinclair followed his brothers in arms out of the cargo door onto the dirt, and he took a look around. In the distance, rising imperiously over the treetops, stood a number of smoke columns; dark, thick smears against the light pollution of Brunei's capital, Bandar Seri Begawan. Dogs barked somewhere, howling at the night in impotent warning.

Sinclair let the warm air hit him – then got moving. He and a band of Gurkhas had separate orders from the main bulk of soldiers, who were heading off to the bottom of those smoke-stacks. He left the throng and hopped on the back of a bus that waited a hundred yards from the paused aircraft. As soon as he sat down on the front seat, his flopping thatch of blond hair was ruffled from behind.

'Easy, junior,' said a voice behind him. 'We've got the special assignment.'

At just nineteen years old, Sinclair was used to all the ribbing and paid it no heed, although he did take note of the second part of the ruffler's statement. Special assignment. To where, and what, he didn't yet know – only that they had indeed been picked for it.

The roads were jammed with a confused public as the bus wound its way through the streets, sounding its horn and veering up onto pavements. Orders were barked by a senior officer who loomed at the front next to the driver, swaying with bended knees to match the bus' movements and, as he spoke, Sinclair was suddenly very aware that him being appointed there was unique. This was no ordinary appointment and instruction. They were on their way directly to the palace, while the rest of the city combusted around them, to extract the Sultan of Brunei himself.

Sinclair wondered what he'd done to get such an appointment.

He'd excelled throughout training, since joining up bang on his sixteenth birthday. He'd received numerous commendations on active duty, even though that hadn't amounted to all that much yet. He was a perfectionist, adhered to every rule there was and operated to the best of his ability with a deference to duty so granite it was practically uncalmable and implacable.

But this? This was all different.

The buses pulled up at a small jetty, the mosquitos in sudden frenzy as the men on board decanted onto two small motorboats, opposite the finest sight Sinclair had ever seen. The white balustrades and gold domes stood proud over the river, which reflected it below with the assured, immaculate touch of a flawless mirror. Moments later, they disembarked on the elaborate stone steps beneath the largest of those vaulted rooftops.

This was the Istana Nurul Iman – the palatial home of the Sultan of Brunei and seat of his government.

The small detachment moved at speed, Sinclair with his Colt M16, the weapon he was getting rather attached to thanks to its substantial handguard, primed, pointed and ready. It was eerily quiet as they approached – a little too quiet, considering the clamour coming from the city itself, somewhere in the distance. It was unnerving.

Approaching the white-washed corner of the building, Sinclair felt his instincts seize and hissed, 'Wait!' to the other men. They obeyed, thanks not to rank but the urgency of the young man. They paused in position, silent once more, the only sound a crane over the water hollering at some unseen threat in the marshes.

One of the older men ahead blew air through pursed lips dismissively and pressed on around the corner – only to be shredded by abrupt gunfire. The night exploded in a cacophony of artillery as the other British soldiers stepped forward to engage the threat beyond the edge of the building.

Sinclair didn't join them.

Instead, his mind raced with how to achieve his objective.

Where would you hide if your home was under siege at night?

Nine times out of ten, it'd be the bedroom.

And if your house backed onto that view, you'd make sure your bedroom was looking out on it.

Sinclair backtracked from the gun battle and looked overhead – and immediately spotted, twenty yards away, the balustrades of a balcony.

How do I get up there? There wasn't time to think, let alone think clearly.

The muzzle flare behind him splashed the building in bright flashes, momentarily illuminating every imperfection – and Sinclair caught it. The white electrical wire pinned tight to the wall, leading to the balcony's edge. The Sultan had a direct phone line to his bedroom. All mod cons for one of the richest men in the world.

The young soldier swung the rifle onto his back, gripped the wire as a rope and started hoisting himself up the wall, one foot after the other, hand over hand, while the firefight raged below.

After hauling himself over the balcony, he was faced by a scene of exotic opulence. Gold was the main feature and colour scheme of the vast bedroom – and that even extended to the man stood in the middle, cowering, looking at the door, his silk robes the colour and shimmer of sunburst.

'Sultan?' said Sinclair as he fronted his rifle. As the monarch turned in swift surprise, Sinclair added, 'I'm a friend.'

The man's eyes were wide. 'British army,' clarified Sinclair, who could see straight away that those words were of some assurance.

'You can get me out?' He asked, his voice faltering through the clatter of bullets.

'I'll have a bloody good go.'

Sinclair looked back over the balcony edge and saw that the firefight had moved directly below them, with a band of irregularly clad soldiers pressing the British army back towards the boats they'd arrived on. Bodies were visible on the ground. Some moving, some not.

Exiting that way would render them both sitting ducks and would do nothing more than lower the Sultan into the arms of the militia. *No*, Sinclair thought. He had a better idea.

'Stay behind me, but stay close,' he told his charge and moved to the bedroom door. He listened quickly, and when satisfied, moved through, rifle high. The sights that met him were of pure opulence, but he couldn't pause to marvel at any of them. They had to keep moving.

Down the marble stairs to the right, the grand balustrades providing cover as they descended, the Sultan's soft footsteps and the rustle of expensive fabric never absent from Sinclair's right ear.

Ground floor, Sinclair's eyes always behind the iron sights of the rifle as it swung. Around the right-hand corner, following the imagined geography in his head.

At the end of the corridor was a grand patio, the doors open to the night, and beyond that, a beautifully manicured walkway, festooned with leaning palms and reaching bushes – and the frantic judder of gunfire.

Out into the night. The corner of the building. The corner he had paused at earlier, only from the opposite direction.

Sinclair moved his barrel around the edge and was facing the back of the militia fighters – and ahead of them? His British army colleagues.

A steady, soft squeeze and the rifle spat. Double tap, centre mass, the fighter on the left fell. He panned swiftly to the back of the next adversary. As soon as his sights hit the middle of the target, two shots again. Another down.

There were three other insurgents visible, and their confusion sealed their fates. In a mix of bullets from the front and Sinclair's from behind, they fell in quick succession.

'It's me, Sinclair!' he shouted, before lowering his rifle and pulling the bewildered Sultan of Brunei from around the corner. 'I've got him.'

His colleagues were dumbstruck and, as they guided the Sultan back to the waiting motorboats, Sinclair knew with pride that he had significantly exceeded expectation once again.

# CHAPTER ONE

I sit in the food court area of the Trafford Centre, northern England's grand tribute to the giant malls of America, with a bowl of cold noodles in front of me, a rattle in my left hand and a baby spoon in my right. High overhead, a synthetic sky washes from crisp daylight blue to a bruised dusk. The space is huge. Walled in by mocked-up ship decks, we sit in the middle at the bottom of the cavern, as if in an amphitheatre – and that same sensation of being on display applies. It's too open for me. I can't say I enjoy it.

But I'm trying.

There are over thirty different eateries here, offering innumerable cuisines – a number of which I haven't even heard of – and I had the bright idea of saying to the five people in my family: 'You can all get whichever lunch you'd like'. Cue a mad, stressful scramble between three fast-food places, a street food vendor and a pizza shop, juggling the increasing pile of food as we went. Only now that we are sat down and Jake, Gracie and Carolyn are all eating, and Jam Jr is halfway through throwing his own lunch everywhere, do I even dare look at mine. But I suppose that's the nature of the parenting beast, isn't it? All the other mouths before yours.

The giant screen affixed to the back of the ship's mock-bridge is playing movie trailers, the boom of which fights with the constant wash of a coin pool below – but neither noise is enough to stop me hearing my phone go in my pocket. I spill baby rice on my trousers as I fish it out; just another stain to add to the litany. It's a text from a number I don't recognise. Simple words.

*Namco Station. Bar.*

My fear of exposure suddenly justified and ramping, I glance around the vicinity. I can't see anyone or anything out of place but that's usually what it's always like before things take a turn for the worse. My unease brings with it a questioning look from Carolyn – and another incoming text. This one containing only one word.

*Friendly.*

'Are you all right?' asks Carolyn.

'Yeah, I'm fine,' I say as I stand. 'Could you take over with the boy wonder for a minute?'

'Sure,' she replies, coming to take my place. 'Supposed to be a family day though, right?'

'I'm sure it's nothing, but I won't forget.'

She knows me inside out and back to front, including what I do for a living. As an advisor to the NCA, in particular the organised crime command, my working hours are so often little more than a guideline at best. However, our family trip out today was a treat and a promise, one that I intend to keep.

I walk to the ramp and drop down off the raised platform we were sat on and spot the neon Aztec cave of the Namco station. Crossing through the entrance, I'm instantly assaulted by swirling neon and sprinting children trailing long ribbons of prize tickets.

All I can see are the arcade games, so I look into the corners for any indication of a supposed bar. I didn't even know this place had one, but sure enough, there at the back, I see a black arch – and through that, I can just about make out a chrome beer pump. I head straight through, careful not to kick any kids as I go.

As it's only midday or thereabouts, the place is quiet. Booths on the right, tables in the middle and a bar on the left, over which sits a bank of flatscreen TVs showing music channels and test match cricket. There are no obvious staff members, but the cold light from an ajar storage room door suggests their hiding place. And there, stood at the bar with his back to me, is a man.

It can't be, can it?

His eyes meet mine in the mirror on the back wall behind the bar and those blues tell me it is.

'You're a long way from Westminster,' I say as I reach him.

He wears a brown suede jacket, navy chinos and work boots and his hair is a swept-back grey. I feel that tightening in my nerves, that squeeze that tells me I'm in the presence of a fellow military man. It's the poise, the width of the shoulders.

'And you are a long way from the soldier I first met,' replies William Grosvenor. 'Three kids, a better half, Sunday afternoons at the local shopping centre...'

'I had to grow up sometime.'

'I should have known you'd be half all right at that too. A beer?' he asks. I can see he's nursing a pint of lager which is about a quarter drunk.

'I suppose I can have the one.'

Grosvenor signals respectfully to the open storeroom door, through which a young barman appears. Within seconds he is pouring a pint of the black stuff on my instruction, and while he does that, I shake Grosvenor's hand.

'I suppose I should be happy to see you, even though this cannot be a social call.'

'There will be social calls for men like us one day, Tom West.' I almost jump at his use of my pseudonym, because he is one of the few who knows who I really am. There's Carolyn, my boss, a couple of others who had to learn the hard way, and that's it. But this is also the man that gave me the chance of a second life so I shouldn't really be too surprised to hear him use it.

'So, what brings you to Manchester?' I ask before frothing my top lip. I'm getting a taste for a weekend beer, usually in front of the sport on telly while Jam Jr bounces on my lap. It's a side of domesticity I had no idea was coming but one I really enjoy. I was looking forward to a similar afternoon today, but that may not be on the cards anymore.

'It's been a success, hasn't it, your work with the NCA?'

'I'm enjoying it.'

'Good. I don't want to affect that, but this is me coming to you for a favour'.

William Grosvenor is a member of the PM's cabinet, a Minister Without Portfolio, and is there in purely an advisory capacity. However, I know his true role is that of trusted overseer of all cabinet activities, who reports directly to the Queen. He's a man of great importance in the country, although few know he exists. Prior to that, he fought all over the world in the SAS. So what could this man possibly need me for?

'I don't know what I can do for you, William. Like you, I don't technically exist either.'

'Which is precisely why you're useful.'

I swig. 'Go on.'

'How politically aware are you, Tom?'

'Not very – on purpose. But with work and everything, I've tried to grow up a bit where that's concerned.'

'So you'll know this is a critical time for British politics – especially in terms of international relations?'

'Are we talking about the EU?'

'Further afield. There is a US presidential election coming up. With the US and the UK both in states of comparable unrest, keeping things on an even keel between the two nations is now more important than ever.'

'I don't know how to hack Facebook if that's what you're asking for.'

Grosvenor smiles. 'My request is nothing so difficult.'

'Tell me, William.' For the first time in my years of knowing him, he looks lost for words. A more poetic mind might refer to him as tongue-tied. 'Shall we move to a booth?' I suggest.

William breaths out, smiles, then gestures for me to lead the way. We take a booth by the wall, away from the glare of the televisions and any prying eyes.

'I need you to pick something up for me,' he says, suddenly fixing me with his gaze. 'And you will be paid well for doing so.'

'Why me? You have the entirety of the British government to send on errands. I'm sure you've got a catalogue of interns only too happy to come running.'

'I can't use any official resources. This one is strictly personal, for me.'

'What's the item?' I've been sent off to retrieve something

I didn't understand before and it nearly cost me everything. When I first met Grosvenor, I was carrying a small vial of a modified botulism isoform, which I'd been sent to retrieve from a plane crash site off the south-west coast of the UK. I had no idea what I was carrying nor the sheer scale of the plot I found myself.

'It's just an envelope.'

'An envelope?'

'If things are as they should be, it is a bog-standard, letter-size, white envelope.

'You know I've got a million questions about this, don't you?'

'I just need you to go and pick it up.'

'You're not going to tell me what's in it?'

'Come on, Tom, you're familiar with the phrase "need to know", a man of your credentials.'

All too well. 'Is anyone else after it?'

'I don't believe anyone else knows it exists.'

'What happens if I'm too busy?'

'I would suggest you find yourself not busy. What I will tell you is that the contents of that envelope could damage the relationship between the United Kingdom and United States governments.'

'Well, that doesn't sound good, does it?' I take a moment to think. The stakes here sound high but what could be kept in a small envelope that could cause something like that? 'What is your part in this?' I ask him directly.

'You know my role in the country is above all the petty motivations of ministerial one-upmanship. And because of that position, and the length of time I've been in it, I've made contacts. One such contact believes this could cause big trouble, that this is something that could genuinely rock the international boat in a very bad way. And I don't want to take a chance on it, hence my coming to you and not any of my political colleagues. If it were to come out, a number of ministers I can think of would squabble over it, betray each other over it, and in turn, jeopardise their own country over it – something we have seen so many times, even in such recent memory as when Covid-19 became a political football, rather than a pandemic to unite against. And through you, I have a chance to stop that from happening. And I have to try.'

'Where is it? The envelope?'

'America.'

'America!'

'You'd have to go over there to get it.'

That has caught me cold. What about my family? My young son? The children who are coming to rely upon me? The partner I keep letting down through these bouts of duty?

'What's the time frame?' I ask.

'ASAP.'

'And it's all solo? No support?'

'Secrecy is paramount. That's a negative, Captain.'

'Sounds really great.'

'I realise what I'm asking – that's why the pay will be good. The best you've ever had.'

'I'm getting paid now and it's already the best I've ever had.' I don't want anything to jeopardise the good circumstances I find myself in. 'What about risk?'

'If you go now, while we're ahead of the intel curve, there shouldn't be any.'

I breathe out hard through my lips. On the one hand, what can it harm if there is no risk? On the other, do I really need this additional hassle now things are going so well at home and at work?

'Tom – Ben – if you do this, you might just save more lives than you can imagine. Will never be thanks for it. But you'll always know what you did.'

Why is it that when the brass wants us grunts to do something, they always play on our sense of patriotic duty? Because we are cut from the same cloth. Patriotically, duty is all we know.

'When do you need an answer?'

'You can have till tonight. If you agree, there's a plane going stateside in the morning. Say yes, Ben.'

'And the money?' It's never been about money for me. I don't even like asking the question. But I want to know that if I get myself involved in this, it really will be worth it for my family.

Grosvenor tells me a figure. My eyes water. 'Plus expenses,' he adds.

It seems I've suddenly got some thinking to do.

# CHAPTER TWO

Soapsuds are on my fingers, the baby monitor is at my elbow and my thoughts are rolling steadily into overdrive. I can hear Jam's breathing across the static, the reassuring to and fro of his tiny lungs, which serves as a constant opponent to any idea I may have about following Grosvenor's wishes to America.

The sink that sits in our small kitchen in Croft, near Warrington, which is halfway between Liverpool and Manchester, is embedded in a worn worktop. Through a wide plate glass window, it faces onto a garden – and in that garden, under the deepening orange of the setting sun, play Gracie and Jake. They chase in the shade of an absurdly tall willow tree. The neighbours have been asking Carolyn to get rid of it since she moved in, but I admire its proud height and the way it sways in any lick of breeze. There is none now, however; the evening so still I can hear the children's conversation through the window. They cavort to a jungle gym on the west side of the garden, which has seen better days. Its joints look dry and worn, brittle as driftwood, as they pretend it's a treehouse they are defending from invaders – pirates, I think.

The dishes nearly done, I come to terms with the notion that I really don't want to give any of this up. This life truly is a second chance for me but not only that, it's a chance I thought I'd never have. People who have done the things I've done seldom feel the warmth and love of family. And I don't want to do anything to jeopardise this.

'You haven't been the same since earlier,' says a soft voice behind me.

'I know,' I reply, grabbing a tea towel to dry my hands. It is emblazoned with pencil drawings of Morecambe – a souvenir from a recent family trip and a further reminder of what I stand to lose. Drying my hands, I turn and look at my partner.

Carolyn.

Our coming together wasn't a simple one, but it was one made of the simplest of things – understanding being the primary characteristic. And that developed, sure as the seasons turn, into a very definite, pure love.

'Do you want to talk about it?' she asks.

'I was going to wait till the kids were in bed, but yes.'

I slump my arse against the countertop and she mirrors me, our knees touching in the galley kitchen.

'It's a job,' I say.

'You and job offers don't sit well with me.' She wears a small smile, but I know her words are genuine. Her understanding of me extends to her consideration of how seriously I take things like duty and responsibility. She knows they are core pillars of my personality, and while they often bend and take new shape, such evolution is only temporary against the granite nature of their founding form.

'It's high-paid. But it means I have to go to America for a few days.'

'America?' she says. I detect surprise but suddenly find I can't make eye contact, so I focus on her high ponytail, which sends her long chestnut hair tumbling to her shoulders beguilingly. I hate disappointing her... but sometimes it feels inevitable.

'There is no risk. Or at least, that's what I've been told.'

'Then why you?'

'Trust. It's me because they trust me.'

'Are they the people you work with?' The people she's referring to here are my colleagues at the National Crime Agency. She knows a mere handful of them, only opaquely, but also knows I have genuine trust in and admiration for that very same handful. But that isn't the case here.

'No, this is separate – from an old friend.'

Carolyn doesn't even ask who that might be. 'When would you leave?'

'Tomorrow morning.'

'Wow,' she blows out, and leaves it lingering between us, before: 'High-paid, you said?'

'Highest I've ever been paid.' I tell her the figure and that makes us quiet again, so I look out of the window and watch the kids play. I'm not Gracie and Jake's father, but I have come to love them like my own. They're good children and will become good people thanks to Carolyn and her selfless efforts as a mother. To my mind, they deserve the absolute best, and the horrible, ever-present bite in my head says I'm not that. I know I'll always try my hardest, but whether I'm what these children need is another question entirely. There are big roads ahead for them and me, but for now, I must protect them in any way I can.

Carolyn slides along the counter next to me. 'What happens if you don't do it?'

'I don't know – maybe nothing. But could be something. Coin flip, it sounds like.'

'You don't have a choice, do you?

It's the first time that I actually concede it to myself and, following a growing trend of the past few years, it's Carolyn who helps me see the truest answers.

'No, I don't feel I have.'

'Then go. But the first thing we buy with that stupid amount of money is a new jungle gym for the kids.'

I look out, the sun nearly gone now, so that the security light over the back of the house fills in the blanks where the orange can't reach. It gives the garden a stage-like quality. Its lack of forgiveness lets me see just how damp and rotted that climbing frame is.

'Deal,' I say, and turn to hug her. 'In case it needed saying, I love you,' I whisper into her neck.

'Get paid and come home, soldier. That's an order.'

'Yes ma'am.'

I make the call at the sink, watching the children chase beneath the willow's swaying canopy, and hope I'm doing the right thing.

Later, when the house is quiet and the children are all in bed, the doorbell rings. My eyes hit Carolyn's, then all pupils swivel to the baby monitor on the coffee table between us. They show a rainbow of dots, starting green on the left through yellow, orange and red.

Green dots flash twice. Jam is moving. I shake my head slowly and feel the ire of indignation grow.

'If it's those bloody kids again…' I say, remembering recent ups and downs with some neighbourhood scamps playing knock-a-door run, which had finally gone away a few weeks back.

The yellow moves along into orange.

I'm up and walking to the door, my stride quickening the closer I get to it. By the time I'm passing the bottom of the stairs, I can hear Jam crying.

My right fist clenches. It took me forty-five minutes to get Jam to doze off.

Carolyn must've heard the crying on the baby monitor and she follows me out of the room, whisking upstairs as quick as she can so Jam's howls don't reach the older two children. The delicate balance of a young family.

I throw open the front door and my face must have been thunder because the besuited man in front of me looks shocked.

'Yes?' I say.

'Tom West?' says the man, all business.

'That's me.'

'Apologies for the late hour. Landmark Couriers. A delivery.' He hands me a large postal bag which contains something rectangular and flat, before immediately turning to leave.

'Nothing to sign?' I ask his back.

He half turns and with a small smile says, 'Not this time.'

I watch him climb into a black, four door saloon and promptly glide away down the street.

Back inside, I head for the kitchen and slice open the plastic envelope with a steak knife. A pink card folder slides out. Still able to hear Jam's crying, I open it and browse the contents.

There's not much, but I slide it all out onto the wood veneer countertop for a better look. First thing I notice is the passport. I haven't had one of these in a long time, and last time I did it was maroon – not this blue effort that sits in front of me. It's unfamiliar and an uneasy reminder of where we are today in a political sense. Nevertheless, I pick it up and thumb through to the thick photo page, noticing that there are a handful of stamps already in place. Barcelona, Belize, Barbados, Tenerife, Chicago – all places I've never been to. Not once. Finally arriving at the photo itself, I see me, Ben Bracken, yet, sure enough, the text to the right of the picture hails me as Tom West. The picture is the one I took at Busby's, the master forger in Norfolk who, a while back, I charged with giving me a fresh start. It looks like his hard work might finally be put to use.

Next is a USA immigration form all filled in, ready to go, credentials checked and signed, followed by a wad of dollars. Then?

Airline ticket. One way to JFK.

It looks like I'm going to New York.

I feel a slight buzz and a small tremor. Excitement and anticipation. I've never been to New York – nor have I been to America at all, for that matter. For a nation that sits so prominently in world affairs, not to mention the fact I've fought alongside so many American soldiers in the Middle East, this trip to the country itself seems long overdue.

Next up is a piece of paper. Nothing more than a small handwritten note, the lettering on which is a short, staccato freehand in blue pen. There are two lines, bold and uncompromising.

Line 1: Third floor, 35 Howard Street, Manhattan.

Line 2: 9.00 pm, Flo-Bar, NoLo. Get a drink.

# CHAPTER THREE

The flight was fine, although I'd become a little restless after the first hour and spent the second hour trying to chill back out again. It had felt weird, foreign, somewhat claustrophobic, clogged through with a nasty kind of nostalgia I thought I'd parked. I hadn't been on a plane in a long time, if you discount the partially submerged wreckage of a jet a couple of years back, but that wasn't airborne. But after that, it was plain enough sailing.

Arriving at JFK, I'd felt that hum again. The air felt different, tasted different, and I wondered if this was anything like what it felt like for those initial settlers all those years ago. The airport was busy, showing that no matter where you are in the world, five in the afternoon is always chocker.

Going through customs, I flash my passport and, just like when I left Britain, there isn't even a second glance from the immigration staff – although the gaze of the staff-member is much more severe on this side of the pond. Papers displayed and passport scrutinised, I'm waved through to baggage collection, where the hiking rucksack I borrowed from Jake's bedroom (last used on a school trip) is already doing the very literal rounds.

I use the bundle of cash I'd been given with my ticket to grab a taxi – a genuine New York yellow cab, no less – and start the steady trundle away from the airport. The cab driver is weathered and sweating, his bald head a varnished walnut dipped in carpet fluff or lint, and when I give him the address, he says with a smile, 'Ah, you staying with somebody? Kinda nice for a backpacker.'

He's cool. When I tell him I've never been to New York before, he tells me how much has changed since 9/11, and before I can chastise myself about giving even my inexperience of the place away, he's into a diatribe about how Rudy Giuliani was a saviour and real leader in those dark days, before he became a government stooge who consigned the city to no more than a pandemic epicentre during the Covid-19 outbreak. He says he felt betrayed. When he puts it like that, I find it hard to argue with him.

The city skyline, somehow familiar already, grows larger as we pass through derelict suburbs, graffiti jungles and loan shops warring for prominence on every street corner. It's hard to reconcile the affluence I see on the horizon, beyond the tired rooftops, with the fatigued poverty we are travelling through. A grand cemetery emerges on a hillside, the background skyscrapers fusing with the graveyard to become obscenely tall tombstones.

Before long, we are sailing across the Brooklyn Bridge, full sunshine scolding the metal-work, rendering it almost black in the hard light, like a cat's cradle of obsidian, and down we swoop into what I believe is the Financial District, thanks to my in-flight analysis of a map of Manhattan I'd bought at the airport paper shop back in Manchester.

The swirl of bridge access roads suddenly turn around and level out and I'm in streets I immediately recognise, despite never having been here. The familiarity is both strange yet welcoming, and it feels somehow like home. I lower the window of the cab to feel the streets, and it strikes me as a city jacked up. The sounds are louder, the smells stronger, the heat of humanity, glass, stone and metal all the more overpowering.

I love it. It's a picture book come to life, a movie I can step into.

It's not long before we drop off one four-lane thoroughfare to a single carriage side street, which has the odd quirk of cobbles beneath the tires. We thrum along for fifty yards or so before we pull to a stop.

'Thirty-five,' the driver says to me, pointing at a glass door. 'Need help with the bags?'

'I'm all right, thanks,' I reply and pass notes up front to him which total more than what is displayed on the red screen above the dashboard, hoping I got the whole tipping thing right.

The driver checks the cash. 'He's all right. Have a nice day.'

I'm on the pavement – sidewalk – taking in my surroundings. The glass door is embedded in a long row of terraces on the top part of a T-junction, facing down another road which joins the first. I can see shops in the distance, but for the most part, it's quiet. The hum of the city feels somewhere else, the high buildings on all sides muffling the sound.

I suppose this is where I'm staying.

I open the glass door to be faced by a simple reception area containing nothing more than a lift and a rack of mailboxes. The lift is already there, waiting, so I step in and press the number three. Nothing happens, except a little light next to three illuminates red. Confused, I press it again. Nowt. I stare at it, hoping nobody comes in and sees the clown who can't work a damn lift. I hold down three this time. Nothing. I tap the little red light, but that doesn't do anything either. I look at the bank of controls, trying to make sense of it. Buttons, next to little light panels, which are no bigger than fifty pence pieces. Big enough for—

'No way.' It's a fingerprint sensor.

That's me buggered then. I'll need someone to buzz me up. I look for a call button but can't find anything aside from a red clicker for "Emergencies Only". Out of frustration, I thumb the red light next to three – and it turns green.

They've got my fingerprints.

Who the hell am I dealing with?

Before I can think any further, the lift is suddenly moving upwards, and I'm questioning what on earth I've managed to get myself into this time.

# CHAPTER FOUR

The lift makes short work of the climb, and as it slows, tension screams to my fingers. I expect a ding or some kind of tone to announce my arrival, but the doors simply part with a scrape. I back into the corner of the elevator and peek around the corner slowly, taking in the detail as I go. The floor is dark, polished wood, and there's an occasional chair a yard or so from the lift doors, back against the wall. I inch around the corner and find myself surprised at the sight of a large, flat-screen TV, its screen black. Beneath it sits a unit hosting an array of black boxes: television providers and DVD players alike. And the more I turn, the more a sofa becomes visible – old-style, sweeping arms, in what looks like a mustard yellow felt. And further around is a fridge.

Confusion takes hold, and I step out of the lift, directly into the living room of an apartment. The lift itself is the front door to a domicile – to which my fingerprint is the key. There's nobody here, but a couple of floor lamps are on, suggesting someone was here recently. Dropping my backpack on the chair, I take stock.

A large open plan living space. Cosy TV area, placed centrally, with a kitchen behind it. Looks well maintained, nice appliances, big extractor fan, expensive-looking cream splashback tiles. It's all in a mishmash of design styles and from a variety of eras – repurposed antiques against bare brick, colonial architraves over high-end tech – as if the owner had picked a few bits from a number of different styles they fancied and put them together in a mad little style of their own. A small dining table completes the room, aside from a corridor which leads away, I'm guessing to a bathroom.

Looking to the right of the lift, there's an imposing set of French windows, through which I can see a large bedroom, easily the same size as the rest of the apartment. A bank of windows looks out over the street and the T-junction below, green fire escapes clinging to the windows as far as I can see, like barnacles grasping on to a giant brick hull. I guess this is where I'm staying.

I can't help but smile. I'm no property expert, but this place must be worth a fortune, at least a couple of million. My smile widens, and I get lost in the moment – before action takes hold. I check my watch. 7.30 pm. I've got to get moving. I need to scope out the bar and the surrounding area before I get there at the allotted time – there's no chance I'm going there into God knows what without having a full plan and exit strategy sorted.

No damn way.

Down that corridor off the living room is indeed an ornate bathroom in green and gold, in which I shower, shave and dress, before I hit the streets. It felt weird not taking a key, but now I'm used to the idea of the key being, essentially, me, it feels really quite liberating.

The streets, once on them, are intoxicating, and within minutes I feel drunk on it. Just so many people, living so many lives, and from the businesses and shops nudging out in every spare square footage, there is something truly for every taste. But on seeing Flo-Bar on Bleecker Street, just a three-minute brisk saunter from the apartment on Howard, even from a distance I can see it isn't going to be to mine. It's neon signed, but not that inviting neon of the old argon gas, glass signs, no, this is decked in neon blocks of blue, like the bar is clad in giant strips of bubble gum Hubba Bubba. Beneath is all glass, and the interior looks gaudy as an art gallery that hasn't had irony explained to it. My lips curl, I eye all exits and entrances, check the alley behind it that leads onto Mulberry Street, and come to the conclusion that if I want out, it's either through the front or back, public or staff. Above are apartments with separate entrances at ground level, and without investigating each door and floor in person, I can't rely on there being any access between the bar and above. The roof, therefore, isn't an escape option.

As I watch the front door, with 9.00 pm approaching, I scold myself for my unpreparedness. This is so unlike me and against all aspects of my training to date. In Afghanistan or Iraq, I'd never have taken an order that was shrouded in such scant instruction – and I'd have instructed anyone under my charge to do the same. Yet here I am.

I'm going soft.

But Grosvenor's instructions hadn't exactly been presented with obvious danger. I'm just here to pick something up. An envelope. I assume it's being given to me in that obnoxious shoebox opposite me, and that will be that.

I check my watch one more time – the battered Casio G-shock that has been with me from the sewers of Lashkar Gah to the bottom of the sea off the Devon coastline, and now to the good ol' US of A.

Go time.

A techno baseline grips my ears as I cross the threshold of Flo-Bar, and any doubts in my original assessment have been sent packing. It's grim in here. The barstools are white, ergonomic ass-supports, and the tables are chrome doors laid horizontally on black legs, thin as a malnourished foal. The bar itself looks like a giant metal suppository, and the only beer available looks to be bottled in fridges beyond the huge pessary. It's proper ghastly.

I'm bang on time, so I scan the room. It's very quiet, with only a barman, complete with twirly moustache and John Lennon glasses (ah, there's the irony), and a couple of people, who look surprisingly normal, at a nearby table.

'West? Shall we ditch this abomination and go for a proper beer somewhere?'

I haven't even laid eyes on the owner of the relaxed male voice, accent thick-as-asphalt Brooklyn, when I'm saying, 'Yes'.

# CHAPTER FIVE

He drops into step next to me, the owner of the voice, and we walk unhurriedly, just a couple of fellas going for an evening beer after a solid shift at our respective grindstones. He's in a tan suit, though the jacket is over his shoulder and his tie is askew. He looks early thirties, a white guy putting in a serious claim to the tall, dark and handsome thing, hair and teeth fresh from GQ, except the nose is more GNVQ – been there, done that, took the bumps en route. He's talking as he's going, his stride brisk and confident. These streets are familiar, this is home turf.

I listen and say nothing.

'I'm sorry, man, in case that place was your thing, but I've tipped, I'm over the crest of thirty, I can't be sitting there shouting at a guy on the other side of the table in the hope he'll catch maybe one in five of the words I've gotta say.'

I can't say I don't agree with him.

'So, I get the call saying I've gotta meet this guy from jolly England, and I'm thinking, does he bollocks wanna sit in a place like that either. Correct usage?'

'Yeah, that'll do.'

'Right, so I'm thinking, he wants a place with ale, real beer, something with a bit of character, not some fuckin' place that could do with a committed arson attempt. So, I had a little think about the stone's throw thing, and bang, it hit me, I knew exactly where to go.'

By the time he's finished his monologue, he's stopped in front of a corner establishment called Bleecker Bar, through which I can see dark wood and polished beer taps.

'Not quite Ye Olde Village Inn, but a step closer, don't you agree?'

I nod, and we go inside. It's a drinker's place. Not a place for umbrella drinks. He heads directly for the bar and raises his hand.

'Two Boston Pales, man.'

'Mine's a Guinness,' I interject. I saw the Harp outside on a fluttering pendant.

My companion turns to look at me with a raised eyebrow, before returning to the barman. 'A Boston Pale and a Guinness.'

The beers are poured (the black stuff, happily, poured correctly), and I follow him to a booth. We sit opposite each other at a low wooden table.

'Slàinte,' he says, raising his fizzing glass.

I clink my Guinness against his beer, a taste for which I was gifted by a Maasai warrior, but that's another story.

'Luca Jones, CIA regional office. I've been tasked with paying you a visit.'

'Tom,' I say, remembering the name on my passport. 'Thanks for sparing the time. You have something for me, I believe.'

'I do,' he says, before breaking into a smile. Some guys' faces abandon the childish wonderment as soon as they're over thirty, whereas Luca seems to embrace his. He can't hide his glee, and his eyes shine. 'Can't say it's not got me fascinated though. What do you know?'

The truth is, very little, but I'm not going to share it that easily. 'Show me one of those posh CIA badges, then we can chat shop.'

His smile somehow widens. 'They told me you'd be like this.' He straightens, takes a beer mat and begins rotating it between finger and thumb. 'I was called by my grandfather. He's ex-CIA. The family business bypassed my dad, so to speak, so it's only ever me and Pops that talk shop, as you say. Anyway, he calls me and tells me that an old friend needs to get something to Britain, so he's sending a courier over to get it. I ask him what it is, and the old gamer says forget it, son. The envelope was sent special delivery to the office, and I've got it here.'

'What makes you so interested in it? An old envelope is just an old envelope.'

'My grandfather never talks about the old days. When I say he talks shop, I mean we talk end of his career, crossover to my career and the present day. When I was younger, whenever I mentioned anything about what he used to do, he'd always brush me off. Once, after a couple of extra brandies one Christmas, he let slip about working with the Brits at some point. So then me, his grandson, gets a job at the agency – Oh, ID, of course.' He pauses to rummage in his pocket, before tossing the open badge onto the tabletop. 'And I get some security clearances. I build up the courage – takes me a while because I don't want to get kicked out having only just joined – and look into it. There's a four-year gap in his resume, fully redacted. Not a word. Not even the option of entering a password to access it.'

I scan the badge and the accompanying picture. Looks legit – says the guy who just entered the United States on a forged passport.

'So you can imagine, when Pops asks me to deliver something to a British guy, connected to his past, I get excited.'

I smile, yet sigh. 'I'm not sure what I can tell you, Luca. My own instructions are vague at best.'

'Yeah, but who instructed you?' I can tell from the chirp in his voice that he's not going to be denied here.

'An old friend.'

Luca actually blows a raspberry, before taking a sup. He then reaches into his pocket and pulls out an envelope. To look at, it's nothing impressive. A5 size, yellow in colour, with the name Luca Jones III printed on the front. It's not old, as I was expecting. 'You're not interested as to what's inside?'

'No.' It's a bit of a lie, but I'm used to being disciplined on need-to-know bases. If my orders call for ignorance, then I'll stay that way.

Luca lays the envelope flat and places his whole palm over it. 'Come on,' he urges conspiratorially. 'I'll throw in another couple of beers.'

'How do I know you haven't already opened it?'

'Because I thought you might be able to tell me straight up. But you can't. So now I wanna know what's in there.'

'For a CIA operative, you're not very discreet, are you?'

His eyes drift down, he bares his teeth with a sarcastic grin, and I've hit a nerve. 'This is family history for me, *mate*.'

The thing in my head is, why does this bother him so much?

He's still got his hand on it.

'Even if it's a family thing,' I say with balance, 'your instructions remain to hand it over.'

He looks at the envelope, his fingers splayed across it like he's going to play that ludicrous stabbing knife game I've seen in countless films, and he smiles in embarrassment. 'Hey, I had to try. I'm not high up in the CIA, even I know I've still got my training wheels on. Don't get me wrong, I want to get there. My grandfather was why I joined the agency in the first place. The chance to know a little more about what Pops was up to was too tempting.'

He slides it over to me and withdraws his hand. I leave it on the tabletop a moment. 'You keep doing what you're doing, you'll reach your grandfather's level and you'll get the keys to all the family secrets you want.'

He smiles again, and I return the gesture.

'Family is tough, I get it,' I say. I can't even remember the last time I saw my parents. Oh, wait, yes, I can. Murder trial, seventeen years… another story.

He tips his glass, conspiracy and the first tendril of bonding flitting between us – two disparate men, bound by the importance of respective orders and bigger pictures.

I feel something. Instinct jars into gear. I grab the envelope and stick it in my own jacket pocket as a shadow looms over the table.

'A word, fellas,' a voice says. It's T-Rex deep, with the Noo Yawk vowels I'm getting used to, only, the intentions behind the ones used here offer scant compromise.

# SINCLAIR

The office was nondescript, a rental. Plywood doors and plasterboard ceiling made from those little squares that you can just pull out and replace. Garish striplight, potted plant in the corner. Function, no form.

At a single desk sat Sinclair, who was facing the officer, one who he'd never met before. They'd certainly never served directly in each other's company, to Sinclair's knowledge, although one could never be too sure about that. The brass often hid in the background, away from the grunting and yelling, although it was their noises that made it happen.

'What is it you want to achieve in the military? You hope for a long career?' the officer asked. His voice was born and bred Home Counties in quality; the cut, green grass of England with a touch of elocution.

The answer for Sinclair was a simple one, even though he'd never been asked nor contemplated the question before. 'I intend to keep going until I feel I've done enough.'

The brass nodded, a smile pulling the corners of his lips. Both men were in civilian clothes. The brass in a charcoal suit, on his way to a business meeting, which Sinclair supposed this was, in a way, while the young soldier wore jeans and a white t-shirt with the sleeves rolled up, the right-hand roll holding a packet of cigarettes like he'd seen Marlon Brando do on the big screen. Either way, there was no uniform nor regalia for this secret meeting in an office building in Maidstone.

'Shall we try a little word association?' said the officer.

Sinclair nodded. 'If you like.'

'Cat.'

'Dog.'

'Fish.'

'Water.'

'Water.'

'Blue.'

'Sky.'

'Blue.'

Sinclair answered without hesitation, maintained eye contact and didn't think too hard about any of it.

'War.'

'Life.'

'Duty.'

'Responsibility.'

'Justice.'

'Occasional.'

That made the officer smile. Sinclair remained cucumber cool.

'Honour.'

'Fanciful.'

'Right.'

'Wrong.'

'Heaven.'

'Hell.'

'You're very much a yin and yang man.'

'A lot of things have common opposites. If there's good, there's bad. One exists alongside the other, it's not something that can be denied.'

The officer nodded slowly, deliberately. 'How do you feel about working internationally?'

'I assumed that would be part and parcel of the nature of my employment. I'm happy to go anywhere.'

'To serve your country?'

'That of course, sir. And to serve good.'

'But you just said that the notion of good made you think immediately of bad.'

'As I said, sir, they aren't mutually exclusive. But I can certainly stack the balance a certain way.'

The door to the office abruptly burst open and before Sinclair could turn, hands were pushing him forcefully over the desk, pinning him down.

'Get down, scum!' a voice bellowed in his ear, as his cheek grazed the rough wood of the tabletop. 'You, on the ground.'

At the periphery of Sinclair's vision, he could just make out the officer standing open-mouthed with his hands up. 'I have no idea what you're talking about.'

'Shut the fuck up!' screamed the voice. 'You're British army, and a traitor.'

'I am not!' shouted back the officer. 'How dare you? I'll have you arrested at once.'

'You've been selling secrets to the Russians – British military secrets!' This was another voice, the pitch a touch higher.

Sinclair's head was swimming. The front of his mind was addressing the immediate, namely, how to get out of this situation, whereas the back was wrestling with his regret for coming to this meeting in the first place. Covert military intelligence, what on earth was that anyway?

'I've sold nothing to nobody, now leave this office immediately!'

The first man moved to seize the officer, and something deep within Sinclair told him to move. That this was wrong, an injustice, and he had to go.

He stamped straight down and hard with his right foot on the top of his assailant's own, which caused a yelp and a momentary relaxation of the grip on his neck and shoulders. He span with his elbows out, once to the left and once all the way round to his right. Both his elbow points caught something hard and heavy. He followed the momentum and turned to see a large man holding his head in pain. Sinclair dropped the side of his palm across the top of the man's exposed neck, which sent him tumbling to the cheap carpet.

'Wait there,' said the other invader. 'Just you wait there.'

Sinclair turned to see a gun come up from the speaker's left side, but his hands moved faster, grabbing the wrist of the gun hand and pulling it towards him. He twisted, pulled and dragged the other man into a judo throw, sailing him onto the desk in the middle of the room.

Sinclair cocked the gun and aimed it at the two intruders – but was caused to pause by clapping.

It was coming from the corner of the room behind him where

the officer was stood, glee on his face, offering applause.

'Well done, Sinclair,' he said. 'Well bloody done, young man.'

The other men pulled themselves to their feet with a groan, and all Sinclair could do was watch, flummoxed.

'Not many people get through these two,' said the officer, 'let me tell you.'

Realisation sunk into Sinclair like an anvil through margarine.

'You passed, young man. You passed. Now, how about something to eat, maybe a lunchtime dram or two, and we can talk specifics…'

The officer's hand clasped his shoulder and led him to the door.

# CHAPTER SIX

We both look up to the source of our table's eclipse, and the first thing I see is a gold chain so ostentatious you could melt it down to fill twenty rappers' grills. The lights behind the man leave his face in darkness, but I can see his head is bald, save for the downy tufts you'd find scattered after a duck has been shot out of the sky. He's in a green tracksuit top and black jeans, both triple XL. The voice booms over us again.

'Well, it can be a word. But the words usually lead us closer to something a little more painful. Or you could just give me that envelope and go back to your drinks.'

I feel flecks of spittle rain as he talks, and I turn my face away, but the suddenness with which the game has changed is unnerving, and we, sat here in this booth, know nothing.

'Why do you want it, mate?' I ask, risking a look up. He's thickset in every possible way, though his eyes are small and somehow kind – like he could be a gentle giant but never learnt how.

'Because, mate, I do. Hand it over or your legs might end up a little broken.'

I've got no weapon. He's got the size, height, reach, you name it, *everything*, advantage. I glance at Luca, whose eyes are wide with fear.

'Do you want to tell me who I'd be giving it to?' I say.

The giant laughs. It starts with a couple of short breaths in, then evolves to a juddering applause. He looks at Luca, then pauses. 'He knows.'

It's that glance away from me that gives me the window I need.

I don't know who this guy is, who he represents, but I've got orders. They didn't sound all that serious at first, but the stakes just raised. And I'm going to carry out my instructions.

The seat below my backside is vinyl, nearly frictionless against my trousers, and lets me slide my legs up beneath the tabletop. The big man can't see, and he's too late to turn back, as the soles of both my feet thrust against his right kneecap, as hard as I can, and his leg bends just a touch the wrong way. It's enough to make him howl in pain. He stoops to hold his knee, so I help him down, crashing his head with two hands, one clamped on either ear, through my pint glass on the table, which explodes in a crack of glass, wood, bone and beer.

But it doesn't bring him down for long. He lurches back up, small prisms of glass wedged in his forehead, and takes a step back, before his reorganised knee ligaments send him tottering again.

Still, the giant, resilient bastard just won't drop.

The momentum is still mine. I charge, blood coursing down the big man's face now, and punch him in the Adam's apple as hard as I can. His breath stops immediately, his windpipe bent out of shape, and finally, he drops to a knee. If you can't damage the outside of the machine, take out the engine room. He's spluttering, clawing for breath, now on his face.

There are other eyes on us as I turn to Luca. 'Thanks for the help,' I say, unable to choke back the sarcasm.

'Do you know who that is?' he asks. His eyes still haven't gone back to normal size.

'Whoever he is, he should have been nicer about the whole thing.'

With abruptness, the wall behind Luca's head suddenly begins popping and chipping, flecks of brick and plaster peppering out at us, and it takes me far too long to realise that we're taking gunfire. I only hear it as I hit the floor, Luca scrambling to join me, screaming 'SHIT' loudly into my ear.

Go. Now.

'Fire exit?' I shout over the onslaught. The gunfire is automatic and suppressed – probably why it took me a moment to compute what was happening. A silenced Uzi, maybe.

'Back door – smoking area!' he shouts in response, pointing to the left, past our booth.

'Wait for reload.'

The gunfire stops – could be for reload or the shooter simply waiting for the dust to settle so they can lock onto us again, nevertheless, it's our time to move. I'm guessing that the gunman is at the front of the bar, near the entrance.

'Go!' I urge.

We run in an awkward crouch as the bullets start to rain again, but the exit door isn't far away, and we tumble through at the same time, shoulder to shoulder.

'Do you have a car?' I ask, the air cooler and infused with crushed Marlboros. We're in an alley under a small awning.

'Don't be ridiculous, it's Manhattan.'

'Then get running.' Bullets suddenly zing and pop against the fire door, a couple of which get through and ricochet somewhere in the empty alley. 'Now, NOW.'

We are sprinting and daren't look back as the door clunks open behind us. We have a head start and it's a relief. Uzis are pure murder at close range. Out in the open air, at distance, they're a lot more hit or miss. That's if it actually is an Uzi. You can silence a Heckler & Koch, and that would be curtains for us both. But I don't think it is. The assault started from inside the bar, and that means the gun would have to have been smuggled in. You can do that fairly readily with an Uzi, not with a Heckler, which is more akin to the kind of rifle that would raise alarm bells. Either way, my mind wanders as I sprint. It's pretty predictable that within mere hours of landing on American soil, I've come into contact with their dreaded gun culture.

'Where to?' shouts Luca ahead of me, and boy can he run. It's either a further indication of my domestic slide, or Luca Jones was an athlete earlier in life.

'Straight ahead!' I command as we break out of the alley and onto the main street I remember being called Lafayette. We're dodging cars, ignoring horns, ducking low, and are on the other side after a couple of near-misses. It's then we realise the gunfire has stopped.

'Shit,' Luca says, breathing heavily as he pulls up – but I grab his shoulders.

'Don't stop,' I say, pushing him on, down the next alley off the main drag. In my head, I know where I am. I've always had this innate sense of direction and geography. I had it as a kid, and it only became more enhanced the more time I spent mastering orienteering in my training. I know now that we need to go south, with a handful of degrees in a westerly direction.

'Where are we going?' Luca asks. He's breathing heavier now as we run along the cobbled surface of the alley, occasionally drifting through clouds of cooking smells and the odd fug of something more sewer-like.

'I've got a safe spot not far from here,' I say as we cross another road onto Crosby, the home straight. Howard Street and the apartment is right at the bottom. I'm now sure we're not being followed, but we can't let up the pace. 'Were you a sprinter?'

'Yeah. Grease lightning over a hundred metres, gassed out at anything over.'

The door to 35 Howard Street is ahead, and I direct Luca to it as the sun finally leaves the city for the night and it noticeably gets a degree or two cooler. Inside and into the lift, and it's only then we check ourselves.

'You all right?' I ask, checking my jacket and jeans.

Luca does the same, and he looks like he half expects to find holes in his clothes. When he doesn't, he puts both hands on his chest. One piece. 'Yeah. Although I'm not sure how. Do you have any idea who that was?'

'I'm assuming I should.'

Luca shakes his head. 'This is a lot more serious than I thought.'

# CHAPTER SEVEN

Once the fridge has been raided for bottled water, we slump onto the sofa and a chair, respectively. The apartment is cool and feels like respite. It's most welcome.

'The big man – the one whose head you made a serious impression on – that's Michael Brutoli. He's a heavy for the Speronis, out of Queens.'

'Is that actually as cliched and on the nose as it sounds?' I say, checking my phone. Only a few people have the number, and each is within that circle of trust that doesn't get expanded often. A text from Carolyn.

DID YOU GET THERE OK, SOLDIER? KIDS SEND LOVE X.

From gunfire to domesticity, in seconds. Back to earth with a bump. It's an ongoing seesaw battle that has taken constant navigation. It hasn't been long since I swapped testosterone, combat and cracking heads with regularity, nappies, night-time feeding routines and school runs. But I know where my head is now. What my heart craves. It's my son, my partner, and the kids I now call family. And with that comes responsibility.

I have to get home to them. They rely on me, and I won't let them down.

'Yeah, you're on the right lines,' Luca says. He's got his suit trousers rolled up and he's massaging his calves, wobbling them from side to side. 'Lactic acid, such a bitch. I'd forgotten.'

'So why would organised criminals want an envelope your grandpa's been sitting on for years?'

He stops jiggling those magnificent chunks of meat. 'I truly have no idea.'

'What is it you do with the CIA?'

'I'm in Budget and Procedures, Administrative Services. New York Regional Office.'

'So, forgive me, how'd you know who the big lummock was?'

'I'm aiming high, remember? And I wanted to know as much about my patch as possible.'

I want to say *bless you*, but I don't think that would help our fledgeling relationship. 'That doesn't demystify the situation. Why would he want it? And how would they even know about it?'

'Your guess is as good as mine.'

I take out the envelope and place it on the distressed coffee table, which appears to have been fashioned from an old shipping crate. It has "Property of NYC Port" stencilled on the side and must have cost anything between five dollars and five thousand. The envelope itself is still in relatively good nick, having survived its hasty jaunt in my inner jacket pocket, and I lay it on the table.

It looks so thin, pitiful. Not capable of causing an incident of an international flavour – and the more I stare at it, the

39

more I feel I need to know. And the more I feel Grosvenor has hugely underplayed the importance of whatever is inside.

'Let's take a look?' I say, my eyebrows raised in question. Luca replies by leaning forward, puppy-eager.

I pick it up and start to tear the easy-peel tab. I don't like going outside instructions, as it usually leads to trouble above all else. But I dislike being stuck in the dark more. When things get heavy, and mortality is on the line, that's when the game changes. We need to know what we're dealing with.

Inside is barely anything save for a slip of paper. Single sheet, A4, folded once. I open it up, the light from the overhanging lamp catching the image of a man. A man with piercing eyes, an intense, accusatory expression, a top hat with stars and a single, outstretched digit in front of him, pointing at the sky.

It's a printout of Uncle Sam giving me the middle finger.

'What the hell is this?' I say, anger rising though I'm not yet sure what at, tossing the paper onto the crate for Luca to get a good look at.

He takes it hurriedly, his eyes roving for a secret he's waited years to be told, but there's nothing there save that famous image edited into something offensive.

'Welcome to America,' I say, giving Uncle Sam the side-eye.

'I don't understand,' says Luca, tossing it down. 'This can't be right.'

I could play this one of two ways. We could put our heads together and sort this out, or—

Standing up quickly, I grab around Luca's jaw with a thumb under his ear and my fingers digging up under his chin. 'What the fuck are you trying to pull, Luca Jones?'

40

The good thing about this pressure point hold is that I can feel his pulse beneath the tip of what would be my ring finger. And his is skyrocketing.

'Nothing, nothing!' he squeals.

'You think it's funny, dragging me out here to America to have me shot at?' I give him a little yank which pulls him forward on the sofa. Two things make this hold unbreakable – one, a good grip. And two? The right attitude. Offer no compromise, and he's desperate for you to let him go.

'I don't know what it is! I've never seen the envelope before!'

'It came from your pocket. What do you call it on this side of the Atlantic, the ol' switcheroo?'

'I promise!'

'I squeeze any harder, Luca, and I can stop blood from reaching your brain, is that something you'd like?' I can't, but saying it has worked in the past.

'No! I haven't done anything, I'm as shocked as you are!'

'Then speak. Who had the envelope before you?'

He starts naming people hurriedly on his free fingers, and it's that no-compromise attitude of mine that stops him from even dreaming of using those hands to try to stop me. 'There'll be Sarah on the front desk, whoever the courier service was, and Pops.'

'There're a lot of gaps in that chain, Luca, anyone else?'

'I don't know! I've got the same instructions as you. Get the envelope and hand it over.'

His pulse is almost a constant throb under my fingers, like a hummingbird is stuck in his mouth, desperate to get out, so I let him go. He gasps and takes a few breaths, like he can finally suck in air. He had air the whole time. I just held him in place. The reason he's relieved? Attitude.

'If you're telling the truth, then we need to track those people down immediately. Starting with the one immediately before us. Sarah on the front desk.'

Luca rubs his neck and stretches his back. 'Shit, man, it's ten o'clock at night!'

I point to the twinkling lights beyond the bedroom windows. 'And there are some gangster's hitmen out there who don't give a shit about victim convenience or murder etiquette – where can we find her?'

Luca gulps his water and tends to his hair, the locks easing back into place with a splash of Evian. 'Yeah, I know where she lives.'

'Luca Jones, you old dog.' I put Uncle Sam back in the envelope, when the lift door in the corner of the room closes and heads down to the lobby.

'Is anyone else in this building?' Luca says, his eyes locked on the joined metal sheets of the lift door.

'I've no idea,' I say.

'Does anyone know we're here?'

We pause and listen. The lift stops, presumably at the bottom, for all of a second, before I hear the door shut again. I wonder if the lift is only programmed to accept my fingerprint.

A ding rings out, as it passes floor one.

Three seconds.

A second ding.

'Do you want to find out?' I say.

'Hell no,' Luca says.

And we're running.

# CHAPTER EIGHT

We're through the French windows of the bedroom in a flash and clambering out of the fire escape as the lift doors open into the living room. We are some sixty feet off the ground and, all of a sudden, looking down isn't the most fun thing in the world to do. We start moving across the fire escape platforms, one at a time, scaling horizontally across the building. Part of me is desperate to know who entered the apartment, but considering how recently we've been shot at, it doesn't seem the smartest move to hang about.

Luca has that speed about him again, and he's agile. It's taxing work, hopping over the railing of each platform, then a short sprint, then doing it all over again. I think we have moved four properties along when a bullet ricochets off the ladder Luca has just gone past.

'Drop down!' I shout, and Luca uses the gap between platforms to drop through, landing with a clatter. I follow him – only to be greeted by a mash-haired woman in a nightdress whacking Luca with an umbrella.

'Steady on,' I say, nipping by her and dropping down to the next floor, which Luca quickly manages to emulate.

One more tinging ricochet off the ironwork and our attacker gives up. We pause and listen.

'No footsteps,' Luca says.

'They've gone for the lift.'

Neither of us needs to utter a further word, and the race continues, down the final two floors to the bottom.

As soon as our soles hit pavement, Luca is pointing to the end of Howard Street. 'That's Broadway, there'll be cabs everywhere.'

We make it to Broadway, unsure if we're being followed but too hyped up to check. Luca was right, there are yellow taxis in every direction. I run to the nearest one, stopped at the lights.

'That's got someone in it!' shouts Luca, and true enough, there's the shape of a person through the back window – but there's a shout behind us.

'Hey!' an aggressive male voice shouts.

'No time,' I say, and throw the rear cab door open. Luca does the same on the other side, and we are suddenly sat either side of, and wedging in the middle rear seat, a somewhat terrified looking clergyman, the knees beneath his black smock bouncing.

'Drive,' I instruct, wedging some notes through the little gap in the window parting front and back. I'm pretty sure there're at least two fifties in that pile.

The driver turns, eyes wide, cheeks and brow sweat-streaked and open with surprise. He catches sight of the notes and jumps the red light, going cautiously at first, but we're suddenly gunning up Broadway.

'Forgive us, Father, for we have sinned,' says Luca, with a heavy breath out, and I can't help but roll my eyes at his corniness. Sat behind the driver's seat, he pulls up his pant legs again to massage those calves.

'Where are we going?' I ask, passing another fifty to the bemused pastor between us. 'For your trouble. At least put it in the collection.' He takes it.

'Sarah lives at 805 Central Park West.'

'That came to you rather easy.'

'Yeah, I've been there before.'

'More than once?'

'Oh yeah,' he says, but I can see he's not smiling. There're nerves there.

As the car slows and rejoins the wider flow of traffic, I roll my eyes again.

# CHAPTER NINE

It's almost full nightfall now as the taxi pulls up outside a huge brownstone apartment block on the opposite side of the street to a row of hedges, beyond which I spy lamp-lit pathways snaking under trees as far as I can see. It must be Central Park. The city has transformed before my eyes as sometime during the short journey, the violet dusk was suddenly crushed by orange-bitten blacks and blues. The taxi sped off with so little fuss that I can only assume it's a regular occurrence, having people in need of a quick escape jump in your cab. America.

We take the steps up to the varnished wooden doors, through whose glass panes I can see a well-appointed lobby area and a desk-bound concierge in a suit. Nice place.

'The secretary lives here?' I ask.

'Old money, I believe,' replies Luca, catching my vibe, before thumbing the buzzer on the wall-set intercom by the door.

A few seconds pass, the cars on the street some feet below paying us no mind as they hiss by. It allows me a chance to pull back and look up, take in the view. It's a good one and must be even better a few stories up. As I look across the treetops of the park over to the high rises on the other side, and on up to the towering skyscrapers with lights pockmarking them all the way to their tops, I'm struck again. What a city this is.

A female voice speaks across static. 'Hello?'

'Uh, Sarah, hi, it's Luca,' he says, looking at the floor. There's a story here, and I feel I'm going to begrudgingly hear it.

'Luca Jones?' comes the reply. There's surprise and scorn there, I'm sure of it.

'Yeah, that's me.'

'What are you doing here, Luca Jones?'

'We need to talk to you Sarah, it's important.'

'We? Who's we? What bullshit are you peddling this time, Luca?'

I find myself giving Luca the side-eye with folded arms.

'It's about the envelope, the one you gave me today. Remember the one from the courier?'

A sigh drifts down the speaker like the flat of a hand across paper. 'Work stuff… can't this wait until morning and, y'know, work hours?'

'Sarah, I know it's not ideal.' He glances at me and looks down sheepishly again. 'But I really need to come in. It's important and it can't wait.'

A pause, then: 'Who's with you?'

Luca looks at me, and after a second, shrugs. It occurs to me he doesn't really know. 'A friend of a friend of my grandpops.'

'For fuck's sake, Luca…' The door buzzes, then the lock clicks.

'Thank you,' he says to nobody in particular.

'Smooth,' I say as we enter.

'Yeah, that's me, super smooth.' He sounds weary and nervous, for the first time since I've met him – and that's including the moments we've had bullets around our ears. He's not bothered about stuff you'd normally be worried about, but this woman? This Sarah has him on the back foot.

In the lift, which happily doesn't need any fingerprint access, Luca presses for the eighth floor and it's clear he's been here before.

'What do I need to know?' I ask.

'I messed up with her,' he says, looking at the numbers rise on the board overhead.

'Messed up?'

'Yeah. I maybe wasn't the biggest gentleman in the world.'

'Nice boy like you, what happened?'

The door pings open, and before we can step out, a woman has stepped in. She wears a dark expression, a shit-ton of make-up, fluffy pyjamas with Thumper from Bambi on them – and she delivers a brutal knee to Luca's unsuspecting bollocks. He drops to the floor gasping.

'Try not calling me, you prick.' She turns to me, and I see her fury, which she cools with a long breath out. 'Sorry. I can't do that at work.'

'I understand,' is all I can say. She's late twenties, radiating indignant fire and spite, looking like she's dolled up ready for a night out, despite the jimmy jams.

'This way,' she says. 'He knows where he's going, he'll catch up when his balls drop back down from his throat.'

I'm not often speechless, and I trot along behind her as she marches down the corridor, like an obedient terrier afraid of getting his own manhood bashed in.

She only lives three doors down and had left the door open. The apartment is dark, lit only by two floor lamps and a slice of

LED strip lighting from the kitchen. It's an all-in-one living space comprising of lounge area and kitchen, spread across one wide room, the back wall of which is a row of windows overlooking Central Park. The air is a soft fusion of incense and fresh garlic. It's luxury.

It's… off.

'You can speak for him, right?' says the woman I assume is Sarah, as she walks beyond the kitchen island to turn down a stove.

'I can try, although I don't know anything about you and…'

'Forget that, why are you here?'

I pull out the envelope from my jacket pocket and place it on top of a large pot on the kitchen island in front of her. 'It's about this. You gave it to him I believe?'

'Yes. I keep it all business at work because it's a great job.' My eyes cast around the room again. It must be. 'And I'm not losing it for that asshole and his fuckboy games.'

I don't know what that last part means, but I'm not going to seek a definition. 'I wouldn't want to either.'

'What do you call a guy who tells you the stars shine only for you, then after he gets what he wants, which was in these pyjamas, no less, he suddenly forgets how to use a phone?'

'I'd probably call that person a bell-end.'

She actually grins a touch, but it's a dark one. 'A bell-end. I like that.'

There's a knock on the door behind us. 'Come in, bell-end,' she says, like she's trying out the word for the first time. Such an obvious Britishism sounds weird coming through her Noo Yawk twang. In through the door walks the shell of Luca Jones, puce and sweating. 'You stay over there, the grownups are talking.

49

Wine?' She holds up a bottle of red, a corkscrew already in the neck, and looks at me.

'No, thank you.' It doesn't stop her from uncorking the bottle and reaching for a glass that looks suspiciously fatter than the usual fare.

'So. Envelopes,' she says. Hand planted on hip, glass coming to lips. Even Thumper carries an attitude when emblazoned across her front.

'Yes, this envelope. Someone dropped it off for him?'

'Yeah, I recognised the guy. It was the usual UPS delivery man that comes to the building. Buzzed him straight in.'

'Straight in? To the CIA?'

'He's been vetted so hard I'm surprised he can still walk straight. Yeah, straight in.'

'Has he worked there long?'

'Been there since before I got there, and I've been there five years.'

'And this was the envelope he gave you?'

She looks like there're a million and one other things she'd rather be doing with her evening than talking to me. 'This was the envelope he gave me. Which I then gave to your bell-end.'

I let the slight awkwardness of translation slide. 'Are you sure?' I glance at Luca, who's dragged himself onto the cream leather sofa. He meets my eyes, despite his heavy breathing. If this is the envelope his grandfather sent, then what the hell kind of game is the old man playing?

When Sarah doesn't answer, I hand it to her. 'Please.'

She takes it with a sigh and examines it, front and back. She looks at the writing for a moment and squints at it just a little. 'One hundred per cent. This is the one. So now we know I've done my job, can you get that stain off my couch and get going?' She points the envelope at me with dismissive accusation.

I take it and turn to the door. 'Come on, let's go.' Luca lops along behind me.

'Nice seeing you, Luca,' shouts Sarah as the door bangs shut.

As we walk back to the lift, I see Luca is managing to walk a little better. 'How're you doing?'

'She's a fiery one,' he says hoarsely.

'I can see the appeal.'

'Where too now?'

I call the lift as soon as I get to it. 'We're going to find somewhere quiet and you're going to tell me everything you know about her.'

'Why?'

'Because she's got something else going on, and she's not off the hook just yet.'

# CHAPTER TEN

Having crossed the road outside the apartment and dropped through the fenced hedgerows of the park, we take a seat on a bench. I'm amazed at the number of night-time joggers there are and the volume of people flitting about. I shouldn't be surprised – this is a hot summer night in the city that famously refuses to go to bed.

'So, Sarah…' I say, leaning back in the seat to invoke relaxation in Luca in the hope that it'll make him spill. 'What do you know? I want everything, and use that CIA brain of yours.'

'I don't know what to tell,' replies Luca, his demeanour almost back to normal after the obliteration of his nuts.

'She said you pursued her, so you must have learned something about her?'

'*Pursue* is a bit heavy. I thought she was hot, so I took an interest, yeah.'

'And did it take a while for you to connect with her romantically?'

'Yeah, a bit, why?'

'That's a pursuit, Romeo.'

'Ah, Christ,' he says, before crossing himself hurriedly.

'What do you pull down a year?'

He straightens, his back suddenly stiff with offence. 'What kind of question is that?'

'A half-decent one, possibly. Come on, give me a figure.'

'Thirty-five k, but I get health insurance and gym membership with that.'

'And do you live like that?' I stick a thumb back over my shoulder to the brownstone.

Luca thinks. And thinks some more. I can almost see the cogs rotate behind his eyes. 'No.'

'So, you're saying the girl on the front desk earns considerably more than one of the actual CIA agents upstairs?'

'No.'

'You see where I'm going with this.'

'I thought she came from old money.'

'Did you see a picture of any family in that place? Any at all? Because if mummy and daddy bought that place from their colonial gaffe up the coast, least she could do is put up a picture of them.'

He falls silent. 'She has an extra source of income. A big one.'

'There you go.'

'Did she look like she was going out to you?'

'Could have been, why?'

'She was cooking. Dolled up. I've seen her in those pyjamas before, and she wears the wildest shit underneath.'

'By wild, I'm assuming you mean something racy.'

He looks at me like I'm the thicko now. 'Yes, I mean something racy. She's waiting in for someone.'

'You think?'

'She did the same routine for me.'

The penny drops between us.

We both turn in unison to the brownstone and wait.

It only takes about ten minutes, maybe not even eight. A sports car pulls up in a red so cherry it looks like a boiled sweet, and he leaves it at the front in what surely can't be a recognised parking space. Luca elbows me, but I give him one strong shush to let him know I've got it. A large man gets out, walks up the steps and buzzes. He's broad, wearing a dark brown wool coat, in which he has to be absolutely boiling. His head is shaved, but I see the dark stubble of regrowth right across the pate, and his walk is like one of those gym-goers who walk with their arms preposterously out to the side, like their guns are so swollen they can barely move in a way that isn't like a barn door.

'Recognise him?' I whisper to Luca.

'Not sure,' he says.

The man has obviously been granted access sharpish and is in and out of sight quickly.

'You think he'll get a welcome knee to the balls too?' says Luca.

'Not if he's paying the rent.'

We settle in, allowing the endless flow of lycra-swaddled joggers to dwindle until, for the most part, we're alone. After a while, Luca announces his hunger and offers to go and get us some sustenance.

I use the moment to type a text to Carolyn.

HI LOVE. MAD SCHEDULE, BUT SOME CITY. ALL OK. BE IN TOUCH SOON. LOVE TO ALL X

I deliberate over one or three Xs at the end, because I haven't really got used to sentimental text etiquette yet. Come to think of it, I haven't really got used to having anything approaching romance in my life yet. Carolyn and I are one weird combination, but for the most part, it works. She's got two kids from a previous marriage to a gangster – who I killed. She wanted out of the relationship, so at least we've got that going for us. We then had a baby of our own, to really fuck that particular family tree up.

But… I love her. She saved me. Those children mean everything to me. And that's all that really matters.

Text sent, I now cycle through the phone to the anonymous contact storage for William Grosvenor and press call. It's around five in the morning back home, but Grosvenor, as a man of military routine, will understand.

Better than that, when he picks up nearly immediately, his voice is bright, businesslike, and it's clear he's already up and at 'em.

'Sorry for the early call,' I say.

'I'm on my second espresso, this is positively leisurely. How are things across the pond?' His tone… there's an edge.

'Were you expecting any trouble with this?'

'None.'

'If we moved fast?'

'Precisely.'

'Well, I don't think we moved fast enough. Not unless you sent me over here to pick up a picture of a photoshopped American icon flipping the bird.'

'I'm sorry?'

'Never mind.' His bemusement answers the question. I felt it unlikely but had to be sure. Covering all bases, as they say over here. 'The envelope has been switched. On top of that, there's an organised crime element who are intent on getting their hands on it too.'

Grosvenor goes very quiet. Something begins to pull at me. 'Who are they?' he eventually speaks.

'My info here is primarily coming from a Luca Jones III. I believe you know his grandfather.'

'Yes. Luca Jones, the original. He was the man sending the envelope.'

'Right. Well, his grandson tells me that the goons that tried to do us in, they're from the Speroni crime family in Queens.'

Grosvenor is quiet, but I can hear a pen scratch. For some reason, I can picture him writing the words Speroni and Queens in the margins next to *The Times* cryptic crossword, itself almost completed. 'I'll get you all I can on them.'

'We're following a lead right now. A Sarah Banners, who lives at 805 Central Park West. She may have been instrumental in switching the envelope and may know who has it. She's meeting with someone now, who we intend to follow.'

I expect Grosvenor to tell me to ease off, that New York isn't his jurisdiction. But he's quiet – and I've never heard him like this.

'Ben…' he says, and I know it's serious because he's used my real name. 'This is unexpected, but not entirely. This was supposed to be a very simple thing, you taking an envelope from the grandson of an old friend. And I very much apologise that it isn't. You're a man who will understand the gravity of what I'm about to tell you. The contents of the envelope – the real contents of the real envelope – is of national importance. Of international importance. It is absolutely paramount you get it back.'

I'm quiet myself now. Initially, I feel disappointed, led down the old garden path by a superior once more, with too little intel and too much danger at the end of it. I've been here, done that, and swore I'd never do it again. But Grosvenor has always been straight with me. Our relationship is one based on mutual respect. He's never led me on before, and I don't think he would do now.

'Why didn't you tell me this in the beginning?' I ask. 'How vital this was?'

'Because, believe me, the less you knew, the better. The safer you'd be. But that's all by the by now. I need to get out to you myself.'

'The apartment you set me up with is compromised.'

'Already?'

'Already. We can't go back there.'

'Jesus Christ. OK. Keep your phone on – and get that damn envelope. I'll be there as soon as I can.'

And he hangs up. It's not often I'm stunned. But, here we are.

Luca catches my disquiet when he returns holding two cups and two bags, all of which are labelled "Five Guys".

'What?' he says, handing me one of each.

'I'm not sure yet,' I say, which isn't a lie at all.

# CHAPTER ELEVEN

I've been awake twenty-seven whole hours now, but, under a cloudless New York sky, below a canopy of soft sycamores, I tap into an erstwhile forgotten sense of alertness. That part of me, that bit that responds to the word *duty*, has kicked back in, and I'm in that mode. It's like sticking on an old jacket from the back of the cupboard, which might as well have "Here we fucking go" written across the back in impact font, all caps.

Luca's dozing next to me, and I envy the simplicity of his sleep – but only a little. His grandfather, the ex-CIA shadow man, is somehow a big part of this, and I'll only find out if Luca stays on board with me. I used to always prefer working alone, but recent exploits have me seeing the advantages of teamwork – plus, Luca's likeable, too, and quick off the mark, especially in a physical sense.

The front door of the brownstone opens. The broad bald geezer steps out. I check my scuffed G-Shock. 3.05 am.

I imagine Grosvenor sipping a Bloody Mary in a business class lounge at Heathrow Airport as I wake Luca. 'Movement,' I whisper.

He's alert fast, and we watch as our target approaches the Ferrari which elicits an absurdly loud and high pitched *bip-boop* as he approaches. He's in and away.

'I don't feel all that special anymore,' muses Luca with sarcastic hurt.

I nod softly, my mind fixed on the smartphone camera in my hand, filming his exit. I zoom as close as I dare before a mix of noise grain and a sub-par autofocus manages to render the recording useless. Still, I'm amazed at how good these have got. Every damn civilian now carries the kind of tech I'd have killed for in the Middle East and takes it for gleeful granted while they do so.

I watch the Ferrari go, change lanes as it accelerates, then suddenly our target must have put his foot down because the red shape becomes a red dot in about two seconds, and it's only when I can't see it anymore that I hear the horsepower, echoing back down the street.

'Shouldn't we tail him?' Luca says.

'Best of luck with that,' I say as the dot disappears for good. I sit back down and compose a quick email, with that very video as an attachment.

From: T.WEST@NCA.co.uk
To: J.SALIX@NCA.co.uk
Subject: Small favour

Jeremiah,

Can you use your fancy facial recognition stuff on this guy, please? And anything on this number plate would be great. I'm on a thing for our mutual friend, and this would help.

Regards,

TW

TW for Tom West, my alter ego. He'll get the rest. He goes back with Grosvenor as far as I do.

'We need a new base,' I say.

'We could go to my place?' suggests Luca.

'You live in Brooklyn? South-east of here, right?'

'That's right.'

'Nah, let's stay in the city. We need to be in striking distance of whoever that was, and he was distinctly heading north. Any ideas? What do you call it, a suite maybe?'

Before he can answer, my phone starts ringing. I'm immediately surprised to see a long-unused app on my phone has been reactivated. Cryptocall. It was developed by a third-party app developer in the Philippines, back when I used to do off the books jobs for Jeremiah Salix, who I just emailed. He's the head of the National Crime Agency's Organised Crime Command back in the UK, and my day to day boss. We used this bespoke app to stay in contact, deep behind all manner of firewalls and phone-line trickery, when sending me info was considered risky to his position. And he's just reactivated it today. Interesting.

'Give me a minute, Luca,' I say.

'I'll go get us something,' he says, before darting off across the road.

I answer.

'What in God's name are you doing now?' my boss says, his northern English voice put-upon, tired and earthen as ever. His words carry an echo I'm familiar with – often when we've spoken at the NCA offices in Birchwood near Manchester, he's been known to make a dart for the stairwell.

'Is this line still secure?' I ask.

'I'm not having this conversation on a bloody NCA line, you pillock.' I imagine Jeremiah, in his chair as always, his dark brown hair every which way, his stubble still at five o'clock setting even though it's not much after eight in the morning back home. I knew he'd be there. He's always there.

'Did you find anything?' As head of the OCC, he's got access to all sorts of fancy tools in his official capacity, and all sorts of other fancier ones that he's finagled along the way.

'My advice to you would be: hands off.'

'I'm not sure I can do that, but go on.'

'He's about as untouchable as you could think.'

'You know that pisses me off,' I say. Nobody is untouchable. Nobody is beyond account.

'This isn't some expat weed farmer, half-pissed half the time on the Costa Del Suntan – this is international big time.'

'I keep hearing that like it's supposed to mean something.' That old stubbornness is kicking in.

'Don't. Ben, I'm serious.' My first name again. These supposed benefactors are breaking all the rules here. 'In all likelihood, you won't come back to that family of yours if you follow this one.' That's the first time a superior has gone for the heartstrings, but then again, earlier in my life, I didn't have any to pull.

'Then explain it to me, Jeremiah.'

The line is quiet until Jeremiah actually shouts, 'God-fuckin'-DAMMIT.'

I wait till he's calm, then put the phone back to my ear.

'Given your obvious location, I didn't even bother with any domestic UK intelligence networks or databases. The PNC, PND, even Holmes would all be useless. I put him straight into the Interpol mainframe and got a big direct hit. Following my nose, I popped him into Europol's equivalent, and wham, a massive deluge.'

'Go on.'

'Goes by Malinki. Russian. Ex-KGB, ex-FSB, mercenary for hire, but only for hire to one office. The one at the Kremlin.'

'You're shitting me.'

'Direct line to the Russian president.'

My heart takes a few big pops. This guy is a Russian operative – possibly with a document of national importance, relating to Britain's domestic security? Jesus. 'Do you have any detail for him?'

'Ben, I'm not going to—'

'This isn't the time for smacking my arse, Jeremiah. Grosvenor says this is vital, and the safety of our country could well be at stake.'

'I hate it when you do this.'

'Have you got any New York addresses for him? Yes or no, or do I have to steal a car as well?'

The line, all three and a half thousand miles of it, is dead. Until—

'The US Marshalls have him holed up in Greenville, Kemper Street, about twenty minutes north of Manhattan, as part of a CIA mandate.'

'The CIA!'

'He's on the records as a government informant. Which means he's on President Connor's payroll too.'

'What the hell?' The idea that he's passing information between both the American and Russian presidencies is both terrifying and all too realistic.

'He's either playing both sides or, as we have suspected for some time, those two are the same side these days.'

Jesus Christ. This is going places. Serious places.

'Send me that address, Jeremiah. And try to forget we had this conversation.'

'Oh yes, of course. I'll do my best. And be careful, you fucking idiot.'

He hangs up, just as Luca reappears.

'I got us a suite over on West 60th. The Mandarin Oriental.'

I can't help my surprise, and he catches it.

'You said suite; we've got one of the best suites in town! You're gonna have to pay, by the way.'

'When I said we need a bolthole, I didn't necessarily mean one with five stars.'

'I was doing what you said!'

I shake my head. 'Forget it. We need a car. Have you got a car?'

'Yeah, I've got one at home.'

'And like what everyone is told about your average God-fearing Americans back in Europe, you have a gun, yes?' Luca clearly doesn't want to conform, but he nods slowly. 'Go and get both. Meet me outside the Mandarin in an hour. We need to make a house call.'

'You're ex-military, aren't you – is that what makes you insufferable?'

'Most likely, now get to it. I'm going to go and see what I'm apparently paying for.'

# SINCLAIR

For a young man who grew up in an English village where the biggest building was the crooked church steeple, itself visible from every north-facing residence window, a skyscraper was a big damn deal. Sinclair wasn't sure whether it was the sheer height of the one he was looking at that got him, or the fact that immediately next to it, there was a construction site over which hung a vast billboard showing an artist's depiction of an even bigger one. And there was one on the other side of the street too, while they'd already passed two more just moments ago. What was this place? How were they doing it?

He'd heard America was the land of opportunity. Elvis himself had sung that he was 'riding the rainbow, hitting the highway to happiness'. Sinclair could empathise, as they swept along a wide street in a car with chrome bumpers so polished he could see himself in them. The colours burst from every street corner and the sky was so blue you could swim in it. It was the scale that did it. Everything was bigger here, simply because it could be. Everything was taken to the furthest point permissible. Here the only boundary you could face was the point at which you could imagine no further. Opportunity, in its purest definition.

Sinclair was in the back of a Buick Special which couldn't be more than a year old. It was a convertible, in a spotless off-white that resembled coffee creamer, and it rumbled along with the authority and confidence of fine engineering. Picked up at the airport by a guy in sunglasses and a Trilby holding up a cigarette and a sign, the latter of which had the young man's name written on it, followed by the usual quick identity check on both sides, Sinclair went along for the ride in every sense.

There was no urgency to the drive, and for a while, they were just boys on a jaunt. Small talk was free and easy.

'Where've you come in from, kid?' asked the man, his neck craned slightly over his shoulder as if he could throw his words like salt for luck.

'Plane in from Heathrow,' replied Sinclair.

'Cigarette?' asked the man. 'You got Marlboros across the pond yet?'

'I don't think so.'

'Here,' said the driver, who took one with his lips then tossed the pack onto the back seat. 'Keep 'em, they'll change your life.'

'Thanks,' Sinclair said, mirroring the man's actions before swapping the packet of Benson & Hedges in his shirt sleeve for the far more exotic promise of the white and red packet he'd just been given.

They moved from the grey shadows on the immaculate pavements of downtown, out into broad sunshine and leaning palms. Sinclair thought the new cigarette he was trying was all kinds of cool, as they cruised a highway alongside other showroom examples he'd never seen before. He tried to catch the names on the lids of the boots. Trunks, he reminded himself. Cadillac, Buick, Ford, Pontiac, something wrought and beautiful called a Chevrolet Camaro…

The car slowed and pulled into a roadside motel which had a huge sign overhanging it in silver and orange paint, reading The Sun Trap Motel. It was two stories high, in an L-shape with a pool in the middle, and it looked like a party was going on. The smell of sizzling meat wafted over to Sinclair as they parked up, but it wasn't the bad kind he'd experienced too many times before. He'd heard about these barbecues, this outdoor practice of grilling meat that hadn't caught on at home at all yet. But then again, back home they didn't quite get this enormous sunlight under which to cook.

'They're so predictable,' said the driver, hoisting himself from the car. 'Give them a little sunshine and it's runway season. The boys in your new unit.'

Sinclair followed the driver's gaze to the pool area, where young guys were sat at some bamboo-lined shed that had a bar in it, while girls flittered in and around. One or two of the men looked like soldiers, like him, all lithe, coiled muscle angle-poised, ready for hurt mode. Others didn't, but they appeared to regard each other as equals.

'You go over and introduce yourself, grab a beer, and I'll go inside and make the arrangements,' said the driver, who then didn't wait for any discussion on the matter.

As he looked, the guys at the makeshift bar, having noticed their arrival, offered a wave. One even held his head high and beckoned Sinclair over. Sinclair did as he was told and passed through the small iron gate into the pool complex. There were high fives, handshakes, and before he knew what had happened, he had a beer in his hand and had been nicknamed Brit Brando because of the damn t-shirt. All of this would work for him.

'I'm Luca,' said the guy next to him, tilting the neck of the Bud bottle he was holding in Sinclair's direction, which he met with his own in a solid clink.

'Sinclair,' he said.

'Welcome to heaven.'

# CHAPTER TWELVE

Luca is precise. No sooner have I stepped out of the lobby than I see him parked on the other side of the street in a bona fide crap-mobile. A dark brown Lincoln with rust spots that make the colourway look poodle-like.

Before long, we're off up the road alongside Central Park, scooting past the duplicitous Sarah's brownstone on the left as the Lincoln runs with surprising smoothness and acceleration and the dash clock reads 04:30. It's no red Ferrari tiny-manhood-substitute, but it will certainly make the drive north no problem – which had been my initial concern when I first saw it.

We stay quiet, no words needed for now, the growing gravity of the situation beginning to weigh ever heavier, and before long, we are out of the city grid and cruising through suburbs. Some are rundown, their wooden fasciae spotted with green mould, the corners of the windows fogged and dirty, the yards out front with grass left long. But that slowly changes, and the market goes noticeably up. Colonial style pillars start to appear on the odd house. They begin to be made of stone and brick, the entire landscape well-manicured and the epitome of leafy, and as we turn onto Kemper Street, as Jeremiah had instructed, we see the red Ferrari almost immediately.

It's parked up next to a stunning home, the kind that definitely supports the notion that the resident might be in receipt of not one but two government-sized cheques. The pillars are in place, all four of them this time, like soldiers guarding the front door, which is a quaint light blue with a heavy iron knocker. The windows are framed by shutters in that same soft blue, and the lawn is the perfect length for wiggling your toes in. A sprinkler shushes the cicadas, if they are even there at all. You'd get a good night's sleep here.

'The gun,' I say to Luca with my hand outstretched, my eyes never leaving the house.

'It's my—' he starts to protest, but I cut him off.

'You're staying in the car, so you'll have no need for it. Hand it over.'

'I'm coming in.' He looks sure of himself, so I waste no time in denting it.

'Categorically, you're not. There's no discussion to be had. You don't want to go in there against some Russian untouchable and neither do I. But I've got so many more hangovers from my back-catalogue of grim situations, while you're a young pen pusher with your whole life ahead of you. Give me the gun so I can sort this out and take a step towards getting this all over and done with.'

'You're an ass,' he says, pointing at the dashboard. I follow his finger – the glove compartment by my knees. On opening it, I find a pistol that looks old but well-maintained – ish. A Luger. Long barrel, black metal, wooden grip. I haven't held one of these before, and as I take it in my hand, the weight of the handle settling into my curved palm, I realise how heavy it is – a comforting heavy.

'Another of grandpa's?'

'No, this is me – I'm a fan of the classics.'

I check the sight. 'No arguing on this occasion.'

'Would make a welcome change.'

I open the door and step out into the cool night. 'Keep an eye out. You see anything out of the ordinary, two pips on the horn.'

'Yes, Captain.' He gives me a mock salute then looks out the windshield with a sigh, like a kid who's been told to wait in the car.

I stick to the path and walk only on the lighter parts of the pavement, the dry bits where the sprinklers can't reach. I walk up to the door and spot a small lizard scurry along the stone flags ahead of me. That's a new one on me.

The lights are off inside, and our man has clearly gone to bed. I need to work out if he's alone – for all I know he could have a wife and kids in there, though I extremely doubt it. The front garden is immaculate, no sign of any untidy offspring, and the house is devoid of any kind of outside decoration, save for the elegant lines of expensive architecture. Without meaning to adhere to the obvious stereotype of the phrase, the house looks like it could use a woman's touch.

The porch has two steps up. Both of which are wooden. Too much chance of a wayward creak with those. I don't need to mask my sound too much because of the swish of the sprinklers, but I take it cautiously, nevertheless. So, I stay low and trace the outline of the house, avoiding windows and the moonlight, which is so bright out here away from the light flooding upward over the city. As I get around the gable end, after one last glance at the car and Luca, I notice that one of the windows on the side of the property is open. I'd read about this of course. It's

70

pop-culture folklore, windows being left open in areas deemed too safe for crime. It has always struck me as weird and stupid, a thought which echoes all the louder as I hoist myself up over a bed of some weedy looking ferny things and in through the window, kicking off my shoes as I go, leaving them to land softly on the grass.

Remembering the steps at the front door, I adjust trajectory for a shorter drop than the climb and lower myself easily into a lounge. It's spotless, a show home. The floor is a polished wood which bounces fragments of moonlight. A couch and two armchairs face each other in silent acknowledgement, while a flatscreen rounds off that quarter, and a dark wood desk sits behind in the opposite corner. There's no bric-a-brac, no chintzy touches, no hint of any true character. There isn't even a proper indentation on any of the seats where an arse has regularly sat. It looks staged – and weird.

I pad through in my socks, but the sterility of the room kicks off a doubt which has me pulling the Luger out. Barrel up, eyes scanning, I check the desk. No laptop on top, no computer tower beneath. No drawers. No papers. I can't even see a pen. Nothing to even investigate, never mind root through. My senses tighten, sharpen, pull focus.

The living room has no door, merely an arch leading into the hall, which I take. The floor is more eager, spotless wood, but the stairs to my left are carpeted. Eyes up and rotating around the space above me, I climb.

White balustrades as the stairs spin a one-eighty onto a landing. A plant stands off to one side, some wilted thing which looks like a deflated balloon version of itself. The one sign of life in the house and it's dead with neglect.

This place is barely lived in.

The landing has four doors to choose from. I want to get it right first go, so I listen at each in turn. There isn't something I can put my finger on, moreover, it's a skill you get from years of breaking down doors to drag people out, but I know he's behind door two.

The handle opens with greased ease, and I enter the room.

# CHAPTER THIRTEEN

The bedroom is all white, two windows overlooking the street beyond, and I spy, in the expansive bed, the humped outline of a large man. The moonlight that's been guiding me steps in once more and pings off his shaved head. It's our man, breathing low and rhythmically. Nobody's with him.

I'm careful, because I don't know who I'm dealing with. Usually, those in government employed at the level we are talking about aren't your run of the mill dogsbodies. These spots are usually only given to elite operatives, so with that in mind, I'm cautious as all hell.

It's a good job too, because beneath his pillow is a loaded Glock, which I take. And under the other pillow on the opposite side of the bed is a knife you could fillet a bear with. As I pull it out, the man wakes, and a hand grips my wrist with hydraulic-like pressure.

'There's a Luger four inches from your temple, comrade,' I say. 'Best let the hand go.'

He does, then lays back on the bed. He makes a bad go of checking for the pistol.

'It's here,' I say, wiggling the little finger on my left hand which, while training the Luger with the rest of it, dangles the Glock upside down below it by the trigger guard. 'This would usually knock my aim off, but at this range, I don't think it'd be a problem.'

'It's not here,' he says immediately, his accent thick with sleep and eastern vowels.

'I haven't even asked you yet.'

'The envelope is already gone. And before you say, I don't know what is in there.'

Dammit. 'Where is it?'

He seems to take stock of me for a moment, and his immense shoulders, with their curving tribal style tattoos, release tension. 'You are British?' I stay quiet, and he smiles. It's a flash of perfect teeth, a further small reminder of the high wage packet they've got him on. 'The British involved too…' he muses aloud.

'Where is it, Malinki?'

'And the British are informed.'

'If you don't have it, you don't really need to be alive, do you?' I click the hammer on the Luger right back, and it sounds like a snapped tibia in the sparse room.

Malinki puts his hands out in front of him. 'Easy, man.'

'Is there a reason you need to be alive at this point, Malinki? There any reason to keep you breathing?'

'Lots of reasons, man. Lots of reasons.'

He's very cool for a man with a bullet primed for his forehead, but that's what you'd expect from someone who sleeps with knives and guns in his bed.

'Give me one. And make it a good one because I've got an envelope to track down.'

'I've seen a really good video of the president with lots of prostitutes in the back room of a famous fast-food restaurant.'

'I'm not the *National Enquirer*.' Although I'd love to see that video get out. 'Ten seconds.'

'This is a nice neighbourhood. And that Luger is too big for it. We have neighbourhood watch, and they are very good at keeping their eyes and ears open.'

'None of you are that great, plus I didn't catch the attack dogs when I climbed in here.'

'But still, they'll hear that.'

And there it is. Eureka and irony. The single piece of decorative touch that this place possesses is a throw cushion in purple that's resting by my feet, presumably tossed on the floor when Malinki got in. In one fluid motion, I grab it, press it against the outline of Malinki's right knee beneath the sheets, and press the Luger's barrel deep into it. Instant suppression.

'They might miss this though,' I say.

Malinki's eyes widen, the balance fully swung.

'The hand-off was very simple,' he suddenly gushes. 'Nothing complicated.'

'The girl. Sarah. Where does she fit in?'

'She took it. Held onto it. I picked it up tonight.'

'Tonight?' Sarah. She had it the whole time we were there. It was right under our noses. 'The girl's in on it?'

'No.' He mustn't like the way my jaw has tightened because he's started spouting. 'She's a civilian. I've spent a long time... turning her.'

This Russian has a mole in the CIA, albeit not at the highest level. That said, if Jeremiah's intel is to be believed, the Russians could well have a great big mole in the Oval Office, so I shouldn't be surprised. But, remembering how adeptly Sarah played us tonight – I mean, I had no inkling she wasn't telling the truth – and the venom precision with which she assaulted Luca's bollocks, I wouldn't like to be in Malinki's shoes when she finds out she got played.

'Does she often skim mail for you?'

'She's been in position for a day just like today.'

'Think very carefully about this next question. Where is it now?'

'A man met me after.'

'Already?'

'Yes, yes. A gas station on the way back.'

Jesus Christ. We may have passed whoever had it en route to this wild goose chase. I thought it'd be too late at night for anything like that – which only serves to underline its importance once more.

'Who did you give it to?'

'I haven't met him before.'

'Oh, come on, Malinki.'

'I'm serious, I've never seen him. He's not one of the usual guys.'

'And you're a usual guy, aren't you?'

'Yes, yes.'

'What is it you actually do, Malinki?'

'Nothing, I'm a message boy, that's it.'

I can see Malinki's worked up. But I can also see that he is lying.

I move the cushion up to his gut and press down hard with the gun, so that he can feel the pointy end next to his belly button, right through the cushion.

'My instructions, Malinki, are to kill you.' They aren't.

He lets out one big, shaky breath that I catch an unwelcome whiff of. That garlic from Sarah's place.

'It literally won't touch my conscience in any way to pull this trigger.' It won't. I don't think.

His hands go up from his sides.

'Gut shots are slow and nasty.' They are. I know that only too well. 'Especially when the velocity is compromised by suppression. A bullet from here will worm its way in nice and slow and you'll feel every single second of it.' I've got no idea about that, but it sounds suitably awful.

'I'm a utility man. Freelance. Mercenary. Nayemnik.'

'For whoever pays the best?'

'Yes.'

'For both sides?'

'For any side.'

'So who hired you to get the envelope?'

'These orders are from my usual Washington guy.'

Washington. 'Was he the guy who met you here tonight?'

'Yes.'

'And who is he?'

'He's a regular.'

'Who does he work for?'

'I don't know. Not my job to know.'

Washington. 'But he's from the Capitol, you must have some idea.'

'I don't, I'm telling you.'

He's telling me all right. And for the first time I can see for sure it is the truth.

Does this guy really not know who he actually works for and answers to? Does he genuinely not know that he is protected by the governments of two of the world's biggest superpowers?

'Where can I find him?'

Before I can finish the sentence, his hands are moving fast. From behind his head, forward to me – and I can see the barrel swinging down to face me. Idiot, Ben. He must have had another firearm hidden behind the headboard. In the darkness, I missed it.

I drop my head as the gun fires, the crack of the report deafening and, while inches from my left ear, disorientating. The bullet must have caught my earlobe because despite it ringing, it feels like a hot razor has just been taken to it.

I throw myself forward, jamming my forearm into Malinki's throat and pushing the Luger barrel into his eye. 'The neighbourhood will be up now, so we don't have to worry about being quiet,' I hiss. I can feel his throat gasping for air beneath my arm.

'I don't know for sure, but he's government. Highest level, Oval Office – Secret Service.'

Secret Service. The president's own protection detail, now working with a Russian operative to reclaim – what?

'You must know how to contact him.'

'He contacts me.'

'Then how does he pay you?'

'Cash.'

An idea. 'Where's the cash?'

'You're a common thief now?'

I push the Luger into his eye, hard, and he screams. A few drops of blood leak from beneath the barrel point and slip down his cheek. It looks like an oily tear in the bleak blue light.

'There!' he gasps, pointing at the bedside table. I release my grip on his throat to open the drawer, and sure enough, there on the top is a fat white envelope. I take it, and as soon as my fingers curl around the edges and notice the obscene thickness of it, I sense movement, bad intentions, decisive action, and I clock the lamp swinging towards my head from the right. I can't avoid it hitting me, but I can avoid it giving Malinki the upper hand.

The barrel still in his eye, I pull the trigger – just as the lamp he'd managed to swing smashes against my skull.

It hurts, but not as much as I thought it would since it broke on impact, jagged porcelain shards littering the bedspread. I take a second to let the blow pass, and as soon as my head isn't swimming, I open my eyes again.

Malinki isn't going to be doing much for anybody anymore. But this is a pretty distinctive gun, and probably very traceable. Not many murders take place in the New York suburbs with a '60s Luger, I'd wager.

I've got to move fast.

The barrel still in Mailnki's eye, I shift him to the right. The headboard is plastered in all sorts of bad red and even worse grey, but I find the bullet easily, impacted right into the wood. In the bedside drawer, I find a pen at last, and I use it to prise the impacted bullet out. Carefully I take the extra gun he'd had behind the headboard and put it back in his hand – before turning the hand around and firing it point-blank into the wood. If anyone heard, there'll be some debate about the number of shots, but I'm hoping this looks enough like a suicide not to draw too much scrutiny. A fresh bullet now in the wood, I step back to look at the scene. To a casual eye, it looks like poor Malinki just had enough and blew his own brains out – he just needed a few goes to get it right.

I'm probably thinking too much about this, and the more it courses my mind, the more my confidence increases that this won't make the news with any scrutiny – because to do so would admit the existence of an American-Russian spy. I can't imagine such news would be popular on either side of the divide.

I quickly leave the house, back out the rear side window to pop my shoes on, the Luger, the bullet and the package of cash in my pockets. As I round the side of the house, I catch sight of someone in a dressing gown ringing the doorbell, and freeze. Neighbourhood watch. Peeking round, I see it's a middle-aged man with glasses and slippers on, and behind him the road is empty. Luca and the crapmobile – both gone.

The sky takes its first orange prompts of daylight, and I'm wondering how the hell I'm going to get out of here when the sun suddenly flashes. I think my eyes deceive me when it happens again. Turning to where it's most bright, I see it's not flashing at all – moreover, it's Luca on the road behind the house, flashing his headlights at me.

You fucking beauty.

I jag between houses to run to him as the good old Neighbourhood Watchman starts banging loudly on the front door of poor Malinki's house.

# CHAPTER FOURTEEN

The sun streams in through the plate-glass windows, the stunning day promised by the dawn sun in Westchester having burst into full fruition over Central Park below. I sit at the window of my Mandarin room, in a pleasingly firm armchair (I hate that saggy shite that near enough drops you down on your arse, knees up by your ears), overlooking the junction at the south-west corner of Central Park, which has a grand metal globe perched right on its roundabout. People are everywhere, dressed for a hot day, as the treetops of the park roll back for as far as I can see. I sip coffee, a brew so rich I can feel it wobble my stomach, and just watch.

I can't deny it – I'm falling in love with this city.

The suite Luca arranged has a connecting living room between two separate en suite rooms, both of which are big enough to accommodate a family of ten. Any bugbears I had about wanting to pay for it were immediately dispelled when I saw Malinki's envelope was stuffed with hundreds. So this suite can be on the generosity of whoever saw fit to hire him.

I saved the note on top though. Put it to one side. It sits on the occasional table next to my coffee cup.

It's 8.00 am, give or take, and when we got back, I gave myself an hour of sleep. Somehow, that has given me backbone and respite. I'm ready to go. It's afternoon in the UK, and I need to get some calls moving. Plus, Grosvenor should be well on his way by now.

The door clicks behind me, over my left shoulder, and a voice follows immediately. 'Goddammit, do we really have to get up now?'

'Do you want me to answer that?' I'd knocked on Luca's door minutes earlier and told him we were leaving in five. 'I need you to run out and get me a couple of things while I make some calls.'

'What like?'

'Fingerprinting stuff. This note here was the top one in the package. When you put a wedge of notes in an envelope, I imagine that nine times out of ten, your thumbprint is on the top one. If we're going to get that envelope back to the older gentlemen in our lives, we need to find out whose print it is.'

'You got any more of that coffee?'

My patience is running thin already this morning, and I uncharacteristically offer a rare prickle. 'You really need a pick-me-up at a time like this?'

'It'll only take a second.'

The coffee grinder on the bureau against the back wall is stocked full of beans, and Luca goes over and starts grinding away. He keeps grinding, and I turn to face him. Grinding and grinding. I look at him, and I can't quite stop my frustration beginning to show. Every telly programme shows Americans devoted to coffee in the mornings, but this is plain ridiculous. He goes for one huge grinding sprint, really putting his back into it, and the whirring gargle of the machine has me ready to snap.

'Enough,' I command.

He stops and takes his cup from the grinder platform. He holds his hand up by way of apology and joins me – then tips the entirety of the coffee cup on the banknote.

'You fucking clown!' I shout, before I see that it is finely crushed dark powder covering the note.

'Calm down, Captain,' he says as he gets on his haunches and ever so gently blows across the surface of the note. More and more, sweeping the fine particles away to the floor, floating off like gothic dust motes in the sun shafts.

'No chance,' I whisper as, plain as day, a crystal-clear black fingerprint appears just left of centre on the hundred-dollar bill, right next to Ben Franklin's face. 'I apologise.'

'Not just a pretty face and a sub-five-second forty metres,' he says while taking his phone and snapping a picture of it.

'Photoscanner will have this as a PDF in a jiffy… and voila.' He turns the screen around, and it's there. A perfect black fingerprint, every whorl visible and canyon clear. 'So, who are we sending it to?'

'You're a genius, Luca,' is all I can say.

'Can I get an actual coffee now?'

'Be my guest.'

# CHAPTER FIFTEEN

The fingerprint sent to Jeremiah, I asked Luca one more thing. He looked at me like I was insane, told me I was on my own, but gave me an address and a luck-loaded pat on the back. As I sit in the taxi en route, I ruminate that it's not really an address he's given me, but a junction. He said if I show my face there, I'll know where to go.

He let me keep hold of the Luger. I'm getting kind of attached to it now, so much so, I might make him an offer when all is said and done.

It becomes apparent from my spot in the back of the yellow cab that we are heading to a different part of the New York map entirely, having crossed a bridge that had far less glamour than the one I came in on yesterday (how is that yesterday?) and far more trips whizzing by underneath it. It's cool, and a feat of engineering inspired by lack of space that you don't see too much of back home in jolly old England. Once over the bridge, it's different. I can feel the city hulking behind me, stretching out like a beached whale made of jagged points, while the homes here are altogether more modest.

'How close do you want me to get?' asks the woman up front, her bindi I see in the mirror another reminder of the vast cultural sea this city floats on. She looked at me with concern when I told her where I wanted to go and shook her head softly. Maybe she knows where I'm going and who I'm going to try to see. Maybe she thinks I'm one of them.

'Close as possible if that's OK?' I reply.

'How about I drop you two blocks down and you can walk up, is that OK with you?' There's a knowing smile there, the raised corners of which are the only thing I can see in the rear-view mirror.

'That'll do fine, as long as you point me in the right direction.'

The car abruptly pulls to a stop on the side of the road, outside a convenience store and its fruit stalls which push out onto the pavement. I smell coffee and fried onions. And paprika.

'Two blocks straight ahead. You see the house with the green roof?'

Up ahead, sure enough, visible through the haze rising from the bonnet, there's a townhouse on a corner with a green roof. It's a soft mint ice cream green.

'Yes, I can see it.'

'Stand on that corner and you'll suddenly find yourself very popular.'

'Thank you.' I pay and get out, and as soon as the car door clangs shut, the taxi is pulling a U-turn right across the middle of the road. I watch it go.

Those onions have got my taste buds singing, so I drop into the supermarket. It's one of those corner shops that have every-thing – and in this case absolutely everything. I can see mobile phones, ammunition, rotisserie chicken and sanitary products – and that's just on one side. Next to the counter, behind which is a man and wife pair who look baked and worn into their roles as the marital owners of a Queens convenience store, there is a street food stand with a hot plate.

'Can I have whatever your special is, and a cup of tea, please – in a soft drink cup.'

The man stands to attend to my order. 'Earl Grey, m'lord?' he says in a mock aristocratic voice, before looking at me more questioningly. 'In a soda cup?'

'Breakfast tea if you've got it, Jeeves, and yes, his Lordship likes to sip in comfort.'

Moments later, I'm walking to the green-roofed house chewing on some spiced chicken wrap thing which is the absolute business, carrying a very hot drinks cup by the rim – and as I approach the corner, I immediately see how the atmosphere changes. There're no shop fronts on this corner, the residences on each side well maintained. The vibe is different too – not the visual one, but the airborne one, the one that reflects that things are going on between the lines.

There's a street sign opposite showing that this is where Booth (which I was on) is run through by Montauk. I lean against its metal, chew and let my eyes wander.

Each building on the respective corners faces out centrally. All the shutters are down on each window, despite their clean and loved appearance. Cars happily pass through the junction, but none of them stop. In fact, there're none parked on any side of the street, the nearest being much further along, almost the distance to where my nervous taxi driver dropped me off moments ago.

It's clear, no matter how you look at it, that the people round here give this junction a wide birth indeed.

A door opens behind my left ear, and I keep still. Luca was right – it didn't take long. It's the mint house, and I can hear footsteps. Three sets dropping down the short porch steps I can't see but know are there – no, four.

One more bite of chicken.

They appear in front of me, in a line. Three men, a disparate group if ever there was one, and at the front, fists tight and white, that big ox, with plasters all over his face. Brutoli.

'How's the knee, Michael?' I ask. He's seething, specks of spittle escaping through his teeth. 'I'd like to speak to whoever's on the other end of your leash.'

'Fuck you. I mean it, *fuck you*,' Brutoli spits.

'Before we all fall out, I don't have what you're looking for, but I have information. So, I've got a proposal.'

Nobody speaks a word. I assume they're considering my words.

'Which of the four of you is best placed to make a decision? Come on, gents, I haven't got all day. Places to go, people to see and all that.'

The man next to Brutoli juts his chin out. 'I am.' I don't recognise him.

'You in charge here?'

'Right this second, yeah.'

From the non-committal back up around him, I can tell that might not be the complete story. Good. 'OK then, well, a contest. You give me face time with the decision-maker around here – and I don't mean you, I'm talking the real big boss – if I can get through Michael here. Does that sound fair?'

Brutoli smacks one fist into the other. Good God, the macho bollocks works everywhere.

'You're on,' says the man.

Brutoli wastes no time in charging me, and his approach is so big, so fast, so overwhelming, he's like the onset of a very sudden eclipse.

'Hold my drink,' I say and toss the cup up to the onrushing Brutoli. Seeing it's a soft drink container with a straw in the top, he goes to catch it – and as soon as his fingers touch the thin cardboard, he yelps in confusion and sudden pain, palm scolded.

Misdirection and small advantages are everything in a close-quarters fight – especially against someone with a big physical edge – and at the end of the day, nobody likes their fingertips burned.

I step forward just seconds behind the cup and front kick it, crushing the cup and fingers against his immense chest, causing the boiled liquid to spray up and out the top, all over his face. Poor bloke – glass one day, hot tea the next, he's never getting a break.

He throws his eyes up and his palms go to his face, dazed – then I smash the butt of the Luger down, right on top of his cranium. Like a fat tree, he crumbles, unconscious.

I step round him and hand the supposed leader the gun. 'I'll need this back once I've seen him.'

'Her,' he says, still looking at the big man at his feet. 'Once you've seen her.'

'She inside then?'

'After you, troublemaker.'

I walk up the steps to the mint house, as the two other men try to scrape Brutoli off the asphalt.

# CHAPTER SIXTEEN

It always feels weirds conducting a meeting of great tension in a family home. Something off-putting about high tension while surrounded by pictures of grinning toothless kids and crap bowl cuts.

'Straight through,' says the guy behind me. 'I'm Gus.'

'Hi Gus,' I say, following his outstretched palm.

The kitchen door is ahead. No lights are on in the hallway, but it feels hot and close with some fragrance. No, not a fragrance, a kind of slow-cooked odour. Aftershave – cologne. And not of the high-end variety.

The kitchen door swings open with the soundlessness of constant use, and again, it's the family home vibe that feels off-kilter.

A woman sits at the table, and she genuinely reminds me of an aunt of mine who I haven't see in twenty years. She's in light blue jeans, brown boat shoes and a flannel shirt and sporting a short haircut with blond highlights that betray dark grey roots. Wide framed bifocal glasses complete a very normal, very unassuming look.

'Good morning,' I say, unsure of what else to say.

She doesn't look up from the newspaper she seems intent

on, but I get the feeling it's a hasty prop rather than anything else. 'I used to worry about Michael, all the time.' The voice is a high-pitched smirk through lips so pursed it almost comes out as a whistle. 'Then, when I realised I couldn't settle him down, couldn't control him, I just gave up. The injuries are constant, but they're always quite manageable for a big boy like him. But you, you nasty, limey shitwipe, you're a bad fuckin' sort.' Ah, she's his mother – but how she fired that thing out of her tiny frame, I'll never know.

'It's always the big ones that try to start something – and I've always been happy to finish things on their behalf.'

'A smart fucker too,' she says, finally looking up. She ain't your typical family figure. Her gaze is sub-zero, ice down her veins and lizards up your back.

'Who am I speaking with?' I say.

It's not a pleasant smile, the one that she gives me. 'You came into my home, and you don't even have a fuckin' clue, do you…'

I don't answer, just keep it straight and firm.

'A rare bad fuckin' sort.' If hate had a look, it would be this thing she offers me.

'You tried to kill me and my friend last night. I'd like to know why.'

'Oh, it's the usual stuff, don't flatter yourself. You have something I want, you piss me off, I tend to try to put a full stop to it. You ain't the first and you ain't the last.'

'And I bet none of them not only got away but fucked up your big baby and came back to knock on your door.'

She looks at me like I just shat on the carpet but managed to spell my name with the output. Disapproving, but oddly entertained. 'You've got me there.'

'Why did you want the envelope? And just to be clear, I don't have it.'

'Oh, I know you don't have it. We were all played like fiddles, we were one big string section running around south Manhattan. You wouldn't be here otherwise.' She gestures to another seat at the table, and I take it, the legs squeaking on the lino below my feet.

'So why do you want it?'

'Let me ask, why do you want it?'

'God's honest truth, hand on heart and hope to die, but not today – I don't know. I was sent over here to pick it up. It wasn't supposed to be this much fun.'

She looks at me as if trying to gauge the swing of my honesty. I place my palms on the slightly sticky, thick rubber table cover – the kind of thing you'd do jigsaws on.

'Francesca Speroni,' she says, offering a hand. Her face hasn't thawed a centigrade, so it's strange to accept a handshake from someone who quite plainly doesn't like you. In the interests of self-preservation, I take it. 'I'm feeling there could be some mutual interests here, so let's look at it that way. It'd be a bit more civilised. Gus! Get in here and get that lemon cake out the refrigerator. It's about time for – what do you limeys call it – elevenses?'

'I could go for something…' I play along.

Gus comes in and starts fussing with plates. He clearly doesn't like me very much either by the way he thunks a side plate down in front of me.

'Gus is my youngest,' Francesca says, waving a hand at him as he passes. 'He's a good boy, does as he's told. Looks after his mama.'

91

Gus interjects. 'He's on the steps, nursing a headache.'

'Jesus fuckin' Christ, the amount of times that boy has sat on those steps with a headache,' Francesca says, shaking her own cranium. 'Obviously, as the biggest, and because you don't get much bigger than him, he does the heavy stuff. He's not the cerebral type, not like Gus here.'

'You had two boys?' I ask as a wedge of lemon drizzle cake the size of a man's shoe is dropped onto my plate.

'I had four boys total that made it. Lost two more, and a girl.'

'Hazards of the profession?'

'Miscarriages.'

'I'm sorry to hear that. We just had a boy of our own, he's getting on for seven months now.'

'How fuckin' lovely. The envelope. What do you know?'

I'm not sharing anything of real importance with this woman, but a little could bring me a lot in return.

'I know there're a lot of people who want it. You weren't the only people going after it last night,' I say.

'How many?'

'Well, there were you guys at the bar and our apartment—'

'I didn't send anyone to your apartment.'

That genuinely surprises me. 'You didn't?'

'Michael and Gus followed you from that shithole bar to the other one. When things got heated, that's when they split.'

'Then there was a third party I didn't even see – who came to our apartment, which was supposed to be completely secure, and managed to get in. Fired shots at us.'

'Interesting.'

'Then there's another one, who we think orchestrated the

switch of the envelopes in the first place. He's got more of a political flavour.'

'OK, and what happened to him?'

I remember the headboard with all that red and grey stuff. 'He's not troubling any of us anymore, and he doesn't have it either.'

She stares at me as if assessing me inside out and upside down, as well as every inflexion of the words I've just said. It was all the truth, so I have nothing to worry about. 'And who do you work for?' she finally asks.

I open my mouth, but nothing seems to come out.

Francesca Speroni doesn't exhibit the same reticence. 'You're cucumber cool and you sound like James Bond. You're British government.' She waves a fork at me, cake crumbs spraying.

I look hard at her, try to assess what I can glimpse of her motives. What truth is to be had in there? All I see is enjoyment. Revelry. She's rising to this game. There's something big going on and she wants in.

I'm not government. The British government, aside from the very man who sent me, would have kittens and shit their pants immediately after if they knew I was here. But... maybe it wouldn't be so bad to let her believe what she wants to believe? I lower my eyes as if she's right, while never committing. I'm on my own here, and God knows what's coming my way, but the last thing I want to do is incriminate myself in any way by swanning about pretending to be an operative working for the British government.

Then... it hits me. What if I am? What if Grosvenor is acting on behalf of the establishment? What if I'm an expendable pawn, a number that doesn't correspond to any spreadsheet. What if they had a problem but needed someone to sort it off the books. What if Grosvenor put his hands up in some dark meeting room of Westminster, secreted far away from the House of Commons, and said he knew a guy? Was this the reason he gave me that second chance, all those months ago?

No… he wouldn't do that to me. Plus, acknowledging I exist would plummet him directly into the shit.

'So what do our colonial forebears want with this envelope?' Too late, the ruse is running.

'No idea. I do as I'm told.'

'Do you always do as you're told?'

'No.'

'If you ever get bored of yes sir, no sir, three bags full sir, I could use hands like yours.'

'I'm not for sale.'

'Men like you never are, until they're sat in your kitchen eating lemon cake.'

All I can do is chew the giant wedge I spooned into my mouth as she speaks. I take too long to compose myself, which amuses Speroni a great deal. 'What is it that a woman of your' – I cast my eyes around the room and alight on Gus for just a second – 'industry and resources would want with this envelope?'

'We all answer to somebody. And money is money.'

'OK, so who's financing it?'

'You'd be surprised.'

'I really wouldn't. The other guy, the one that's no longer an issue; it seems he handed it off to the Secret Service. Can you compete with that?'

To my amazement, that actually stuns her. After a moment's

silence, as she blinks the information through a couple of times, processing it, she chuffs out a solitary *huh*.

'Quid pro quo. What do you know?'

'My cheques are signed by the FBI. I mean, I wasn't going to tell you, a good upstanding American citizen like myself, but…' She looks away and puts a hand under her chin.

'Why would two separate governmental agencies go their own ways, using their own illicit means, to get their hands on something – unbeknownst to and independent of each other?' Let alone the unspoken notion that the Federal Bureau of Investigation would actively employ a New York crime boss to do its dirty work for them, by any means necessary.

'I don't know.' She looks troubled.

'I don't like it.'

'Neither do I.'

We are silent for a moment, and Gus clears our plates, giving us time to our own thoughts.

This is turning into something preposterously big. The FBI, the CIA, the Secret Service, maybe Russia and perhaps my own countrymen back home – all wanting the contents of one little envelope.

One thing I know for sure – possibly the only thing in this grand inflating shitshow – William Grosvenor is going to answer my questions.

'I've no skin in this game, not really,' she says, and there's no hint of play or scheming. Just an elegant, middle-aged woman telling me what she's really thinking. 'But I don't like being used either – and that's what's happening. Something is suddenly valuable, and these people, on all sides, are using people like us to get their dirty work done for them – without telling us a goddamn thing.'

I don't want to believe this to be true about Grosvenor, but it certainly looks more likely with every revelation.

Suddenly, there's a crash at the front door. A bump, and a couple of raised voices. Gus leaves the room immediately, while Francesca looks at me with dare in her eyes.

'I came alone. I promise,' I say, palms up.

Footsteps in the hall, quick clomps getting louder, and the kitchen door swings open forcefully. Luca Jones is thrown into the room, followed by a red-faced and blister-marked Michael Brutoli.

'This yours?' he says to me.

'Shit. Luca,' I say. I hope this doesn't mean the cordiality is going to come to an abrupt end. Francesca's hand turns to a fist on the table, and I worry we're about to go south very fast.

'He came alone, it was me that fucked up,' Luca spurts while on his knees, trying to tuck his crumpled shirttails back in. 'I told him where to find you but told him there was no way I was coming down here. That started to make me feel a little less than honourable, so I came down here as backup.'

Francesca looks at me, to which I shrug. Gus takes out the Luger and points it at Luca's right ear. Luca promptly goes still as a lamped rabbit.

'He was loitering by the plant pots at Mackie's place,' says Brutoli, apparently keen to earn back some favour.

'Across the street?'

'He was either some nut job with a hard-on for flowers or something wasn't right.'

I can hear the tremor in Luca's breathing from my place at the table, which reveals itself even further when he speaks shakily. 'I'm telling the—'

'Shut your mouth,' says Gus, pressing the Luger barrel into his earlobe.

I interject. 'I didn't know anything about it, Mrs Speroni. I do know this man, and what he says is true. He was trying to help me, but at the end of the day, we're both as lost as each other in this. And that seems to go for you too.'

Luca looks at Francesca with pleading eyes.

'It's Ms Speroni,' she says. 'Take him outside and give him a coke.'

Gus lowers the gun and crosses to the fridge, pulling out a soda bottle with a clank. Brutoli and Gus march Luca back out of the kitchen, the latter of whom throws me a look of pure confusion over his shoulder.

'That's not a New York euphemism for something bad, is it?' I ask as soon as we're alone.

'No, poor kid looked like he was gonna shit his pants and die from the sudden loss of blood sugar.'

This is all kinds of messed up.

'You keep me in the loop, I keep you in the loop. Understand?' says Francesca.

'Understand.'

'I don't want to be used, and I'm getting to think whatever this is should never be found.'

I neglect to inform her that Luca, the young fellow outside being treated to a soft drink, is unwittingly part of this plot via his grandfather. I don't think he could stomach another face to face with Ms Speroni quite yet.

'Where are you staying?' she asks.

'The Mandarin Oriental.'

'And who do I ask for?'

'Ben Bracken.'

'I'll be in touch.'

# CHAPTER SEVENTEEN

Having left Speroni's, I find Luca on the stoop of the mint house, a coke in one hand and a hard-bitten mobster on each side. Gus gives me back the Luger and I feel Michael Brutoli's eyes on me, right until we manage to hail a taxi. I fill Luca in as we return to the Mandarin.

'Thanks for having my back,' I say, as we walk through the lobby of the hotel. I mean it too. It was brave, what he did. Even though it nearly got us both killed.

'You got it,' he says, but his voice lacks conviction.

I check my watch. Just about to hit eleven in the morning. 'I'm not usually one for this, but shall we see if we can get a drink?'

Luca blows out. 'God, yes.'

The hotel bar is up high, overlooking Central Park. It's as ornate and elegant a hotel bar as I've ever seen, with smart leather chairs, polished walnut, warm lighting and floor-to-ceiling windows looking over Columbus Circle and Central Park. We order a couple of double Taliskers which set us back fifty dollars. Excuse me – set Malinki back fifty dollars.

As I drop into the leather and glance over the treetops, marvelling again at the inherent uniqueness of this city, I realise that, although any old speakeasy would have done, this is pretty bloody nice.

I raise the crystal tumbler, the sunlight catching the contents, rendering it a block of polished amber. 'To you, mate.' We clink glasses and sip. God, it's early for that kind of hit, but so much has happened already today, it doesn't feel like it.

We sit for a moment and watch the people mill about below us.

'This is mad, Luca. Truly getting mad. The FBI wants that envelope. The CIA wants that envelope. A British guy – ex-SAS, current government – wants that envelope. The Russians want that envelope. So… what the hell is *in* that envelope?'

'Something that could change the course of history.' The voice isn't Luca's, and it damn well wasn't mine. I turn to where it came from, behind me, and he's stood there, holding a flight bag, dressed in a polo shirt, cream chinos and some orthopaedic looking trainers.

'You made it,' I say, standing. Ordinarily, I'd shake William Grosvenor's hand, but I can't. Not considering the predicament he has put me in. He puts his bag down on the nearest chair. Like any good soldier, he travels light.

'I am sorry, Ben. Very sorry. I thought we had time. Turns out, we didn't.' He walks past me and extends a hand to Luca Jones. 'Luca, I know your grandfather well, have done since we were much younger men. He's always been a good friend to me and remains so to this day. He speaks very highly of you, and it is very good to meet you. For what it's worth, I'm sorry that you ended up in this mess too.'

'The pleasure's all mine,' Luca says, standing to take the elder man's hand, rising to meet the respect Grosvenor manages to instil in people so effortlessly.

An immaculate waiter appears. 'Another of those, please, looks very good,' Grosvenor requests. 'May I join you?'

I nod, but I've never seen him like this. Slight nerves, playing the secondary role to the commanding presence he usually occupies. He pulls another chair over and then there were three, overlooking the park.

'You both deserve an explanation, and I'll give you as much as I can while protecting you. Ben here will know the value of not quite knowing everything, from a deniability and accountability perspective.' A whisky is placed in his hand, and he takes a cursory sip. 'My God, you boys have good taste. Expensive, I'd imagine, but excellent.'

I keep staring out of the window. 'I don't think you can afford not to tell us everything. We've come this far on your instruction.'

'Be that as it may, there are some things you're really better off not knowing. Luca, you're a CIA officer, I know you'll understand just like Ben here.'

'Is Pops in it as thick as you are?' Luca is clearly wasting no time, and I sympathise. He's far younger, much less jaded than I. He's wanted to know what his grandfather did for so long that now he's got face-time with a man that might have actually worked with him back in those days, it's no wonder he'd take the opportunity. I don't begrudge him, and let him speak. If there's something I need to know shortly, I'll bloody well ask.

'Thicker, I'm afraid, Luca. It's something that he's carried around for a very long time.'

'How'd you know him?'

Grosvenor sighs, but when he opens his mouth to speak, you can tell very easily this isn't a tale told often. If ever. 'He was part of a joint intelligence attachment that I had the occasional dealing with. USA and UK combined. Very hush-hush, very need to know. The Cold War was raging, the world was imbalanced, and a covert unit was assembled to handle extreme incidents of joint interest at the very highest level.'

I turn, enough to see Luca flush with pride, and his eyes go misty as he finally, finally hears some answers. 'I knew he was CIA, but that's all.'

'Yes, he was CIA, that's correct. But he did take a few years out to be part of this group.'

'Did they have a name?'

'I don't think you want to know that. They worked on a few things that were extremely covert in nature. Some things that certain governments didn't even know about, for that same reason that if you don't know about something, it can't come back to haunt you.'

'So why now? What's changed?'

'Nothing, but at the same time, everything. I know that's not much help, but I'm trying to protect you.'

I'm a bit tired of the filibuster, and I know a politician's hot air when it's blown at me. 'I've had enough of hearing this already. Luca, this man is a Minister Without Portfolio in the current government. He's a part of every cabinet, regardless of party, on the Queen's instruction. He's the level head the Queen looks to in order to keep our MPs on track and on side. What is in the envelope, William? We've been shot at and forced into some bad situations already, and we haven't even got our hands on it yet. What is in there?'

Grosvenor breaths out. 'Evidence of a particular operation which has the potential to change the dynamic of world politics.'

I was aware enough of that, but it still doesn't fail to shock and awe when it's put like that. 'More. Why are people killing for it?'

Grosvenor maintains his address to Luca. 'Has your grandfather spoken to you yet?'

'No. He just told me to pass it over. Been trying to call him since, but in retirement, he's got a busier social life than I have.'

'Then certain things are not for me to say. But as far as I know, he's the last surviving member of this covert unit, and we vowed we would take the contents of that envelope to the grave. It is evidence of one of this unit's missions that, trust me, nobody wants to get out.'

Thinking laterally, I stumble across something. 'Why haven't you destroyed it? Why haven't you got rid of the evidence?'

'There's an insurance element to keeping it safe. Something I believe you're familiar with, Ben?'

He's right, and all I can do is nod. Sunk at the bottom of the Manchester Ship Canal, three and a half thousand miles away in Manchester, is a sealed dry-bag containing prison guard uniforms covered in a dead inmate's blood – part of a blackmail plot to secure my freedom from the prison I was stuck in at the time. Back then, as long as I kept the evidence safe, they couldn't touch me, because it would bring down the entire corrupt institution. I don't know how Grosvenor knows about that, but yeah, I get the notion of insurance in such matters.

'So how does everyone know about it?' Luca asks. 'Why is everyone suddenly chasing it now?'

'I can only assume that your grandfather wasn't as careful as I thought. At some point in the last God knows how many years, word has leaked gradually, and Luca Jones Senior has become a person of interest to more than one party – but his lofty role in the CIA had him protected. Upon retirement, and this is all guesswork until I get to speak to him, surveillance on him has obviously not just continued, but ramped. And when it became apparent that some evidence would be on the move, the intelligence world started moving too.'

'Are you sure you can't tell us exactly what this is about? Forewarned being forearmed?' I say.

Grosvenor drains his glass and bares his teeth at the peat fire in his throat. 'I promise you, you're better off not knowing. And that should tell you how seriously we need to get it back.'

'Oh yeah…' I pull my phone out, remembering I'd put it on silent for the visit to Speroni's. I didn't want any rude interruptions during what was always going to be a delicate conversation. Sure enough, as I unlock the screen, there's an email from Jeremiah. I open it up and bingo, he's got a print match. 'I know who's got it.'

'Then let me get a room sorted, and let's go.' Grosvenor stands, and I pull out some of Malinki's notes.

'Here, use this. And don't forget to buy yourself something pretty.'

# CHAPTER EIGHTEEN

We head up to our suite as Grosvenor checks in, and I read Jeremiah's email in the lift. He's not a happy bunny.

Decryption protocol:

From: J.SALIX@NCA.co.uk
To: T.WEST@NCA.co.uk
Subject: Fucking idiot.

I don't know how you got that print, but it worked. Hits on ViCAP for a couple of solicitation and DUI arrests. Brent Sleatham, 2299 Heritage Drive, Washington. He's in the system, but for nothing more than that. Slaps on the wrist all brushed under the carpet because of what it says in the employment column. He's White House staff: official role, Administrations Liaison, which sounds like made up bollocks. Mugshot attached.

Further info. He used his credit card early this morning to buy two nights at Bill's County Line Bar and Grill in

Maryland, just off the I-95 highway. Guessing he's heading home but took a break. With his track record, maybe he's got something extra going on in Kingsville, because his credit card suggests he stays there quite a bit. Rental car receipt from two days ago says he's in a silver Dodge Charger, reg 89384.

Give my best to Grosvenor and delete all this immediately.

J

I open the attachment. Standard mugshot of a guy whose jowls promise a degree of scale below the frame, with receding hair swept back from his forehead. The fact that he's in a shirt and skewed tie suggests he gets up to no good on company time. His skin is ruddy and slick, and he has the injured eyes of a hurt deer. In short, he's got government stooge written all over him.

It's getting on for midday. We have to go catch this guy before he moves on.

'We're checking out, Luca,' I shout.

His head pops round the door, his hair wet, suggesting I must have interrupted him mid-preen. 'Now?'

'Now. Need to call work?'

'Nah, called in sick this morning.'

'Then grab whatever you've got and let's go.'

He pauses and looks back into his room. 'All right then.'

While he picks up his gear, I check Google Maps. Bill's County Line is about two hours from here, maybe two and a half. Could work nicely for an afternoon beer.

Crossing to the coffee table, I grab the phone and wait to be connected to the front desk.

'Hi, yes, this is 717. I'm looking to hire a car.'

Minutes later, we are knocking on Grosvenor's door. He answers holding a coat hanger, looking like he's just getting turned around before it's time for canapés and Aperol Spritzes on the back terrace in five.

'We're going. Grab your stuff.'

'Bugger it.'

# CHAPTER NINETEEN

I asked for the biggest gas-guzzling, super-SUV road-churner they could find, which it turns out is a Chevy Suburban, and it was like the parting of the Red Sea getting out of New York. I paid in cash and took the wheel and told the rental car company I'd drop it off at their Washington offices. No dramas at all, save for navigating Columbus Circle and all the people. We scooted past Sarah Banner's brownstone and the onboard satnav had us whisked under, through and out of New York in no time.

I click on cruise control, having managed to clean the windscreen and the rear windscreen a couple of times each, and even find that the wing mirrors have little wipers on them too.

America, the land of serious fuckin' opportunity.

The interstate, as I'm getting used to these big roads being called, sounds appropriately grand for this sixteen-lane runway I'm cruising along at fifty. The M25 it ain't. It's spectacularly easy driving, with the air conditioning tuned just right as the midday sun bakes away the last of the frothy clouds, and my arse nestled so perfectly into this armchair serving as a captain's seat that I could be settling in for a weekend afternoon of Grandstand.

Grosvenor is next to me, up front, in an equally plush recliner, as I note that Luca has deferred himself lower down the command chain in our newly formed triplet. I can feel his energy from up here though, and I like it. He drops in bits of info to us both like a tour guide, but when we hit the interstate and he's run out of things to talk about, he starts getting down to business.

'William, what happens if we can't catch this guy and he gets that envelope to Washington?'

Grosvenor, who did have the seat set back and dozing – like all military men do when we've got a spare minute; you have to catch that sleep where you can – pulls the seat upright and focuses. 'I would imagine that the contents would be initially confusing, especially if you didn't know what you were looking for.'

'OK, but say, for example, whatever's in there gets seen by any one of these parties that want it. What happens next?'

Grosvenor considers his answer for a moment as I drive past a huge dead white crane on the side of the road, its once pristine feathers beginning to smog darker with the constant exhaust pipes whizzing by its corpse. 'They'll wonder what they are looking at. Then someone will twig. That will set off a chain reaction and a further race against time.'

'And there's no other copy of this?'

'Absolutely not.' He points with a weathered digit to the horizon ahead. 'It's this or nothing.'

We are quiet again. It's very hard to be told something is of huge value and importance and accept that as so, while not having a single clue what you're dealing with. The natural state of the human condition is to wonder and fill in the dots.

So, I begin to do so, carefully.

Switching lanes, I ask with as much nonchalance as I can garner, 'This operation that it pertains to… does it look bad for certain people?'

Grosvenor takes a second. 'Yes.'

'I know those involved were following orders, but would it be embarrassing for certain parties if this got out?'

'Very much so. Two in particular.'

'But that doesn't apply to all the parties after it?'

'Correct.' He's answering carefully.

'So, the parties wanting it have got their own reasons for doing so. They want different outcomes.'

'Yes.'

'Then how has this situation befallen us three in this car? How are we the ones at the centre of this plot that could change everything?'

'It's somewhat quaint and endearing that you think we're the only people on this motorway in pursuit of this thing.' That silences me and I'm suddenly aware of every other visible vehicle. 'If this group in this car are looking for it, having followed a certain sequence of events, there will be others too.'

I put my foot down just a little more and take us up to sixty.

After a while, buildings are swapped out for high trees on the sides of the highway, as the satnav tells me to take the next exit, exit seventy-four, labelled 'Joppa and Fallston'. As I take the exit road, I'm offered a menu of fast-food eateries in the immediate vicinity, which makes my stomach restless. I'll wait though, I know we're not far from a place that, according to the website, prides itself on the best home-cooked plates around. My stomach is proper agitated now.

Only yards off the interstate and it feels like we're off the beaten track, the houses set back from the road like neat blocks, tight into the trees. It reminds me of just how much space there is in America. Miles of it. There're huge spaces between each house, yet every bit of it is neatly maintained. It's nice.

At a junction with a tiny fire station on its nearside corner, we turn right, and the traffic picks up. I feel Luca and Grosvenor sit up straighter in their seats, anticipation charging them up. We travel a silent mile down the road and see it in the distance.

'There we are,' I say. It's a two-story building that resembles a barn, with strange patchwork signs dotted across it. Set by itself just off the road, with a car park on either side and across the front, you wouldn't know it was a bar at all if it weren't for the glass patio door wedged in the brick frontage which says, in simple white lettering, "Bill's County Line, Bar and Grill". Above that is a sign promising karaoke every night of the week.

'Is his car here?' I ask anybody, while pulling up. As soon as we stop, Luca jumps out and rounds the corner of the building to look at the overflow car park.

He turns back almost immediately. 'Yep, it's there. He's here.'

My eyes lock with Grosvenor's, just for a second. He nods.

We leave the Suburban out front and enter. Thanks to Jeremiah coming through with the intel yet again, we know just who we are looking for – and it takes us all of eight seconds to spot him.

# CHAPTER TWENTY

It would have been quicker if it weren't for our eyes adjusting from the glare outside to the dimness of the bar – and no sooner have we entered do we have one of those Wild West moments I've always wanted, where every pair of eyes in the place (maybe five in total) turns in unison to see who enters. I nod like just another goldarn cowpoke and head to the bar, which is furnished in light wood with brass taps and a row of empty barstools.

'What are we having, gents?' I ask.

'The coldest beer they've got,' Luca says.

'Same,' says Grosvenor, taking a barstool, placing his sunglasses on the counter, playing that touristy version of himself that works so nicely. It's a well-practised cover, one only I can see through because I know the man, whereas most will look at him and think "Wow, that old guy keeps himself in decent nick, good for him", not knowing what he's capable of. Or what I hope he's still capable of.

The bartender, who was one of the five who turned to catch our entrance, moves over to us in long strides, wearing a navy t-shirt which says "Bill's" across the pocket in white. 'Gentlemen, the special's the surf and turf, which today is catfish and chicken, and we've also got unlimited Buffalo wings for fifteen ninety-five. You order all that, you get a beer of your choice on the house.'

We look at each other. 'Three, please,' says Luca.

'My kind of people,' says the barman. 'I couldn't help but overhear – our coldest is this one.' He points to a beer pump which actually has frost on the outside of it and a little temperature gauge built in. It reads 0.1, no unit of measurement. 'Three?' he says. He gets a bank of nods in return.

Furnished with three tall foaming pint glasses, we can't help but clink.

'To… whatever it is we're doing,' says Luca. I find myself smiling at him. He's a good lad.

Turning to face the bar, we take stock. Pool table opposite. Clean, well furnished, plenty of space. A couple enjoying lunch at a central table, the elderly man positioned to look at the wall-mounted flatscreens above the bar, which he simply can't take his eyes off. Another man sits at a back table, eating a plate of something big, thumbing through stuff on his phone. He's got a navy shirt on too, so he must be staff. And then, round the side corner, to the extreme left of the bar, is a row of booths – in one of which sits Brent Sleatham.

I hatched a brief plan on the way down, and now I put it into cool, easy action. My colleagues might think one thing, but I definitely think another.

'Excuse me, mate?' I say to the barman, who turns around, amused.

'Yes, mate,' he says with a smile, that last word Dick Van Dyke'd to ribbons.

'Can we get three rooms for the night?'

Luca and Grosvenor just sup and listen.

'I can't do three, I'm afraid, but I can do a twin and a single, would that work for you?'

'Yeah, that'll be fine. Luca, you're in with me.'

'Not again,' Luca sighs under his breath. He's getting good at playing along and he's a fast learner.

'Dry your eyes.'

The barman smiles and retreats to the far end of the bar.

'Watch our man,' I hiss to the other two. 'If he moves, let me know.'

The barman gives me a couple of keys. 'Entrance to the rooms is by the side door, back around the far side of the building. You're the two at the end of the corridor, can't miss them.'

'Cool.' I turn to the guys and make a show of it. 'You guys just relax, get that beer down you, and I'll get our stuff upstairs.'

Grosvenor tips his glass at me, while Luca says, 'I can handle that.'

I leave the bar and go to the car. There's no luggage to really speak of, except for Luca's backpack and Grosvenor's wheely case – hell, my own flight bag is still in the apartment in New York – so it's an easy trip. Bags in hand, I walk around the side of the building. It's devilishly hot, and the sound of crickets is nearly overwhelming. That sound would take some getting used to, Jesus.

There are only a couple of cars in the side car park, one of which is our man Sleatham's, although there are empty spaces for a further forty or so. And in the wall of the building it faces? A single glass door, just like the front. One of the keys on the fobs opens it, and I'm up a short flight of stairs into a corridor with a red carpet and the eye-stinging smell of recent bleach. I walk to the end, eyes up, listening. There's no camera up here monitoring the corridor. Or at least, none I can see. I take my phone out and look at each door in turn.

Now, which one belongs to Brent Sleatham?

# CHAPTER TWENTY ONE

This is a nice place – far nicer than it looks from the outside, I shamefully must concede –but I hope they haven't upgraded their doors in a while. I run some probabilities through my head as I stalk the corridor. I can hear no sound from any of the rooms, no TVs burbling away, no voices, no giveaway of life. At this time in the early afternoon, especially on a weekday, I'd imagine that anyone checking in might not have done so yet. So that potentially leaves Sleatham as the only other staying guest. I walk down, taking one room at a time, listening, and then stop in my tracks. The next door has a "DO NOT DISTURB" sign hanging from the handle, stuck in such a way that the corner is jammed in the door and from where I'm standing, almost pinned out of sight. This must be the one.

I check my phone – no change.

I look down the corridor – nothing.

On checking the door, I find it locked. I trace my fingers around the edges of the frame and find no obvious point of weakness. I'd half-hoped I'd be able to use a credit card to jimmy my way in – we are in the fatherland of cop show cheese, after all, but there's nothing to suggest that will work here. I drop to the floor and check under the door to see if I can peek in. I can see the same shade of red carpet but nothing else. My eye suddenly goes dry, however, and prickles.

Air. A draught. He's got the window open.

I'm up and in one of our rooms in seconds. Mine and Luca's.

It's simple. That red carpet lays beneath two single beds and an en suite, with all the stuff you'd usually come to find in a roadside motel. A kettle with coffee mugs. A mirror and dressing table. A TV. It's all clean. I cross straight through to the back wall and the window, tossing the bags down on one of the beds as I go.

The back garden is a series of picnic tables facing a small stage, all of which is unoccupied, and to the right of that is a garage, tight up to the back of the establishment and with a pitched roof I can walk along to get to Sleatham's open window. I can see it, four windows along, the curtain sucked out into the breeze and wafting gently like a fairy-tale maiden beckoning me in from strife. Taking care not to make any noise, I hop out and lower myself onto the tin roof of the garage.

It's not the strongest structure in the world and gives a little with my weight. I really do need to be careful here. Crashing through into whatever lies underneath wouldn't be the smoothest move in any covert ops book. I keep low, staying below the sills of the windows I pass, and gently ease into the room.

No wonder he's put the "DO NOT DISTURB" sign on. This place is... different.

As a simple hotel room, it's a carbon copy of the one I'm to share with Luca just a few doors down. The layout is identical and from what I can see of the fittings and furnishings, it's all the same. What is different here is the disarray – and the additions. Four bags of Cool Ranch Doritos sit on the dresser, two of which are yawning open at the ceiling while crumbs litter the wooden surface. With them are two family size pop bottles of something lurid pink and radioactive and a half-empty litre bottle of Jim Beam. Beside those are some Pedialyte rehydration sachets. Looking at that, you'd think he's set up for a particularly draining Netflix binge, but then I see the clothes on the floor, all his by the looks of it, and the unmade bed – which is rumpled, stained and has a couple of handcuff restraints poking out at the top and bottom ends, hanging loose on black cords under the mattress. A small mirror sits on the bedside table with a couple of white streaks across it – I'm guessing where he's wiped away the last of whatever powder he and whoever were enjoying. A case sits open on the chair in the corner, waiting to rehouse this travelling decadence kit, and I half expect that if I click my fingers, all this crap will jauntily dive back in there like in a particularly sleazy untold chapter of Mary Poppins.

Enough gawping, Ben. Where's the envelope?

I check the bathroom. Nothing.

The case. Nothing.

Same goes for beneath the mattress, all the drawers in the room, the wardrobe, behind the headboard. Nothing. I even check the kettle, but the only things in there are chunks of limescale like blocks of unburnished jade.

I think of cliché. The cistern's got nothing. The bath panel pops out easily, but there's nothing aside from a disarming collection of lint. There isn't anything even tucked between pages of the room's designated Gideons.

It must be on Sleatham himself.

At that, my phone vibrates in my pocket, and I scurry back to the window, checking the room is as I left it. As soon as I'm back on the roof, I check it. It's Luca.

'He's moving. Not upstairs. Behind the bar. Office.'

# SINCLAIR

Another night, another plane. The former with no clouds, the latter with no seats.

Well, there was a bench on one side, along which five men sat, knees bouncing, all except for one pair. Sinclair. The drone of the aircraft prohibited conversation – that and the fact that the door was open and the air was whistling heavy, low and thick. All the men could see were stars and the officer held in place by the door with a harness and carabiner, the silver clasp of which was caught in the invading moonshine.

'Ninety seconds,' said the officer. The guys knew him as Gilman, and he was a World War Two vet who'd been over to South East Asia – and even now, he could never resist the chance to pull on the camo once more. Born and bred for the thick of it, and he wouldn't let years change that. Sinclair knew him as one of Handshake's handlers, all of whom frittered in and out. Some were there, some weren't, like memories you could barely piece together. Even now, Sinclair couldn't remember outside of the present when he'd actually seen Gilman and where, only that he'd seen him. He supposed, working for a top-secret trans-military unit, that was the idea.

Sinclair stretched his neck and, from his position at the head of the line, looked along at the unit. G-Man was next to him, who he'd learned quickly was the other Brit. Despite that, they weren't as thick as thieves as one might picture. He felt more brotherhood with the man next to him, Luca, who was staring granite centre, a smile heavy on his jaw. Then there was Jinks, the crafty little guy who you'd have thought would have no place in the field, but quickly proved you otherwise with a knife in his hand and a bee in his bonnet. And on the end was Lee. Super quiet, yet super cool. Dependable.

'OK, we are live, gentlemen,' said Gilman, who braced, adopted a wide stance and gestured Sinclair forward. Having parachuted a number of times before, Sinclair felt no fear whatsoever. That is to say, he had no fear up here. He had plenty of fear for what lay down there. 'On green, soldier.'

Above the doorway, a light flashed green, and Sinclair hopped out with no need for further invitation. He got his bearings, assimilated to the updraft and spread his limbs.

The view was breath-taking. Soul-affirming.

All around was the deep dark of the sea, reflecting the moon in giant white shards, for almost as far as he could see, although there was a soft orange hue on the horizon a long way ahead. Florida.

Below, the spread of the sea abruptly hit land, and to the right, a hive of lights. Havana. Some sixty kilometres away. Which meant he needed to stick westerly.

Just south of the hills, on this course, directly below. That's where he was aiming.

Given the accuracy of his position, he could coast his way

in. The operation, while constructed in haste, was thorough. But when you have five of the best, brevity can be better than wallowing in detail.

He sank to earth with a feeling that was somewhere between leaf and stone, before deploying his parachute. The hills began to grow from the earth below, mere dark shapes that started to reach for him. He glanced upwards and saw the underside of four chutes. Clockwork. Perfection and clockwork.

He landed on the grassy hillside on his feet, the incline giving him purchase. He never even dropped to a knee, just took the chute off and left it. It didn't matter if that was found, all that mattered was what the five of them had come to seek. A parachute found tomorrow morning would mean nothing in the grand scale and scheme of what had become known as the Cuban Missile Crisis.

Having all arrived with similar ease, the five men regrouped and fell into a ranked approach, down the hill, into San Cristobal. Only hours before, a U-2 reconnaissance plane had sighted what had been deemed to be an SS-4 construction site.

Nuclear bombs. Soviet nuclear bombs.

For use on America.

And Handshake had been deployed from Tampa, where they'd been stationed since the beginning of the crisis. The five guys had been at a margarita-themed beach party only two hours prior to placing the soles of their feet on Cuban soil.

They'd been sent to find out if nukes were there. Sinclair felt, if you're gonna start a nuclear war, might as well have something to go off.

He had half a mind on some of the girls he'd seen at the party and wondered if, knowing how such things went, the party might still be going when they got back.

Wordlessly, with music and sugar-rimmed glasses forgotten, they walked down the hill. The site on the surveillance images was coming up fast.

The terrain rose slightly and gave them the perfect view over an undulating forest of trees, broken occasionally. Scopes raised, they took stock.

'Tents to the east,' said Luca, his eyes trained on a clearing a quarter of a mile away. 'Enough for a workforce.'

'Intel checks out so far,' replied Sinclair. 'You see those missile sites yet?'

'No,' replied Lee, his own gaze far away to the south. 'Should be just down there though.'

'Shite,' said G-Man. 'In the trees. Torches.'

They all dropped to their bellies, rifles forward, eyes behind scopes.

'They saw us come down?' mused Sinclair aloud.

'Must be a tip-off,' replied Luca, his words followed by a thick wad spat into the grass.

They watched a line of torch beams approach up through the tree line, the lights glowing stronger with every step. There were ten of them, at least.

'We haven't got what we came for,' Sinclair hissed.

'We've got enough,' replied Lee. 'What else would they be guarding, a battalion like that?'

'He's got a point,' said Jinks.

'Then help me confirm,' Sinclair said, before crawling back down the hill from where they came.

He crab-walked and shuffled until he was back down the rise

and travelling around its base to the trees, circling around the oncoming security party. On the hill, though he could only see them because he knew he was looking for them, were the rest of Handshake. Waiting, watching, rifles ready. He nodded firmly enough that they could see his movement and entered the trees.

They were talking, their pursuers. Chattering away in bold tones. They were local accents, as opposed to Russian, which didn't make him think he'd find what they were looking for. It must be a construction site of some other kind.

It only took three minutes and a couple hundred yards of walking to know he was wrong, and the surveillance pictures were unerringly, and worryingly, right. There, through the trees. Unmistakable. Scaffolding, posed cylindrically, for missiles. Excavators and diggers dotted the building site.

Jesus Christ, Sinclair thought. This is a missile site to launch nuclear war on America.

He needed to get this word back to command. He needed this discovery to be known. The Russians were ready. And Cuba was in on it.

The whip-crack snap of gunfire chased from the woods behind him, abrupt and all-encompassing.

The hill. His men. His friends.

He turned and ran, drawing his rifle up to firing position.

# CHAPTER TWENTY TWO

The back window of the building is facing away from the street, pointed at the rear garden, picnic tables and stage, but its most crucial characteristic is that it's open, allowing a soft lick of breeze into the dark office space. It's a standard back room affair, littered with a lot of crap from the bar front that no longer has a place, paperwork filed in a method only decipherable by the filer, and the dank smell of a hot body with too little air. I can see through a vertical portion at the side of the window frame, a slit afforded by the gently swaying Venetian blinds that have been dropped down to keep the sun out and thus cooking the room any further.

Sleatham is in there, furiously typing on his phone, pacing the small space between the desk and the overflowing shelves. He keeps looking up intermittently to the space I can't see to my left, which must be the door. I can see his tension, his shoulders wrought, the sweat on his upper lip glistening repulsively. He reaches into the back pocket of his slacks and pulls it out, simple as that. The envelope. White, small. Still shocks me to think that all of this is about that.

He turns abruptly and his back is to me as he sets about a task I can't decipher. I can see from his shoulders that his hands are moving fast, and with the envelope out of sight, it's making me nervous. A click and a robotic whirr make me tense further when, above his head, suddenly, I see headlights pan across the ceiling from outside.

Only… it can't be. Mine is the only window into this room that's backed by garden, and it's the middle of the day. What can—

As soon as I realise, I've dived into the room and have my arm round Sleatham's neck, the crook of my elbow deep into his throat in a chokehold. 'Don't scream,' I hiss, but I can feel the tremor of his windpipe against my arm, which betrays that he's really damn trying to. I pull him back so I can see, but it's too late – the photocopier on the small side table, which was out of sight before, spits out an A4 piece of paper that's blank save for three smallish squares of drying ink in a horizontal line from the top right corner. I can't make them out at all, as the paper sits there in the out tray – and whatever it is, whatever secret it holds, is now doubled in magnitude and danger.

The envelope is in his right hand, its seal open. 'Put everything back in the envelope,' I say, and he opens the photocopier lid, breathing heavily like he's just run up a flight of stairs. He pulls three small squares from the glass that are thin and plastic-looking, judging by the way they bend under his fingertips, and puts them back in the envelope.

'Now – out the window, round the back of the building and up the stairs. Unlock your room and enter. I'll be right behind you, and don't make a fuss because although you can't see me, I've got a great big gun lined up at your great big gut, and if I have to pull the trigger, it won't leave me with sleepless nights. OK?'

He nods shakily, and I take the envelope from his juddering fingers. He takes his cue and climbs out of the window, which he manages with all the grace of a bag of cement channelling the Marx brothers. One step behind him, I follow him upstairs, the gun still in my waistband.

'Are you going to kill me?' he asks as we walk along the hall to his room. His voice sounds like plastic being rubbed together underwater.

'Depends what we talk about,' I say.

He unlocks the door and as soon as the door is shut behind us, I shove him to the bed and cuff him to it, using his very own sex tools. I spot a necktie on the floor and wrap it around his face, stuffing the fabric into his mouth and tugging it tight. Then, his arms and legs splayed, I pull the cords under the bed tight.

'Be back soon,' I say as I take the room key and lock the door behind me, ensuring the "DO NOT DISTURB" sign is visible.

I feel the envelope and that photocopied sheet in my jeans pocket and take out the latter. I know, having seen him make the photocopy, that all that's in the envelope are those three little squares. Under the wall light, I hold up the paper and try to make it out.

Three small square pictures.

Very similar to one another.

Grainy, hard to establish what's going on in them.

But it looks to me, if I strain very hard, like a crowd.

There are the outlines of people, I'm sure of it.

What the hell is this?

# CHAPTER TWENTY THREE

I rejoin the gents back in the bar, now ensconced in a booth a couple down from where Sleatham the sex-fiend was lurking before, and judging by the rising steam licking ceiling-wards over the table, it appears our food has just arrived. Suddenly, catching a whiff of the fish and meat seasoned in something I've got no clue of but can only assume is bad for you, I'm famished. Luca scoots up so I can sit next to him, and nobody says a word – I merely give them both a curt nod to let them know all is in hand. Grosvenor ploughs back into his dinner and again carries that unmistakable military attitude. Chow time. Get it down you, and don't talk. It's infectious, and we eat.

The food is big. America big. Big in flavour, big in filling – and it doesn't take me long to murder it, and I somehow finish before them. I spot our glasses are empty, signal for three more beers and take out the envelope, just as the other two are wiping their mouths on paper napkins. I place the offending article on the tabletop in front of me, and Luca and Grosvenor lock eyes on it in quiet weighty reverence.

'You've got it,' Luca can only say.

'He had it, now we've got it,' I reply. The beers arrive, and I briefly palm the envelope like a crap street magician, before placing it back down.

Grosvenor is staring at me. He won't break eye contact, and I know what this is. He's asking me, wordlessly, if I've seen it.

I tell the absolute truth. 'I don't know what it is.'

It's the awkward part, and suddenly, silently, the three of us know it. Luca was supposed to give it to me to fly it home to the man sitting opposite me. But it's caused us so much trouble and danger, and Luca is desperate to know what his grandfather was into.

'Will you let Luca have a look?' I say.

Grosvenor looks at me with a firm jaw, then at Luca. He appears to soften before: 'I can't recommend that.'

Along from me, I can feel Luca's whole body tense through the bench seat, and those calves of his start to bounce in place.

'William, you worked with his grandfather and pulled him into this mess. Don't you think it's the least we can do?'

Grosvenor is a reasonable man. An honourable man. It's that side I'd like to appeal to. However, I suspect that at the end of the day, there's the code. The code he can't be separated from, despite the years that have ticked on since it was ingrained in him in the beginning. The steady pull of duty, regardless of border, boundary or pressure. Obligations, borne out of a calling you once deemed higher than anything. You alone know what that means to you and how far you'll go to protect those principles. Principle is the word, and as I learned some time ago, you can't be part-time with your principles. You just can't.

I should know all this because, while some forty years younger, I am exactly the same. No matter how often I feel like those days are behind me, when a matter of safety, security and duty presents itself, I still find myself when told to jump, asking how high. That's why I'm sat here, after all.

Grosvenor interrupts my train of thought. 'I can't. It's not for my benefit that I say that, Luca, but for yours. If you knew the contents, I believe your own life would be in danger.'

The thing is, my journey has not been a normal one, up to this point. I've had to bend rules more than many would, in adherence to keeping those principles in check.

Which means I find it surprisingly easy to turn to Luca and say, 'The only things in the envelope are three miniature pictures. Looks like a crowd scene. I can't tell much under the conditions. Would need magnification to establish what's really going on. I haven't got a clue why it's so important, but for whatever reason, it is.'

Luca looks at me like I just pissed on his Christmas presents, whereas Grosvenor gives me the hard stare.

'He had it open when I apprehended him, the images were in his hand.'

'What was he doing with them?' Grosvenor asks urgently.

It's strange, but I'm feeling my own insurance policy coming on. 'Nothing.' I don't like lying to Grosvenor; he may find it useful to his own hand to know I have an extra set of those images, however small and uneventful they look. But, because I don't know how this game is going to play out, I'm going to keep that quiet.

'Where is he now?'

Luca has drifted off, his gaze still on the envelope, but not daring to grab it. His disappointment, however, looks heavily etched on.

'Shall we have these beers and go meet him? He's just cooling his heels while he waits for us. Maybe he can tell us why suddenly these pictures are the hottest property on the East Coast.'

Luca nods. He's back in the game. Grosvenor puts the envelope back in his pocket and purses his lips. I don't think he's best pleased with me. Unlucky, mate – you aren't the first and you definitely won't be the last.

# CHAPTER TWENTY FOUR

I walk the guys round the back while the bar begins to fill up. Workmen clocking off and stopping in for a swift one or two before they worryingly hop onto the interstate just a couple of miles away, which hums softly somewhere behind the treeline of the car park like the fattest cicada of them all.

As we step out into the afternoon sun, I see that the car park itself is now littered with flatbed trucks and vans, and bikes lined up by that rear garage. Proper hogs these, no Vespas. This is Harley country, Triumph land – and the riders all seem to have congregated in the rear garden where, on that small stage that looks like a cottage trailer back home in the UK, a band is setting up. I can see Fender guitars beyond the chrome of the bike handlebars. Rock and roll, baby.

At the room, I open the door with the key and leave the "DO NOT DISTURB" sign in full view.

Before I've even got in the room, Luca has seen what's trussed up on the bed. 'Jesus Christ,' he says.

'This is his room,' I'm quick to point out. 'All this shite was already here.'

Grosvenor walks around the room in that upright way of his, before looking out of the window. I can hear the test notes of the band, all twangs and screeches before the amps have been plugged in. In a telling move, Grosvenor closes the window, but in doing so, I almost feel the heat rise instantly and the room suck closer.

On the bed, where I left him, is Sleatham. His dress shirt is up over his pot belly now, suggesting he's been wriggling all over the place during dinner. I walk to the head end of the bed and catch a whiff of him as I pass, an odour sharply grim. Taking the tie, I notice it's wet from all the saliva that's leaked from his mouth and seeped across the fabric. I force myself to hold onto it while all my senses want to let it go and pour bleach over my hand.

'If I untie this, will you talk sensibly? As in, you won't cause a fuss?'

His eyes rotate like pool balls in his sockets, and he nods once.

'Didn't want to leave you like this,' I say. 'But I wasn't expecting to have to restrain anybody today and, well, these were my best bet.' I point at his binds. 'Velvet handcuffs. What is the world coming to…'

I pull the end of the tie which immediately loosens the Half Windsor between his teeth, and he shakes his head like a puppy to free himself. Short breaths flourish, which deepen and slow, while I step into the bathroom to wash my hands.

When I return, I see Grosvenor is leaning against the closed window, arms folded, while Luca stands at the foot of the bed, quite clearly unsure of where to put himself. I look at Grosvenor in a question, a question that only men who've done it will interpret. With a flick of the eyebrows, I silently ask: are you happy for me to take this? He nods once in reply. I think he knows my history more than he lets on, and he'll know that I did a touch of interrogation during my time in the Middle East. A touch might be underplaying it, but when you know it won't appear on any official records, who's counting?

In my hands is a bath towel, which I took from the bathroom rack. I stand over Sleatham. 'I'm not from round here. But you guys love a bit of waterboarding, don't you? It was your big show stopper. I saw your chaps do it, over there. Nasty business. Horrible to watch. But I did. And my God did it get results. Couldn't believe it. They'd spill their guts, then they'd spill their guts some more. So, I practised. I had a go myself, and I've got all right at it. The problem with me though, Brent Sleatham, is I'm not that good with the stopping part. I can never read the signs, and I've got it wrong a couple of times. What was it Gary Player said? The more I practise, the luckier I get? Well, I'm a lot out of practice. So, if I got going, who knows where we'd end up.'

Luca passes me one of those bottles of toxic cherryade, the top already off. He's catching up and playing along again.

'It was easy enough to brush my failed attempts under the carpet over there in Afghanistan, Brent, but it won't be so easy here. So help me. Let's not have to do any of that stuff, OK?'

His chin wobbles up and down, and I can't help but pull his shirttails back over his wobbling belly fat. Whether it was to ease his dignity or my nausea, I'm unsure. Bit of both maybe.

'You're White House material, aren't you, Brent?' He lies still and looks at each of us in turn. At this rate, I could have left him ungagged while we had a few beers, such is his quietness. 'We know, Brent. We have our own intelligence. So, speak now, please.'

This gets a small nod of agreement.

'OK. Who sent you on this errand to Malinki and the big city?'

Eyes wide, jaw clamped shut.

'Brent. We talked about this. You piss about, we get the fun stuff going. Who sent you to play fetch?'

He looks at each of us in turn. He seems scared, but not totally losing his mind scared.

Grosvenor has noticed it too because he speaks. 'He's playing for time.'

I look from Grosvenor to the man in the bed, whose features really betray terror now. I march briskly to his bedside, which causes him to scream, 'No!'

'Voice down, dickhead,' I say while I put a hand over his mouth, grab his earlobe and twist it. Ears are funny little things. Wobbly bits that appear to do bugger all, but that give you a choirboy falsetto if you play with them wrong. 'Have you alerted anyone?'

He holds fast, and I twist harder. I feel gristle separate in my hand, but he still doesn't relent. A shred of surprised respect blooms between my ears but fades just as abruptly.

'Luca, check him.' He goes through Brent's pockets.

'Nothing,' he says.

'Fuck…' Brent gurgles under my hand.

I twist harder. 'Safe words won't work with us. Who have you told?'

'Got it,' Grosvenor says. He's at the small bureau, holding Brent's phone. 'Text message outbox, unsaved number, simply reads "EXTRACTION REQUEST, 386009BAC, CODE: BLACK, LOCATION: SIM".'

This guy's a big fish. 'When was it sent?' I ask.

'Soon after two.'

135

'Shit.' He made us in the bar earlier. That's why he was in the office, he was plotting his escape.

I draw the cherryade near and raise it high so Sleatham can see it. I pull in close so the government mule can hear my every utterance. 'Listen here, you little shit. This won't be pleasant, but you'll talk. They always do. Speak now, and we don't have to go that far. And remember… I'm not very good at this.'

I cover his face with the bath towel and shove a couple of wads of it into his mouth. His body starts churning beneath me. Luca sets his jaw so his lips are a tight line, and I look at Grosvenor one more time, asking a silent question: is it worth this?

He nods, and I begin to pour the bright pink liquid into the little towelled well where his mouth is. At some point, later, I'll have to have a word with myself about how it got to this, but sometimes your hand is forced. There're goodies, baddies, your side, their side. Winners get to go home, losers get dead.

And I've got a family I need to get back to.

As soon as the first neon flow really hits the fabric, he relents. 'I'll speak!' he chokes through cheap, wet cloth. I pull the towel over his chin to reveal his mouth, and he gasps for air as words suddenly start to spurt.

'Secret Service is en route to pick me up. The package is for them.'

The Secret Service is the president's personal security service. We have hit four corners bingo here with this guy – if we can keep him talking.

'On whose orders?'

'Oval Office.'

'And Malinki?'

'I was the go-between. I'm the president's man in Manhattan.'

'Bullshit,' I bark, putting the towel back over his mouth. 'No president's man lives like this.'

'It's the truth! I swear! He needs an odd-job doing in NYC, I'm the man he sends!'

'I'm still smelling bullshit. Time for more liquid.'

'I promise! The president has been advised that the contents of that envelope could swing the next election. He's down in the polls; he needs control of the contents, to play it how he sees fit. The CIA heard it was on the move and intercepted it using Malinki.'

'The CIA robbed itself? Dream on.'

'It's the truth! The CIA has so many layers you don't know about! I swear on my kids' lives, the CIA hooked the Secret Service up, told the president they knew where it would be and when. All we had to do was get Malinki to get it for us.'

'Why didn't the Secret Service just go and get it?'

He goes quiet and still for the very first time, and that stills my hand. 'You don't know what you're dealing with, do you?' Sleatham's voice has taken on a soft note of wonder, and it makes me loosen my grip on his face. 'This, if it's true, could change everything. Everything.'

'He's right.' That voice came from behind me. Grosvenor. 'It could change everything. But only if the president gets his hands on it.'

'You know what it is? What is it?' Sleatham carries that wonder again, like Grosvenor might finally be able to give him some measure of peace.

'I caught you looking at it, Brent. You know what it is.'

'I don't. I wasn't told. But obviously, the myth around this envelope has been building in the halls at 1600 Pennsylvania

Avenue for a while now. I couldn't *not* have a look at it. But I'd need a projector of some kind to get a proper look.'

Projector.

Shit, those things in the envelope are film frames.

Back to business.

'So why were you photocopying them?'

His voice drops in volume. 'I wanted a copy for myself. And then I thought, when all is said and done, they'd fetch a bit on eBay.'

'Photocopying them?' Grosvenor exclaims, suddenly upright.

I pull the folded sheet of A4 from my back pocket and pass it to Luca, who opens it greedily, then give Grosvenor a look of stone. 'Now at least two of us are on the same page.'

He returns with brimstone. 'Ben, your orders are to give that to me.'

'My orders were the envelope. I've fulfilled that. And your orders keep getting me almost killed.'

'Ben, you don't know—'

'What I'm dealing with? I'm tired of hearing that but nobody wants to enlighten me.'

A spotlight suddenly fills the room from beyond the window. The band suddenly stops. We are caught in the whitest light. Spielberg Close Encounters levels. Unable to see anything. And then the glass breaks and bullets start to split the air.

# CHAPTER TWENTY FIVE

Of the three of us in the room on our team, Grosvenor and I are already on the deck by the time of the first ricochet, those instincts from years of thunder over our heads clicking into gear just in time. Luca, green as an Irish meadow, stood in full panic mode, but I was able to grab him as I went. The three of us lay there as the room around us pops with bits of plaster and glass, raining onto us all. God knows what's happened to Brent Sleatham on the bed – poor bastard couldn't dive for cover. I can't imagine the sight of him now will inspire many good dreams.

I take the Luger from my jacket and scurry round the side of the bed as the bullets fly in disparate spurts, but all in clusters of three. Three shots. Pause. Three shots with a different sound. Pause.

That tells me there're multiple shooters and they're all well-trained.

The wall around the window looks OK. Nothing coming through. I crawl up to beneath the sill. Grosvenor has the same idea, and we're next to each other.

'Multiple shooters,' he says, pulling his own Glock out and into the mix. 'One spotlight.'

'Range?' I ask, as more shots sail over our heads, taking out a cheap framed sunset on the opposite wall.

'Fifteen yards, garage roof. Slight height advantage our side.'

Grosvenor got just enough of a look at them before he dropped from sight. It really does never leave you.

I look above me at the window frame. The curtains are long and hang down over the sill.

'Take that,' I say, gesturing to the curtain hanging by Grosvenor's left ear. I crawl to the wall on the opposite side of the window, stand and ready myself. 'Now.'

Grosvenor tugs on the curtain, causing the fabric to billow up and down – when three bullets split the early evening air and tear the curtain to ribbons. As soon as the first shot leaves the barrel, I'm aiming from between the curtain and wall on the other side.

Aim for the light and think logically. Think where they'll be. The spotlight. The person pointing the spotlight. And at least two more nearer, in formation, down front.

I fire once into the light. Easy enough. Don't wait for my eyes to adjust. Then move up and left by a fraction. Fire again. I'll go for my own cluster of three. Lower the sights, think of the roof layout I saw earlier, pick roughly the front edge, where someone would be ready to lead the assault. Squeeze the trigger.

And back behind the window before I can see what I've done.

An anguished shout lets me know I got at least somebody.

I hear someone shout in a thick accent that's considerably different from what I was getting used to in New York. 'What the fuck is going on?'

The gunfire stops for a moment, the only sound being the guy

I hit gasping quietly and moaning through gritted teeth. I can't have hit him badly.

'Up there, they've got a government employee hostage!' shouts someone. Oh crap. I peek through that same gap between curtain and wall, and in the dwindling light can see one man down on the roof, a shattered spotlight next to him, blood from a devastating head wound slowly beginning to pour down the corrugated undulations of the garage roof to the gutter. That's definitely one down. Another is trying to lower himself off the garage roof, down in front of me. A splash of red like a paint spillage marks the roof he's leaving. I think, for the purposes of the fight, that's two down.

And now, behind the apex of the garage roof, I see three heads. The rest of the Secret Service unit, I'm guessing, having retreated to regroup. It's amazing what three well-thought-out shots can do. Down on the ground, where the band were playing, stand a group of bikers, beers in hand, all jeans, boots, leathers, bandanas and beards.

'You mean Brent?' comes the reply from below. This voice, the one I heard first, belongs to a tall guy with a black bandana which is trying unsuccessfully to hold still a mane of fire-red beard and hair, so big and unruly on his face, I can only see a bent nose and a couple of eyes.

'Yeah, they've got Brent!' comes the answer from above. This is recruitment, nothing more.

It's working, as someone else hollers from the back of the biker group, 'Brent's my fuckin' boy!'

'Brent's the man!' shouts someone else. Sleatham has been making friends on his errands, it seems.

I look at Brent finally. He's a shredded sack of meat, held fast in velvet handcuffs. It's not a pretty sight, but that's what indiscriminate fire from an automatic weapon will do.

'They're holed up in room five,' shouts the Secret Service operative who's been doing the talking.

'Tool up, boys. Let's give these fine gentlemen a hand.' With that, the grizzled bikers start running towards the entrance to the upstairs suites.

'Gents, we've got incoming,' I say. 'The stairs. Does Sleatham have a weapon?'

'Yes,' says Grosvenor, pulling apart Sleatham's wheelie case. From the front pocket, he extracts a .22 pistol. A travel gun. Good at close quarters, but more than that and we're squirrel hunting. I give Luca back his Luger.

'OK mate, time to use this for real. You riled up?' I jump over Sleatham's body and grab Luca by the shoulder. 'Let's scrap our way out of here and find out what Pops did for his country, OK?'

He nods, takes the gun and blows out a hot breath. 'Ready,' he says. Since the moment I met him, he's never looked so young. Well, it won't be the first time I've been in a firefight with a young man at my side.

'Grosvenor, cover fire at the door. Stay low. Spare the bikers if possible. Don't worry about those guys outside the garden.' The older man adopts a crouched stance by the bathroom door, facing towards the main door of the room. 'Luca, check the wall behind the bath.'

I look back to the window and fire three cursory shots over the garage roof with the .22. Not aiming to hit anybody, just to keep them occupied.

'They're here,' says Grosvenor as he pumps two rounds into the door. Six shots are returned, ripping chunks of the door away. These bikers came to fight.

'Luca, the wall?' I shout.

'Tile and plasterboard, I think,' he shouts back.

I join him. 'Keep that cover fire coming, sir,' I shout, then curse myself immediately. I couldn't help that last word from slipping out. I stand in the bath, shoulder braced at the wall. 'Luca, on three, everything you've got.'

He mirrors my stance. 'One, two, three.'

At the same time, our shoulders impact the cheap pink tiling, and it gives surprisingly easily in a parting of plaster, grout and porcelain. It jars the muscles across my back, and I feel a ringing in my collar bones, but we must 'Go again!'. We crash it again, and structures on both sides of the wall divide between the adjoining rooms begin to give.

'Push through,' I instruct, then, covered in dust and chunks of wall, join Grosvenor – but a bullet whizzes by my head and lodges in the bathroom door frame.

Shit, I forgot about the Secret Service outside. That was nearly game over.

I drop, then scoot to Grosvenor. 'Go through the bathroom with Luca, then do the same on the other side.'

'There're at least seven,' he says, before making a crawling retreat around the corner. I aim at the door and see immediately it's in bits. It's barely on the hinges, plates of wood held together by very little but somehow standing. Through it, I can see the occasional gun poke into view and fire a pot shot. These bikers, they're eager, but not especially well drilled. I don't want to take these guys out. This isn't their fight at all, and I wonder how it would fit in with their rebellious sensibilities if they knew we were trying to stop a pivotal conspiracy from getting out. I'm pretty sure they wouldn't align themselves with the Secret Service, acting on behalf of the government itself, but I'm not sure they'd align with me either. I pump a couple of rounds into the corridor wall behind them, let them know they can't stick their heads round for a proper gander just yet.

There's a metallic thud behind me, clanging off the mirror over the dresser. I retreat to look and clock it immediately – a matte black cylinder, as big as a pint can of stout, only this one has a pinhole in the top.

Before two and two are even getting anywhere near each other in my head, I'm up and into the bathroom. Luca and Grosvenor are halfway through the bathroom wall, and I throw myself at them – as the room behind me rips apart in a floor-shaking explosion.

# CHAPTER TWENTY SIX

My momentum takes all three of us through the remaining pieces of drywall and sprawling into the bathroom on the other side, forced through on a cloud of debris and furnishings. It's an ugly landing, since the bathroom in the room next door mirrors the one we just left, and so we tumble half into and half out of the bath. It's painful and cacophonous.

'Grenade,' I croak.

'All fifty-two?' Asks Grosvenor.

'What?' says Luca, dragging himself to his feet.

I stand and realise Grosvenor isn't up yet, so I hoist him up by the shoulders. 'Fifty-two playing cards. Are you a full deck, Jones?'

'I think so,' he says as the three of us shamble into a spotless bedroom, which is worlds apart from the one we just left, which is now presumably filled with wreckage, gore and probably more men on our tail. 'We've got to go. Move. Move.'

I support Grosvenor as we get going, since I notice he has begun to limp. 'What's hit?'

'Nothing, just. Knee replacement three years ago. Something feels loose.'

'You're getting too old for this.'

'I think you might be right.'

The hotel room is empty, which I already knew, but it's still a relief to confirm we aren't dragging anybody else into harm's way.

Luca suddenly starts firing back behind us with the Luger. 'They're coming through!'

I let go of Grosvenor and run to the window. Our change in position reveals our pursuers. Three Secret Service operatives, on the side of the garage roof, advancing across the roof in the direction of the wrecked room.

'Hold those bikers off!' I shout back to Luca, before turning to Grosvenor. 'The Glock.'

It looks like he's trying to whack a dislocated knee back into its socket with the flat of his palm, but he pauses to toss the Glock from his waistband. I check the magazine. The Glock carries seventeen rounds, and there're nine left. Enough. I turn to the window and raise the barrel.

One to break the window. The glass falls like a dropped curtain. Lock shoulders.

One-two to the man at the rear. Aim for centre mass both times. Rotate right.

One-two at the man in the middle. He's paused because of the first shots. Dead simple, centre mass, squeeze twice.

Rotate right and down. The last one's dropping from the roof.

One – hold fire. A spark off the iron shows me I missed.

Don't waste ammo. The roof is clear. Three bullets left.

'Luca, William, this window now. I'll cover you.'

I head back to the bathroom, while the other two men hop out of the window. Luca is right. The bikers are taking it in turns to try to force their way into the bathroom. One gets halfway through, but I put one in his thigh. He crumples into the bath.

'Same happens for anyone else coming through!' I shout. 'And we didn't kill Sleatham.'

The bathroom beyond goes quieter, so I drive the point home. 'I really don't want to shoot anybody else.' It sounds ridiculous, because it is, but I don't, so it's not.

'Then what the fuck happened up here?' shouts a man I can't see, but all I can picture is bike culture's answer to William Wallace bellowing through the hole over the bath.

'Those guys outside are using you. They killed Sleatham when they opened fire.'

'Then why's he tied up?'

Good question. I don't answer it and go for the window, hearing that same guy shout, 'I said, why the fuck is he tied up?' at the top of his lungs.

When I catch up with Grosvenor and Luca, they are walking along the roof towards the car park. We've got three guns up as we clamber. There are eyes on us from over by the stage, including the band's, but I know there are at least two of these Secret Service fuckers unaccounted for. There are three dead on the roof, spread-eagled and appealing heavenward for safe carriage.

Dropping down into the car park, I let the others go first, and as I lower myself down, I catch sight of the bikers emerging from the window we left a moment ago. They see me, just before I can drop. Damn.

Luca and Grosvenor already have the right idea of running round front to the Suburban, and I sprint after them – but I can hear Braveheart behind us shouting from the roof, 'Catch those bastards! Those fuckers shot at us!' His grievance has changed slightly, but he still isn't letting us go – so I don't wait to hear if we're being followed.

I round the corner at the front of the bar, just behind the other two, to find our Chevy has been joined by a number of other glorified monster trucks, as well as one big blacked-out people carrier that must be the imposing transport for the Secret Service. But thankfully, the coast appears to be clear – yet, as soon as my idiot brain thinks that, I know it's not and stop.

From the recess of the front door emerges one of the Secret Service guys, gun up. He's fixed on Grosvenor. 'Freeze, old man,' he instructs.

This is the best look I've had at any of them so far. All black, attack vest and jet combats. Tactical sunglasses that don't do anything apart from make you look a proper twat, and for all his supposed ocular advantage, he hasn't seen me. I'm paused prey-still at the corner of the building.

Grosvenor, by the SUV, stops, hands at his sides. He doesn't turn his head.

'Do you have it?' the shout comes again.

Grosvenor doesn't flinch.

'Do you fucking have it?' The agent shouts again.

No response.

The agent loses his cool and marches to Grosvenor. 'Listen, you geriatric bastard, or have you lost your hearing? Do you have—'

'I've got it!' I shout, drawing his attention, and immediately a gunshot blasts out. It confuses me because, while I'm holding the Glock, I didn't pull the trigger.

The agent drops to his knees, before slumping onto his face.

Luca stands up between two cars a couple of yards away, the Luger smoking in his hand.

All that green is gone.

# CHAPTER TWENTY SEVEN

We waste no time in bundling Grosvenor into the car since it looks like that knee of his couldn't make the step up into it. I toss Luca the keys as bikes begin to spit diesel from somewhere in the car park behind us.

'Start the engine,' I command, then run back to the corner of the building. The bikers are running onto the tarmac and hopping onto their steeds, strangling them to noisy life and movement.

And then, around the side of the building, in a determined sprint, is another Secret Service agent. One from the roof. From his stature, I think it was the leader, but now he's ditched his tactical helmet to reveal a too-perfect tan and wayward brown hair at all angles.

Shit. That one round left in the Glock isn't going to solve any of this, save prolonging the agony.

I look around the car park for something, anything, and see the post for the overflow lot has a chain coiled at the bottom of it, with a battered tin sign attached. It reads "BILL'S IS CLOSED" in nothing more than rust.

Something sparks in my head.

I run for it.

'Go, Luca, back to the motorway,' I shout.

'The what?' he shouts from the open driver's window of the Suburban.

'The fucking interstate!'

I'm sprinting past him as he catches on. The great thing about these monster SUVs is the automated doors. Luca has obviously thumbed the release on the dash, as the rear passenger door slides open. I sprint as the vehicle moves away slowly down the road, dragging the chain behind me. The bikes are getting louder, growing in bass. We're going to have a swarm behind us any second, and I don't fancy our chances against all of them.

'The post, Luca!'

Luca picks up speed, I hop in and the chain begins to tighten. I throw it over the post as we swoop by, before suddenly it goes taught – right across the front access to the overflow car park. The bikes, angling to follow the SUV, seemingly miss the chain in the failing light and plough straight into it. Bodies somersault over handlebars into the road, before the chain breaks – but the melee is too complete, the tangle of metal, rubber and bodies too dense, for anyone to get through.

We made it, and I watch back out through the now softly-closing car door at the dwindling lights of Bill's County Line, the lights of the car park bleeding harshly into the deepening blues of the Maryland sky.

'Tell me you've got the envelope,' I say, as the door shuts with a quiet click, and I face front.

'It's here,' Grosvenor replies, holding the envelope up for us to see. It's streaked, crumpled and a shell of its former self, but it's intact.

For the first time in what feels like an age, I breathe out.

# CHAPTER TWENTY EIGHT

We drive for an hour before stopping at an all-night Target shopping Mecca, fifty miles outside of Washington, where, on Malinki's coin, we each buy a backpack, some toiletries and a couple of changes of clothes. From there, I look for the nearest river on Google Maps. We are somewhere beyond Baltimore, near a place called Avalon. I'm thinking we definitely need to get off the beaten track, that this car we're fleeing in is far too hot. But right now we need distance, so I take over the driving and angle us into the inking humps of hills above the Patapsco River.

The sun finally sets in the summer sky, and the darkness out in the hills becomes ever more complete. The sky takes impossible depth and infinity never felt so close. Grosvenor dozes, while I feel Luca's calves bouncing behind me again.

'How are you back there, mate?' I ask, swinging the car along ever-narrowing roads, the headlights catching the boughs of arching trees that seem huge and overpowering.

'I'm OK,' he says. In the rear-view, he looks supremely troubled, eyes drawn out the window, his mind anywhere but in this car.

'He's asleep, Luca. Talk to me.'

He clears his throat softly but doesn't initially say anything.

'Was that the first time you've shot someone?' I ask.

'No, it's not that. It's Pops. The more we find out here, the more I'm not happy about this. The more I wonder what my grandfather was really about. What he was really into.'

I know what he means. Grosvenor isn't my grandfather, but I trust and respect him. I can't pretend that these emotions haven't been ruptured somewhat by the revelations of what he knows, and how he has drawn us into such danger.

'What do you think is on these pieces of film?' he asks.

'I really don't know, mate. But I feel we deserve to. I'll be bringing that up, don't fret.'

'You know when you have built up someone in your head, and they might not be the person you imagined after all?'

I do know that. I didn't build up my mum and dad as such. We were normal, northern people. Not great with overt displays of emotion and good with getting on with things. But we worked, and they were proud of me. But when I left the army with a dishonourable discharge, they suddenly didn't want anything to do with me. There was no preamble, no begrudging acceptance that I was their son no matter what and that every son deserves guidance, from their father especially. They were simply no longer there for me and no longer a part of my life. So yeah, I get the whole bit about people you love letting you down.

And then I think of Grosvenor. I wasn't in the market for another father figure, having seemingly subconsciously decided not to bother. But Grosvenor is the closest I've come to that hand on my shoulder.

Is he going to let me down too?

I sincerely hope not.

But then again, everything in the last day has suggested things are far from what they seem, and I'm frustrated at my lack of a true grasp on the situation.

I see a sign for Ellicot City, a mile away, and slow down. I want to get rid of this car before we enter another suburban area, with all those CCTV cameras and eyes eager to dob in a band of conspirators. Going off the satnav, we've been following the rather unimaginatively named River Road for a while, so I wind down the window. I can hear it, close by, gurgling along with a rich cadence that suggests depth.

'William, time to get up,' I say. 'Grab your things and hop out.'

Within moments I'm coaxing the car through the sparse trees off the now empty road, as the river grows slightly louder. It doesn't take long before I see it burbling by in the immaculate moonlight, the surface inky yet pierced by ready white caps.

The riverbank is undramatic and eases to the water's edge, and after an embarrassing moment trying to get the handbrake to stay off so the car will roll (they really thought of everything in this oversized go-kart), I finally wedge the pedal down with a stick. The grand metal beast slides into the murk of the water with barely a whisper, and I'm left in the cool quiet. Just the water, the stars and the trees. It's beautiful.

The land of opportunity is a phrase that suddenly feels so real.

After a quick hike back up the road, checking that there weren't any obvious broken branches or tyre tracks to give us away, I catch up with the guys. They're talking and I catch the end of it.

'…well, I am grateful, Luca,' says Grosvenor.

'You and Ben saved me a bunch of times back there, I only got one.'

'Ben has been trained by the best. And at one point so was I. You saved us both with that shot. And it's not the first time a Jones has fired a shot that has saved my bacon. Your grandfather would be proud.'

'Come on, you two,' I interrupt. 'And don't let that go to your head, Dirty Harry.'

The walk into Ellicott City is a pleasant one, and it's one we spend alone in our respective thoughts. There are big conversations to have, plans to make, and we universally seem to agree to conserve our energies for those very moments.

We enter the city, which I quickly realise should really be in inverted commas, under an iron bridge that wouldn't be that out of place carrying the canals of Lancashire, before entering onto a Main Street that looks eerily like it could be in the Cotswolds. I'm struck at the formative nature of the country and how comparatively young it is, in terms of history. All of what I look at right now – the light stone cottages and shops lining the road – were most probably magpied from Middle England. That sort of notion would once have had me feeling proud of Britain, my home country, but that's not me anymore. A lot has happened since I was misty-eyed and hopeful, not all that much of it good.

In amongst the blocky houses are wooden edifices that immediately recall more of the colonial perception I had of these areas, and it leaves a rather bizarre but not unpleasant hotchpotch of styles. And suddenly, there in the distance, like a beacon, I see a swinging pub sign just like back home.

In instances of uncertainty, there exists another very useful British maxim.

If in doubt, head for the pub.

The streets still have people on them, and for all I feel about how much has been jammed into this wild day, it's only ten o'clock at night, proving once again that time has a funny way of behaving when you've got a lot on. We enter the Manor Hill Tavern at just gone ten, and it's mercifully quiet. I instantly feel like I can settle, conserve and restock for the next phase.

'I think I should get these,' says Grosvenor. His limp has all but gone now, and it's a funny plight of his knee replacement that such pain can come and go. I thought he was bound to be crocked for a while, but it turns out you actually can knock metal back to where it's supposed to be, even while it's inside your body. That and a handful of budget anti-inflammatories from Target.

The bar is long, the wood is dark and the atmosphere is close, candle-lit and quiet – although there is the obligatory flat-screen TV showing ESPN on one wall, at which a couple of guys sit and watch baseball while eating nuts from a massive bowl in front of them. At the bar, I pick a beer that has a huge sturgeon on its label, because it reminds me of the pike I enjoyed catching on the River Bure down in Norfolk, before my second chance. It's called Hardywood: The Great Return, and it is cool, tall and godly.

We sit at a table at the back, and Grosvenor must have caught the underlying pressure in the air because he tackles it head-on. 'That was some scrape back there. We all did well to get out of that one. Thank you both, for getting us out of there – and for getting this out of there.'

When he pulls out the envelope, it seems to carry even more weight since last I saw it, but he merely puts it on the table like it's just another beer coaster. 'We won't need this anymore,' he then says, before bringing out the folded photocopy sheet and holding it over the tea light candle on the tabletop.

Luca puts out a hand immediately, as if he can't bear any chance at knowing the truth evaporating, but Grosvenor steadies him. 'This copy is meaningless. There's nothing on it that would help answer any question. The items in question are pieces of film and need backlight and projection to see. Useless on mere paper.'

'I think you owe us a full explanation,' I say.

'I think you might be right,' he says with a sigh. Then, after a quick glance to the bar, he lays it all out for us in a quiet voice.

# CHAPTER TWENTY NINE

'It's about a young man called Sinclair,' says Grosvenor, his shoulders wrought, high and tight with his elbows bunched on the table, giving him the sudden presence of a vulture. 'And the part he played in the unit that Luca Jones Senior was a member of and I had dealings with.'

'Operation Handshake?' asks Luca, the eagerness on his face painfully obvious to see.

'That's right.' I've never seen William Grosvenor like this. He's always been the very definition of unflappable, with a composure you'd stake your mortgage on. This version of him is genuinely unnerving. 'I haven't breathed any of this for getting on sixty years, so please bear with me.'

I sip and resolve to give him the time he needs. I'm bursting to get at the truth of things now. Grosvenor continues with his gaze rooted to the grain of the wooden tabletop.

'Handshake undertook a number of different operations and were comprised of a seemingly disparate group of men who all had only one thing in common. They were highly trained and highly impressionable. Prone to idealism, I think is another way to describe it. And the powers that be that assembled this group knew only too well that they could press certain buttons, say certain things, play on those very pure notions of doing good in a broad sense, and they would usually convince those poor saps to go and do pretty much whatever they wanted. No offence, Luca.'

Luca waves it off without blinking. Grosvenor continues.

'We are talking about the shadow of the Second World War – which in itself was in the shadow of the First World War. The Cold War sat large over all of it, and nobody – nobody – wanted to go back to the awful periods of fighting which so stained our very species in the early part of that century. So absolutely everything was done to stop it. The greater good was deemed greater than absolutely anything else. So the operations Handshake were sent on were rooted in good intentions in the eyes of those undertaking them – that would be the chaps on the ground like Luca Senior and Sinclair – but they were so easily played by those behind the scenes.'

'Were you one of those people that used them?' Luca asks with no shortage of accusation.

'God no, my involvement was much later. And if I'd have known, of course, had I the power, I would have done something.' He takes a long swig of the cold Virginian draught, followed by an even longer moment of reflection, before resuming.

'It's very fair and accurate to say that sometimes Handshake did things it shouldn't – although they were convinced they were doing right. After all, that is what they had been told. And as Ben will know only too well, and myself for that matter, the chaps on the ground are only as good as the orders they are given. You follow them, or you are surplus to requirements. And in the military, my God, you follow them.'

I nod in agreement. I understand that position and the plight it causes at times.

'Those three frames of film in that envelope are, as far as I know, the only evidence of Handshake's involvement in an assignment that should categorically never have happened.'

'What assignment?' says Luca. Family pride is at stake for him here – he now knows his grandfather was involved in some extremely shady military shit, even if his heart was in the right place when it happened.

'Some things aren't very simple, Luca,' Grosvenor replies.

'You're going to have to spit it out, William. We get that in hindsight these soldiers had to do stuff that probably looks bad, and you're right I understand the weight of orders. What are those frames part of?'

He is so still, there's a chance he may have had a very subtle heart attack and died right in front of us. Eventually, he grabs his beer with both hands like a life preserver and says, 'Have you ever heard of the Zapruder footage?'

A cold hand seems to grab the entire back of my head. My hands tingle with sudden uncontrolled fire.

No fucking way.

'No,' says Luca.

I'm too stunned to make a sound.

I know. Oh, I know all right.

Grosvenor voices the words I daren't believe are true. 'It's a famous film clip, recorded in 1963. Of JFK's assassination.'

Luca's gaze becomes instantly unmoored, like the attachment between body and conscious has just been cut. 'Pops…'

'Handshake was there that day. And the only evidence of their presence is on those three frames.'

Jesus Christ. Jesus. Christ.

The jumbled people in the picture. The crowd. The sequence.

'There has been a long-mooted and oft-trotted out conspiracy theory that the Zapruder footage, which was taken by Abraham Zapruder, a father who was there merely recording the president's visit for nothing more than the family album, was tampered with before it was sold to the world's media.'

This is the most famous sequence of grainy footage you're ever likely to think of. Right up there next to the moon landings. It's an iconic series of images in not just American history, but international legend.

'The truth is, gents, it was tampered with. When things went the way they did, they had to clear out. Had to make a clean getaway. So Handshake got to Zapruder before the Dallas PD did, and looked at the film. There was only a problem with three frames, at frame 132, just as the president's motorcade was straightening out onto Elm Street. The way Luca Senior tells it, they had to snip three out to save their skins, before recompiling it for the media. The story goes that Luca Jones had a white envelope in his jacket pocket that day and put them in there – and he has held on to it ever since. This envelope.' He places an index finger on it, and suddenly it has taken on the sheen of intense pricelessness. 'And inside? Frames 132.a, 132.b, 133.c of the Zapruder film.'

The weight of his words hits me like a ton of breeze blocks. The notion that JFK's murder was an inside job has long been rumoured, but proof? Never. Yet... here it is. Incontrovertible proof that President Kennedy was killed by an internationally composed military unit.

I look at Luca, who has gone deathly still. He just found out a beloved family patriarch was not only present at one of the darkest incidents in his nation's history, but that he may also have had a hand in it.

'And what do they show?' I ask grimly.

'The young lad, Sinclair. In the crowd. Like all the other guys in Handshake, like Luca Jones Senior. They show a young lad, thinking he was part of the right thing.'

# SINCLAIR

The trucks reversed without so much as a word. No adios, no preamble to what was to come next. Drivers with jobs done and other stuff to do, other trips to make.

The handful of young men looked at each other, their bond having grown to the point that they could all pretty much get what each other was thinking. Here, in the middle of nowhere, the city long gone. What was this team of elite operatives doing here at the arse end of some industrial street? They were amongst the greatest their nations had ever produced, their chests puffed with the mere knowledge of it.

One of the warehouse doors opened, and out came a short, compact man in a polo shirt tucked in to reveal a physique that certainly didn't spend its post-work hours in some local dive bar. His hair was swept and trimmed with equal professional rigour and his eyes twinkled as he beckoned them over with a folder.

'C'mon in, fellas,' he said, with an accent redolent of southern drawls, and the easy coercion of long being a superior.

The men filed in, infantry once more.

'I'm Hector, and I'm the reason you're here in Dallas,' he said smoothly, as they all entered the warehouse. There were foldout tables positioned ready in the centre like there was going to be a cookout. Whiteboards, sparkling, ready to be filled with whatever it was they were here for. The rest of the area was lined with crates, and at the back was a truck covered top to tyres in tarp, although the outline was unmistakable.

'Do you know why you're here?' said Hector.

'No, sir,' came the response in unison, except for one lone voice.

'Handshake doesn't need to know, sir.' Sinclair smiled. Lee. He loved this shit. Belt, braces, britches and boots – loved this shit.

'Excellent, gentlemen. There's a cafetière in the office adjoining through there.' Hector pointed with his fanned-out papers, which Sinclair could now see were rudimentary personnel one-sheets. 'And there's a loft above with some cots. It isn't the fuckin' Ritz, but it'll do you fine for the next couple of weeks. Grab yourself a coffee, or tea for our British contingent – yeah, I know how you transatlantic boys love that breakfast shit – and come on back out here so we can get started.'

'Yes, sir,' they replied in chorus once more.

'And at ease gentlemen. We have serious stuff to discuss. Stuff that's gonna, we hope, stop a president from getting killed.'

Even though the young soldiers had been told to relax their attitudes in Hector's presence, the words spoken put any sense of chill-out to bed.

An operation involving presidential protection. That pride flushed in Sinclair's chest again. It wasn't the Queen, but damn, it was close.

# CHAPTER THIRTY

It's almost too much, what we are being told. Like what we thought and presupposed has suddenly broken away and crumbled, and the overhanging threads left behind could never meet again or be resewn.

'Who was Sinclair?' asks Luca.

'A young guy, not dissimilar to yourself, Luca, or your grand-father. He was a good guy doing exactly as he was told, but this footage placed him, to the rest of the world, in the exact wrong place at the wrong time. You see, Handshake operatives had lives prior to recruitment to the unit, and they'd been recruited because of that. Your grandfather was in the Marines, for example, so there was a trail of people he had worked with – influential people, military people who, if they were watching, slack-jawed, a film of the president being assassinated, then saw one of their old military charges on the footage... well, it wouldn't look good, would it?'

'It would look very suspicious,' I say.

'Sinclair was no different. If he was placed in the vicinity of the president's murder it would be like announcing a covert military presence. A very bad look.'

I get so much of what I'm being told, but then again, I don't. There're still so many loose ends.

'How many did Handshake have there that day?' I ask.

'Five in total.'

'What was the name of the guy they arrested, the guy they said fired the killing shots?' Luca interjects.

'Lee Harvey Oswald,' I say, finding myself phrasing it as an accusation at Grosvenor. He catches my tone.

'Oswald was Handshake,' he replied.

'And these boys were instructed to kill the president?'

'No. But the bare facts of the matter, which these frames can prove, is that there was a covert military group in Dallas that day, and one of them shot the president of the United States twice with what can only be described as extremely well-trained and well-organised precision. Again, it doesn't look good, does it?'

We can't refute that. Nobody would believe that the unit wasn't instructed to do exactly that.

'So what's the truth? The truth that really happened?'

As if there can be any versions of the truth except the only one.

'The truth…' The words come loaded with sadness, fed through a smile so bitter it sieved them to near inaudibility. 'The truth, as I understand it from my old friend Luca Jones Senior, is that they were told that they were going to be an additional layer of protection for Kennedy, that there had been a threat that even the Secret Service didn't know about but was still credible.'

I think of those Secret Service agents who had come to take us out back at Bill's and their almost direct vocational lineage to those operatives in Dallas that day. It's almost like they'd come to find the truth for their forefathers, like they were there to try to lay to rest an ugly family secret, purge the ultimate skeleton in the Secret Service family closet.

'There was a credible threat all right. Handshake itself, although not all of it.' Grosvenor looks so torn now, and I've never seen him look so old. The weight of telling this is adding years to him but stripping him bare at the same time. He's carried this for decades, this knowledge of this plot. 'Oswald was the eye in the sky, the guardian angel with the high-powered rifle looking out for the supposed incoming threat. Luca and the three others were ordered to get him and the rifle safely into the Book Depository, which they clearly managed, and then were to adopt positions to cover the president. What they didn't know was that while Oswald was indeed Handshake, he had different orders – and he carried them out to the letter. The other boys were left as patsies, a convenient, unexpected covert military presence watching as one of their own turned. They were a bunch of kids sent to kill the president, but only one of them knew that was the real job. The rest thought they were there to protect him. I can only imagine what they felt. I've sat on this secret for years, and it's been a near-unbearable burden. How they must have felt… How Luca Senior must have felt…'

I feel terrible for him – and all of them. Imagine being involved in this, but not knowing until it was too late.

'How did they find out they'd been used?'

'Well, we all know that Oswald got the job done. The remaining boys went back to the extraction point at the operation headquarters, which was some rented retail warehouse a couple of miles from the Grassy Knoll, and, on arrival, they found it gutted. Completely cleaned out. No trace. No superiors, no nothing.

167

Just an empty warehouse. They were on their own, abandoned. Oswald was arrested. The police were tipped off to the warehouse and converged there. I believe it was the boys' superiors who did that too – in fact, there's always been a lingering question as to the police's involvement that day, but there's never been anything to prove it. Luca escaped with the envelope, and it has stayed with him, until now. The other boys, I don't know what happened to them. If they were picked up by police, they never resurfaced.'

'Where do you come into this?' Luca asks.

'My career was already varied but was also elite, much like these boys. Luca remerged and reinvented himself in the CIA, forging a long career. He never told me as much, but I believe they'd reached an entente, so to speak.'

'A what?'

'An agreement. He was where the CIA could see him, and he'd have a good career if he didn't talk. It was during this long career that I got to know him. An SAS man turned politician, a Marine turned intelligence operative, on either side of the pond. You can see how a relationship like that may well be mutually beneficial. That's when he told me about the big, dark secret. And you can imagine how horrified I was, to learn of British involvement, however unknowing those British lads on the team were – and you can further imagine the international outrage it would create if it ever got out.'

I can. Doubtlessly.

'Luca eventually retired to Florida, and we'd not seen each other since, until we made contact again in the late '90s. Ageing men, getting back in touch. But time… time has a way of weighing down on you that you don't expect. When Luca told me he still had the envelope, and its contents, I was initially furious. Imagine, the only evidence of a plot that dastardly, which has the potential to do your own nation monumental damage… But as time progressed, I got to thinking about those frames more as evidence of one of the greatest cover-ups the world has ever known, which only he could set straight.'

'Who was in charge of Handshake? Who would be upset to find this out?'

'It was, of course, unknown to his fellow operatives, but Lee had defected. A Marxist with Russian sympathies, so it turned out. But the CIA had their own motives. Kennedy's political direction was not aligned with their own, and I've long thought an agreement was formed between the CIA and the Russians, away from the eyes of the government.'

'Malinki,' I say.

Grosvenor nods. 'When a man on the direct payroll of the CIA and the Kremlin comes into the picture, working to get his hands on those frames, then… well, for me, that's suspicions confirmed, regardless of how much time has elapsed.'

'But why would he then give them to some White House stooge?' I ask.

'That, Ben, is another big question.'

Luca asks his own question, his mind coming back to life now, knowing that his grandfather was not directly to blame for the president's assassination. 'How did they know about the missing frames?'

'Come on, Luca – even amateur conspiracy whack jobs noticed that something was slightly off with the film when it was played back. Most thought it was a quirk of the technology at the time, that it would be somewhat jumpy. But Zapruder was an AV obsessive – he kept everything clean and smooth on his kit. So if Joe Public could notice the film had been doctored, the CIA bods definitely could – only they had something to lose. They've wanted it back for years, I'd imagine. And the events of the last few days only confirm that perception.'

'But why didn't Zapruder say something?'

'Fear, I imagine. Luca Senior must have taken those frames and outlined just how serious the situation was. How he too could be in danger if he spoke out. Then… he died before the scales could be balanced. With his own tortured secret, I should think.'

I'm spent, emotionally, just listening to this. We have to keep this hidden. We have to keep off the tracks. And we have to find out why the government wants it so badly. The CIA wants it hidden, the Russians want it hidden and the current administration plain wants it. How the hell does this fit together? I drink beer and wallow.

'Thanks for telling us, William,' I say.

'Luca, I firmly believe your grandfather only did what he thought was right. He thought he was doing something so patriotic, but in the end, he was betrayed. As was Sinclair, the other boys, even Oswald. Don't think badly of him.'

Luca has a tear in his eye, and I sympathise. His world just got fried. As for me? Well, it certainly puts a different slant on… everything.

# CHAPTER THIRTY ONE

The Tavern has rooms and by the time the conversation has been reduced to embers, we take one each. Broadsided and weighted down by the sheer magnitude of what I'd heard and the enormity of the challenges that face us tomorrow, I'm suddenly exhausted and spent. As soon as I get into my room, which is a box of waxed pine that makes up for its lack of floor space with sheer cosiness, I drop onto the bed and plummet to sleep almost immediately.

I wake with a start, what feels like minutes later, and take a moment to work out what woke me. Listening hard, I remain still, but hear nothing. The clock over the mirror reads 12.20 am, so I've been out for an hour, give or take. Satisfied it's just my whirring thoughts – seriously, how the hell do we get out of this? – I try to settle back, but I can't. It's strange, I've not struggled with sleep in years – soldiers take rest as soon as it's offered because they never know when the next time will be. But this situation is so big, so overbearing, I can't shake it. I feel like sleep is cheating.

The window is covered by a set of Venetian blinds, and beyond and below that is the street we walked in on. Every now and then, a car cruises past and I tense, imagining we've been tracked down, but the headlights sweep slatted bars across the back wall of the hotel room while passing.

Rather than lie here and let my mind wander, I start to think proactively and ask the big question. We know this is serious, but what's the end result? At the minute it's just a question of keeping the frames out of the wrong hands, but that can't go on forever. What about after that? Where do we want them to end up?

I'm half-tempted to walk into Grosvenor's room, snatch them up and destroy them. Tell William to get the word out via his government connections that they are no more, and life can go back to normal. But doing that would acknowledge they existed in the first place. And admitting those frames existed means admitting one of the biggest conspiracy theories of the human era is also real too. So what do we do?

I can't work it out. It's still too far from my grasp.

The CIA wants it as it proves they had something to do with JFK's murder, and would surely want to suppress it.

The Russians want it for that same reason. Helping murder the American president is bad, whatever era it took place in.

The British want it, via Grosvenor, because it confirms British involvement in JFK's death. As a Brit myself, I'm ashamed just hearing it, even though I know Handshake was tricked into it.

The current administration wants it for… what? Why does the present US government want this? Is it for power? Control over the CIA? What does it give them? Maybe it's the chance to show something positive? President Connors and his administration get a constant kicking from all corners – maybe this would be a chance for them to show they got to the bottom of something for once? Or is suppression the aim of the game for them too? There are long links between the presidency and the CIA, so oft-documented they would be very hard for anyone to ignore.

By the time I've played this out, over and over in my brain, looking at all the variables and where they may lie when the chips are truly down, I see the clock hands have crept to 2.00 am.

It's about seven in the morning back home, so I grab the phone and call Carolyn. It takes her a little while to answer it, and I start to feel guilty when she picks up.

'Hey, it's Daddy,' she coos breathlessly, and I can just imagine Jam has been scooped into her arms so she can pick up the call. 'How are you, wanderer?'

'I'm sorry,' I say, 'I didn't think; you're right in the middle of it, aren't you?'

'The usual morning chaos, nothing new there,' she replies, and suddenly I can't put into words just how much I'd like to be there with her now, scrambling eggs and pouring cornflakes, filling lunchboxes and finding clothes. My guilt intensifies, and I feel an acute longing. This is the longest I've been apart from her, not to mention my beautiful boy, since we moved in together. And on the other end of this phone line, the night at its deadest, with the sheer pressure that's outside these walls waiting for us, I feel as far away as ever. I know I always wanted to be a family man, deep down, at some point. And now? I feel its loss.

'How are you holding up?' I ask, finding the words hard to come by.

'We are OK, you know. Kids aren't sleeping great, Jam misses you, I miss you. And the older two might not admit it, but they do too.'

'Tell them I miss them.' I want to keep my relationship with the older children growing and to make them feel like they can rely on me always – which is admittedly a tough ask from thousands of miles away, but still.

'I will,' she says, before pausing to separate the raised voices I can hear suddenly squabbling in the background. When she comes back on, there's a questioning tilt to her voice. 'It's the middle of the night over there, isn't it?'

'Just gone two.'

'Just got in?' There's no judgement in that. We are both too old for juvenile mistrust. She's more concerned with me burning myself out than canoodling with some stray woman in a bar.

'Trouble sleeping.'

'Oh.' She knows me inside out. She knows that's abnormal for me, to say the least.

'I can't say much over the phone, but… it's getting big over here. Really big.'

'Should I be worried?'

'You should never worry about me.'

'That doesn't mean I won't, soldier.'

'Understood, ma'am.' I go quiet without meaning too, before finding my voice. 'We are trying to work it out, it's just complicated, that's all.'

'Dangerous complicated?'

I'm definitely not going to answer that head-on and add fuel to the fire. 'More like delicate negotiations complicated.'

'Will you call again soon, keep me updated?'

'I promise. I just needed a taste of home tonight. Can I talk to Jam?'

'Yeah, but it might be a little one-way.' I can hear the smile in her voice as she shifts position with a rustle of fabric. 'Jam, it's Daddy. He's looking at the phone.'

I can imagine that perfect boy with his blond curls and his immaculate little nose, those crisp baby blues looking at mummy's phone with confusion. 'Hello, son,' I say.

'He's smiling. He's confused, but he's smiling.'

I feel tears build up. 'Daddy's here, young man. Daddy's here.'

I only manage a few more moments before it gets painful, not being able to see him or cuddle him. So, I make my excuses, tell them I'll call home again soon, and hang up, as water rolls freely from my eyes either side of my face, dropping onto the pillow in fat audible drops.

# CHAPTER THIRTY TWO

Breakfast is a subcontinental affair that neither myself nor Grosvenor can touch, but Luca dives into it like a death row inmate given a last-minute reprieve. The older man and I just settle for matching black coffees by the canteen-full. None of us say anything until it gets a little uncomfortable.

'Rough nights all round, it seems,' says Grosvenor, breaking the apparent pact of silence. It doesn't exactly jog conversation along, and the only sound anywhere near the table is the smooth croon of a country singer on the radio behind the bar, who it seems has actually managed to insert the phrase catfish dinner into his lyrics. We are a long old way from home.

By the time the singer has informed us that the catfish dinner is the preamble to knockin' boots in a flatbed truck (of course), I have to tackle the big issues head-on. 'What's the endgame here, William?'

Grosvenor's eyebrows flicker upwards, then droop at the sides, like he's thought of a number of things, but at the end of the day, he doesn't have even half a clue. Same here, buddy.

I'm bulling this one by the horns now. 'Let's talk ideals. The three of us round the table. What are the ideal end results for us all? Let's say we're in control of this, which we are if we stay one step ahead – what is it you both want to happen?'

Luca has one small segment of pancake left on his plate, maybe an inch square, but he waterboards that fucker in maple syrup while he speaks. 'I'm gonna clear Pops' name, even if it's just for me. He didn't bargain for any of this shit; as you put it, Ben – he thought he was protecting his president, and he was used. For me, either that secret stays buried, or we expose who did it. And I don't mean that dipshit turncoat Oswald – I mean the real people behind it.'

'Even if it's high up in your own organisation? Properly shit on your bosses' parade?'

'Especially if it's high up in my organisation.'

'So you're up for following this through?'

He finally stops pouring the damn syrup. 'Yep.'

'You could stack out here pretty easy. Me and William could keep those wishes in mind as we proceed.'

'No way. I'm in this to the season finale.'

He breathes in and out. That settles that. Luca's hand played, he wolfs that soggy excuse for a delicacy in the most belligerent exercise of freedom I've seen since I landed in the states.

'William, you're holding the damn things, you'll go last, because if you decide to flush them down the pisser right this minute, I don't think I could do a good enough job of stopping you.'

Grosvenor's coffee cup must have suddenly got really interesting, the way he stares at it.

'For me, I'm in the same boat as Luca,' I say. 'We clear out. We redress this balance. Handshake was framed – his grandfather was framed. If he hadn't got out of there, he'd have been arrested and sentenced to death, I've no doubt about it. I think we have to go full bore at them. Clear Handshake's name. Expose the real perpetrators.'

Silence again, for a solid minute. 'You sure that's what you want?'

'Yes. I've been up all night on it; I feel like hammered shite.' Luca tips his coffee cup at me. 'But you know me, William, if there's a chance to do proper good, you know I say do it. I'll always say do it. But if we play smart, ruthless, then I'm convinced there's a chance here.'

I let the words waft across the table as Luca, God love him, clinks his coffee cup against mine. He's an infectious bugger.

'You have to understand,' says Grosvenor, his tone suddenly embracing the elder statesman role I suppose he uses in Westminster, 'what you're suggesting is that the three of us can somehow take on the CIA – his employers…' A finger wags at Luca. 'The current president and his government. And Russia – *Russia*, for Christ's sake. And a bunch of men who were powerful in the '60s but are most likely dead now. None of those superiors who arranged this back then will still be alive, surely. We have no one to bring to account. And all we'll do is try to keep one step ahead for as long as we possibly can, while all comers try to take us out.'

'Do you want justice or not? Because the toilet is that way if you're unsure. But if you want to set history right, then now is a perfect damn time to do it,' I say.

He mulls it over. 'God, I wish I had a cigarette.'

'I was unaware you smoked.'

'I don't.'

'How would you propose going about this then? Clearing the decks?'

'Any journalist in the country – hell, any journalist in any country – would want this story. Front page of the *New York Times*, front page of *The Washington Post*, that would get the story out there.'

'But they'd want the proof. And that would put Sinclair in the frame. Where is Sinclair now?'

'I assume he's dead. He's a ghost, but again, he's a recognisable one. And he's British. It could be catastrophic.'

Something is niggling me a bit here, and I'm beginning to work out what it is. 'Listen, you just said that there's likely nobody left alive in a position of power from that time. So who would be around to recognise Sinclair?'

That stumps him, yet I continue. 'What alarms me is that all these parties chasing this down – they must know that there's proof. And they've got a way of proving who it is and therefore proving that the kid in the photo was part of the assassination plot, albeit unwittingly. That means there is evidence of Handshake somewhere. Living evidence.'

'Bloody hell,' Grosvenor exhales. 'It stands to reason that someone, somewhere, has something definitive to prove what truly happened that day.'

'Who's left?' I ask. And sure as a twisting vine aiming for sunlight, our necks turn to Luca.

'Where's your grandfather?'

Luca looks startled. 'Florida.'

'And his testimony, in a newspaper, would seal it, maybe even without the need to print those frames.'

Within three seconds, our chairs are scraping back from the floor in screeching unison, and we are off upstairs to grab our things.

# CHAPTER THIRTY THREE

Sometimes, it helps to have a British government minister on your team, especially when it comes to pulling off minor miracles in the organisation department. They can be damn persuasive. A quick taxi ride takes us the eighteen miles to Suzie Field, an airstrip set in acres of green squares of agriculture, where a light jet is waiting for us, fuelled and ready to tilt skywards. I've never been on a private jet, and my heart takes a sudden pump of endorphins at the ostentatious buzz of it.

The taxi drops us off at the airfield gates, beyond which is nothing more than a flattened strip of dirt amidst oceans of grass, resembling a giant cricket pitch. Sat at the near end is a gleaming white plane that looks like a forgotten toy.

As we walk to it, surrounded by the harsh buzz of insects either doing the nasty or advertising that they'd like to do the nasty, I can't hold my curiosity any longer. 'So, how much did this set you back?'

'Eleven grand, US. So about nine thousand quid. And I've never fiddled my expenses once, so I think I'm due a little leeway.'

I smile.

Luca blows out as we get near and the cabin door opens, an

automatic stairway lowering pointed legs to the dust. 'This is great,' he mutters, with no shortage of wonder.

My smile broadens irrepressibly. There's something about this country that, while I can't quite put my finger on it, I really enjoy. The expanse maybe. The freedom of choice. The sensation that you can have it all. No wonder immigrants have flocked to it in their droves, drunk on the idea of streets paved with gold.

The pilot walks down the steps, and I was expecting a fellow with a starched collar and aviators, but this guy looks like he's about to go on a turkey shoot (not that I've been on one of those, but I'm getting the hang of the culture and vernacular here). He wears wrap around orange-lensed shades, the kind I haven't seen since the mid-nineties, and a camo shirt with a blaze-orange high visibility vest.

He extends a delicate hand to each of us, starting with Grosvenor. 'Val Vincent, of Val's VIP Travel.' His accent is honeyed Texan, from wind-chapped lips, as if he flies his jet with the windows down. I can't see his eyes, but his thick grey handlebar moustache is more expressive than any ocular organs ever could be.

Grosvenor takes his hand. 'Thanks for helping us out, Val.'

He adjusts his belt, yanking it up over his pot belly. 'A usual day is some rich coffin-dodger who wants to go fly a glorified crop-duster over the farmers' markets to see them from the air before the last big ride. But someone calls up looking for the silver service with decent miles on the contract? You say jump, I ask which cloud I'm aiming at. And because of this bad boy, unlike other services, I can get you there.'

He shakes our hands too, then lets us board. It's plush, the leather of the twelve passenger seats only faded on a couple of them, with plenty of legroom and a kitchen at the rear. I take a seat, strap in while Luca walks to the back and sits by himself. The kid is beaming. Clutches his backpack like it might evaporate, the plane and his belongings both, any second. Good for him.

'Just the three of you?' shouts Val as he pops his head in.

'That's right,' says Grosvenor.

Val shuts the door behind him, pulling up the collapsible stairs as it goes. 'Tea and coffee back there. There's some danish in the cupboard. I hope you don't mind but, as I believe there's a time issue here, I don't have the time to play stewardess. Although the uniform's in the closet back there in case any of you fellas want to play dress up. Settle back, seatbelts on when you're on your asses, flight time is approx. two hours thirty, but I believe there's a chance of a tailwind that'll chop ten to fifteen off that. Any questions, come knock on the door. Wheels up in under two minutes. See you up there.'

And with that, he's gone, and we're left to look at each other.

'He's a find,' I say.

'He wasn't for asking too many questions. That's why I liked him,' replies Grosvenor. 'Best get some rest,' he says. 'I don't know how far ahead of our pursuers we are, but we need to be ready for a hectic schedule.'

'Where are we headed again?'

'Naples,' Luca says from behind me. 'Not that one.'

'Mafia country?'

'Not that one.'

I settle back into the seat as we start moving forwards. The pace ramps up, the dirt beyond the window starts to blur, my stomach tilts back and I start to drift, the sleep that I missed last night finally coming back to claim me.

# CHAPTER THIRTY FOUR

I wake when Val croons, 'Arriving on a jet plane' in a sub-John Denver remix over the plane's speaker system, and the jet slumps gradually out of the sky. 'Three minutes,' adds Val. It feels like sailing into a sinkhole as I look out of the window to see tall palms and the bluest seas I've ever lain eyes on. I half wonder if I've been asleep for hours, such is the abruptness of the scenery change.

'Is this your home town, Luca?' I ask, turning. The young CIA man is against the glass like a kid at the zoo.

'Yep. This is where I grew up, all right.'

'Your folks still about?'

'Nah, they moved inland after us kids grew up.'

It's such a completely different vibe to the America I've seen so far. Stucco-lined streets with low terracotta roofs, boxed in by the stretchy green blobs of a golf course and the hard strike-line border of the sea. We start to bank left but as we tilt and my perspective changes, I see the criss-cross runways of Naples Airport like a giant grey plaster in the middle of everything. We aren't headed there, clearly.

'He's dropping us off somewhere quiet?' I ask.

'I think,' Grosvenor says as he checks his phone, 'Wings Park South is more our speed. National secrets don't go through major airports if you want to keep them.'

We're down within two minutes, at an airport that's a horseshoe-shaped cul-de-sac of grey outbuildings, and Val reappears. 'I'll handle everything. There's a car on the tarmac, and the gate at the far end should be open.'

'Val,' I call, and he turns. 'In appreciation.' I shake his hand and pass him two hundred-dollar bills, which I'd taken from Malinki's cash wad.

'The appreciation is mine, brother. I'm gonna go catch a few rays this afternoon before heading back up the Eastern Seaboard. If you need anything, get on the horn, all right?'

'We'll keep that in mind.'

Val nods at something in the distance. 'Keys will be in the ignition. Or they should be.'

On the tarmac is a no-frills Sedan which barely warrants description, only that it is in a crap green like the mould in a turtle tank. Luca asks if he can drive and, as the only native, we let him. The keys are right where Val said they'd be, and we are away.

'Who arranged the car?' I ask.

'A local budget rental company. If you don't go to the big ones, you can get a lot more discretion and a bit more bang for your buck.'

'Apart from in the actual vehicle department, right?' Luca jibes from the front. I notice he's driving in that hunched up owl style, with his nose almost on top of the steering wheel itself.

Grosvenor wipes dust from the dashboard. 'I really meant in the getting a car into the airport and leaving it for us with no paperwork department, but I agree – something from the last five years wouldn't have gone amiss.'

With a nose for direction that can only come from habit and history, Luca takes us through the airport barriers and into the sparse, ambling traffic of yet another broad road that seems a hallmark of every American corner I've been so far.

'How long to your grandfather's?' I ask.

'About ten minutes.'

I watch out of the window, counting the obligatory chain stores that have adopted the local architectural trends, like that Burger King lined by leaning palms, topped with a red tile roof. There's a stubborn permeation to commercial expansion here that seems almost virulent in its determined approach. Everywhere I've been, I see the same signs. Ones that weren't recognisable before, suddenly, after only a smattering of days, have grown in familiarity. I don't know what a Chipotle is, but I know there'll be another in a few miles.

Having eased in and out of traffic for almost exactly ten minutes, we pull to a stop in a parking bay directly next to a two-story building that is covered in a soft red pastel wash, well-manicured and gated just before the doors. Luca gets out of the car and breathes out, and now we're not rushing, the heat really hits me heavy and hard like a broken sauna. We follow Luca, who approaches the black gate and thumbs the buzzer.

'It's just how it's always been,' he says. 'His is the ground floor apartment on the corner there.' He points along the building to where a black door rests buried in the red. It reads "1a" in white vinyl lettering and the only distinguishing mark of personality is a doormat that I can just about read: "No Sales".

I rest my hand on the railing and pull away, skin burnt, the baked metal hot enough to grill a ribeye. We wait, and the drone of insects from the elegant topiary that adorns the walkway beyond the fence is loud enough that it competes with the buzz of the road.

Luca tries again but soon gives up. 'No answer. He must be out. But whenever he was, when I was a kid, I'd go sit over there and wait for him.' He points to an ice cream stand on the other side of the street, outside a grocers. 'We could just chill out with a couple of ices till he gets back. He's never long.'

We head over the road, and I'm treated to the sight of a decorated war veteran and current cabinet minister trying not to get melted chocolate ice cream down his chinos. The tabloids at home would have a field day.

We wait an hour, and the heat is making me restless. Hunkered down in the desert, I endured a lot of waiting, but here, with the sweet smells of urbanisation under oppressive heat, I'm restless. There's a funny discrepancy about that building opposite that I just can't place.

I've got, what I've come to recognise as, a feeling.

'Just gonna have a nosy,' I say, and cross the road, without waiting to hear Luca try to stop me. When I reach the pavement on the other side, I try to look at the building with fresh eyes. What is off to me here? Something is. I know it is. I just can't establish what.

While trying not to look conspicuous, I let my eyes wander every contour.

The guttering is immaculate. The foliage perfect. The security cameras high in the eaves could be winking at me. The entrance gate looking like it could withstand a truck reversing into it.

So why does it not feel right?

And, like an uppercut from the invisible man, it hits me.

# CHAPTER THIRTY FIVE

It's all in the windows. This apartment block appears to offer eight separate living spaces for eight separate sets of residents. I can see all the windows on this side comfortably, as well as the four front doors – and also their windows. All are clean, well maintained, pretty spotless apart from the occasional bric-a-brac on the sills. Except the one on the corner, which is dripping with condensation so much that drops run from the top to the bottom of the pane like the clearest tears.

And that's Luca Jones Sr's apartment.

Without alerting Luca, I walk around the side of the building, following the hot black fence, until I'm out of sight of the guys at the ice cream shop – and as soon as I can't see them I start to climb. Forget the cameras, we'll be long gone from Naples before the tapes are even checked.

'What are you doing?' says a voice behind me, cracked. I look down as I'm cresting the top of the barrier to see a little old lady in a nightdress and slippers pulling a wheelie trolly with a pony-tailed rat-dog on the top.

'Forgive me, madam, it's a police matter.' I only realise after

I've said it that I've put on my best Roger Moore voice.

'Better had be,' she says somewhat flummoxed, before shuffling along, the dog's black, marble eyes never leaving me.

I drop down the other side and see two more windows – condensation rife on both. It's all off.

Getting in will be the hard part, but there's no time for subtlety here. If something bad has happened then we're too late and we need to be on the road again, away from here fast.

I check the nearest window but can't see through it. I assess the pane, but I'm no cat burglar. I don't know how to jimmy it open – so I wait till a truck passes, and precisely as it roars by, I hit the glass with a rock from the shrubbery. The pane collapses, and out blasts air of the utmost putridity.

It's so bad I have to duck, but the assault is so sudden, so hot, so sickly sweet and rancid, I throw up into the flower bed.

No time to waste here. Establish what's happened and get out. I was unnerved, but now I'm expecting the God's honest worst.

I tear off my t-shirt sleeve and slide it over my head, covering my mouth and nose, before hopping in through the empty frame.

I'm in a bathroom. Neat, orderly. A shaving brush on the sink. One bar of soap. It's a man's bathroom and a man's bathroom only. The door is open, and the air is oppressive in its weight. It's that heavy, I feel if I did breaststroke I'd get through it quicker than walking.

I go out into the hall, and again, nothing visually out of place. Luca Jones Sr was clearly an orderly man. To my left is the front door, painted white on this side, and my right leads to what I assess is the living room, judging by the back of the sofa I see. The heat in here is nigh-on absurd. And it only feels like it's getting that bit warmer. I enter the living room, and the mystery of Luca Jones Sr's whereabouts is solved with categorical firmness.

He's sat – or at least, part of him was. I can't really put proper words to what I can see, but this is one of the most awful things I've ever laid eyes on. He must have been in that leather recliner for a few days because it looks like his back is still stuck to it – while the rest of him has drifted downwards, and there's been a parting of his two pieces. Some of him remains in the chair, the rest of him is sliding to the floor. Next to him, pulled close, is an old electric heater, still on full blast, all three of the thin horizontal filaments burning bright red.

The nausea rises again. Where's that damn flower bed when you need it?

I try to detach myself from the horror and look at things coldly – even though, and this is hard to admit, while I've seen some shit in my time, my new friend's grandfather melted to a chair in a hot Florida apartment might be the worst of the lot. Did he die like this? Naturally, I mean. Fell asleep, didn't wake up, and here we are?

I move closer, try to adopt some zen bollocks of putting myself on a separate plane to the here and now. The condition of the body is bad, the skin so unnatural, that I'm sure it would take a clear-headed coroner to find something workable. Just as I get ready to give up and throw up all over again, I see a door ajar behind him, over his shoulder, deeper into the apartment. The door to what looks like an office. A ransacked office, paper spilt and spat all over.

No prizes for guessing what they were looking for. They didn't find it, and Luca Senior paid for it with his life.

I hear the faintest loop of a siren, and I'm already up and running back for the window before my mind catches up. That nosy, wonderfully community-minded neighbour called the police, fantastically caring pain in the arse that she is.

I'm out the bathroom window and over the fence, gulping air that, while still hot, tastes a hell of a lot better than it did just moments ago.

Jogging across the street, I see Luca and Grosvenor coming the other way. Luca looks worried and I am too – for him, more than anything.

This is going to break his heart.

'What's happening?' he asks, eyes broad with fear.

'Nothing, it's empty,' I say, as I turn him towards the car and aim him at the driver's side. 'But the sirens mean we can't stick around.'

Grosvenor climbs in the back but just as he does, he looks at me. One of those looks. Play it straight with me, son.

I shake my head once, and Grosvenor gets it.

We are away from the scene just as the first responders arrive from the opposite direction, and the flush of adrenaline peaks. Then I'm left with the hollow. That vacuum of dread, as I accept I've got to tell this kid what happened to his grandfather.

# CHAPTER THIRTY SIX

We drive south out of central Naples until the buildings can't see us and the sirens can't reach our ears.

'The police will be looking for me,' I say. That plane home to England feels a long way off. 'Laying low is a good idea.'

'Well, we wouldn't have to lay low if somebody didn't break in.' Luca is distrusting of me and biting – and I completely get why. He's sharp – he knows when there's a gap in a story. But how do I doll up what I saw in that living room?

There's careful omission and there's straight-up bullshit.

'We're moving, that's the main thing.'

'He still might come home. Only now he's got the big problem of coming home to a break-in and police at his door.'

I can feel Grosvenor's eyes scalding the back of my head. The longer I leave this, the longer it'll be like deception. I shift in my seat, spare Grosvenor one eye and turn to Luca.

'Take the next turn off, Luca,' I say.

'Why? We need to get movi—'

'Just… take the next turn off.'

I can tell just by the way he indicates, with his whole hand gripping the stalk, he knows.

We pull off into a densely lined scrub lane, which has a grass-choked creek running alongside it. Luca pulls over and kills the engine.

'Dead. Am I right?' His words sound too cocksure, too bold, while his red-rimmed, drowning eyes betray him.

'I'm sorry, Luca. Your grandfather has passed away.'

Compassion is a developing characteristic for me. Death was part of the deal in the army. You were a number, no more. When one number got rubbed out, another was put in its place. But this isn't war, and this isn't the army. This is about a young man and his grandfather. I put my hand on Luca's shoulder.

'Was it bad? Had he been hurt?'

A siege of the most heinous images assaults the space behind my eyes. 'He was sitting in his chair. Passed on.'

'He'd fallen asleep?'

I can't forget that Luca works for the CIA. He might be able to pull in the odd police report. He'll be able to read in black, white and all the lines in between, the condition his grandfather was in when I found him.

But that's for some other time. Not now.

'I don't know.'

'Was he mur—'

'It looked to me like someone had been there, looking for something. His office had been turned over.' I keep my voice even.

'God. This fucking envelope!' he shouts, and punches the steering wheel until his cheeks go red. He breathes through his nose, causing flecks of mucus to dive from his nostrils.

'He may well have died protecting it.'

'Had they hurt him?' Luca looks at me head-on, rage pulsing in every sudden angle of his wrought body.

'I… truthfully don't know. All I know is he had passed. Then the sirens started.'

'I need to go back. I need to go and be with him.'

Shit, mate – you don't want to do that.

Luca reaches for the keys, but Grosvenor settles it from the back-seat. 'If you drive back there, he will have died for nothing, Luca.'

And the poor young man sobs for a couple of minutes.

I glance at Grosvenor in the rear-view mirror. I've no idea the true extent of his relationship with Luca Jones Senior, whether they're little more than colleagues or if there was any true kinship. But he stares out of the window at the rippling fronds of green. He closes his eyes, and his jaw tightens.

There it is. They were real friends.

Feeling as if I'm intruding on their grief, my gaze wanders to the creak, where two little eyes poke above the water. Ever watching. Cold. Reptilian. Otherworldly. It won't be big, whatever it is, but it's there. Watching.

Watching.

That's all we'll ever feel, our whole lives. That's all this will be. Lives on the run, decades trying to stay ahead.

No life at all.

Luca Jones Senior lived it. Grosvenor has too, to an extent.

No, we need to change tack. We need to bring the fight to them. Draw them out.

Luca suddenly speaks, nasally and full of snot.

'All we need to do is drive into another jurisdiction. A crime like that, you just look like a burglar who got more than he bargained for. There'll be no APB beyond jurisdictional lines – we'll be fine if we just stay out of Naples.'

'OK, Luca. What do you want to do?'

He looks out of the windshield and, after a moment, uses the washer jets and wipers to try to ease away the sheer number of bugs mashed into the glass, which I erstwhile hadn't noticed. 'Let's blow this thing wide open and take them down.'

I turn to Grosvenor. His regal air returns to full pomp and he nods once.

We're on.

# CHAPTER THIRTY SEVEN

The Rod and Gun Club is something else. A lost in time colonial pile on the waterfront, the sheer wildness of the mangrove community evident everywhere you look. Situated on the edge of Everglades City, it's a call-back to a much simpler time when men were judged on what they could haul up from the depths or spray bullets into. Whatever my stance on hunting might be, I can't help but dig its Wild East qualities.

'Do you think she's going to come?' asks Luca, absently twirling the fronds of a mini umbrella that had been dunked into the soda he ordered twenty minutes prior.

'She'll be here,' replies Grosvenor, on his second coffee. He's been quiet for over an hour now, these being his first words. The sweat pours off them both, not through nerves but through the sheer humidity. It's like being in a hot tub but free to walk around. 'She can't not be.'

I'm sat just a little down the small bar, underneath the head of a stuffed doe, looking out across the establishment. An old hunting and fishing lodge that has been purposely frozen in the 1920s, it's a bit like stepping behind the ropes at a museum exhibit and getting in amongst the waxworks. Every surface is dark stained wood and festooned with taxidermized catches and trophy busts. A pool table sits beyond a giant copper fire hood, the coals and logs beneath it mercifully unlit. Pool cues, fishing rods and antiquated electrical features complete the look. The Rod and Gun Club remains a functioning hotel, and if I was here on anything other than this, I'd be booking a room and ordering something a little more interesting than the sparkling water that sits next to me – but I'm still, given the circumstances, happy enough. Despite this being only a short visit across the pond, it seems I've actually managed to catch a bit of culture after all.

'To Pops,' says Luca. We clink glass and porcelain.

I hear the heels before I see anybody; a foreboding, take no shit, wobble your Adam's apple click-clack, and in unison we all turn. Into the open bar space she walks with her head held high, a briefcase on a shoulder strap, jeans, white dress shirt and stilettos so high mere mortals would get nosebleeds wearing them.

She sees the three of us and walks straight over, dropping her bag on a spare barstool. 'You couldn't have picked a sweatier ass-end of the country, could you?'

Her tone is brusque but not arrogant – I suppose that's what happens when you get a call offering the story of the century but you've got to get to south Florida immediately if you want to hear it.

Grosvenor stands and immediately acts the statesman organiser. I'm happy to take a back seat.

'Thank you for meeting us,' he says, shaking her hand and turning to introduce us in turn. 'This is Luca, and...' He's always been so good at letting me finish.

'Ben,' I say while receiving a firm shake. 'But that's off the record. Is that the right expression?'

'Nobody actually says that, but it works. And as far as I understand it, all your identities are *off the record*, right?'

Grosvenor answers for us all. 'Yes.'

'But you're the British minister.' She points at him, fingernails immaculately groomed and rendered the hue of a bloodshot cornea.

'Indeed. Shall we go and get something to eat?'

'As long as it's not fried gator, I'm in.'

I thought she was joking, but as soon as we walk onto the all-white, enclosed decking at the back, which appears to serve as the alfresco dining area, I see a specials board offering exactly that. Fried gator, with plantain and creamed grits.

I know what I'm having.

We are ushered to a lone table for four in the furthest corner, lit by citronella candles to ward off whatever bugs might have got through the industrial level fly screening that lines the veranda. And beyond that? One of the most idyllic and captivating river settings I've ever seen.

I fell in love with the river a while back, hunkered down on the Norfolk Broads, and this is a jacked-up version of the same thing. Even the bugs here are more potent, and instead of pike in the river, there're gators that'll pull you under and leave nothing left. The water itself is calm, the flat angle of the failing sunlight lending the dark water an unnerving depth. Gazing out along the tributary, islands of mangroves promise adventure and the untamed.

'Drinks?' asks a waiter in a crisp shirt and slacks.

'A Moscow mule, squeeze of lime, plenty of ice – please,' says

Fiona Villiers, head political editor for *The Washington Post*, having wasted no time in making her selection.

Sounds good to me. 'Same, please.'

'Same.'

'Same.'

As the waiter darts off, an electric snap from somewhere announces the incineration of one of the environment's heftier insects. Fiona puts a small Dictaphone on the table, next to her glass of water. 'For the parts that can go on record.'

'We'll get to that,' says Grosvenor, who has changed for the evening into a salmon polo shirt. I'm still in my civvies from Target the night before, and I'm acutely aware that they may not be as fresh twenty-four hours later. 'For this story to get maximum traction, you'll have to relay some genuine facts.'

She suddenly adopts an air that time is money, and she's spending a lot of time here. 'And what are those facts, Minister Without Portfolio William Grosvenor? What are you doing here in the Sunshine State? And I'll say it outright, I'm not going home with merely a Florida Man headline, or some bullshit about the skunk ape.'

'The tape stays off unless it's you speaking. Our voices never appear on it.'

'Why would anyone believe me?'

'That's why we came to you.'

'You mean that's why your office in London called me.'

'You're still the one we invited to the table.'

The drinks arrive, a thin black straw in each, and Fiona takes a decent sip before immediately asking for another. 'Speaking of tables, cards on it.'

'Brass tacks, we have evidence of a major global conspiracy.'

'Pertaining to what?'

'An assassination plot.'

'Against who?' She starts taking cursory notes.

'It has already happened. And it was successful.'

She pauses in her note-taking and slowly looks up. 'Who?'

Grosvenor leans in and pulls the envelope, now more dog-eared than ever, from the breast pocket of his shirt, and empties the frames onto a napkin. 'Be careful with these. Hold them up to the light.'

Fiona walks to the wall lamp at the corner of the decking and holds one of the celluloid squares up to it. I can see her scrutiny leeching off her stance, but suddenly her shoulders arch tight. 'You're fuckin' joking,' she mutters, but I catch the wonder in there – and any concern that she doesn't recognise the imagery goes the way of the bug zapped moments ago. It tells how deeply ingrained the character of the Zapruder footage really is into the American psyche, but to a Washington political journalist? This might well be her Holy Grail.

She checks the other two, then returns to the table with the napkin. Her Moscow Mule is downed immediately, before she picks up her pen. 'Tell me everything you can.'

# SINCLAIR

It was a beautiful day. They'd had breakfast out on the front of the warehouse driveway, those sausage patty things that Sinclair, only months ago, would have thought fit for nothing more than the bin but was now addicted to. Coffee by the shedload, in between the odd cup of tea to try to not hurt Hector's feelings. They'd even played baseball, which was nothing to Sinclair but cricket for those who struggled with maths but were too proud to say so. All the supervisors were there; the Handshake guys they hadn't seen before, and they'd all managed to bond that morning to let off steam.

As midday approached, the weight of forthcoming events began to press down on each of them. Everyone looked after themselves in their own ways before a job. Sinclair's way was through quietness. Luca got even louder, if that was possible. Lee went into himself. The other boys, Jinks and the G-Man, were studied focus.

Not every day you were going off to protect the president. Not every day you got to be the silent layer of protection beyond even the official lines of security. They were better than the best of the best. They were Handshake.

They called each of their get-ups their uniforms, even though each was merely a variant on civilian clothing. Sinclair was in a charcoal suit which, for Sinclair, worked amazingly. James Bond wore one of these in *From Russia With Love*, which he'd managed to go out and catch at a drive-in theatre just over the state line in Oklahoma a few weeks back. It had blown Sinclair's mind. On the contrary, Luca was wearing a bomber jacket and some jeans. Lee was wearing a white t-shirt, something Sinclair thought he'd maybe got from him, some dark slacks and a dark shirt.

All of them looked unconnected. Which was the idea.

The cars arrived to take them to Dealey Plaza, the location specified in the threat. More Buicks. They climbed in without a word, while Hector was the only one to come out and offer a wave. He was all cheer and smiles, sending the boys off to do their duty which had been weeks in the planning. They knew all the escapes, knew all the avenues of threat, and Lee, as eye on the sky, would be watching over them. Repetition emboldened by training cemented action into habit. They were all ready.

The radio crackled. It was the driver's on the passenger seat. Hector's voice came over the static. 'Ten-four, front door. Just checking in with a little surprise mail.' The tone Hector used was jovial and off the cuff. In the thickly enhanced police and Secret Service presence, they'd decided to use CB radio speak as their way of communication. The three men in the back were rapt, tuned in to this being a message from HQ with a change of instruction.

The driver replied in a similar vein, with the rolling delivery of a seasoned pro. 'Roger, Old Charger, come on.'

'There's a ten-thirteen up ahead, you'll have to angle north.

Copy that?'

'That's a ten-four, Old Charger.'

'Seventy-three.'

'Threes.' The driver suddenly addressed the operatives in the monotone they were accustomed to. 'You boys catch that?'

'Loud and clear, sir,' said Sinclair, before his mind got whirring.

The message revealed that the president's motorcade was rerouting, but just by a single street. It was taking a more indirect route to the expressway. It was easy to imagine that certain last-minute plan changes were necessary when faced with a silent threat, so Sinclair was merely glad their intel networks had kept them in the loop. They had alternate northerly positions now to go to when they arrived at the plaza, but aside from that, the operation would go as normal.

Sinclair watched the streets become choked with people as they got nearer the plaza. He sat in the middle of the back seat, between Luca and Lee and, as the car pulled up to make the first drop off, Luca got out.

He gave Sinclair a nod as he left and said, 'See you on the other side.'

A few more streets along and now it was Sinclair's turn to get out. He stepped from the car and turned to Lee – who was smiling. As expected. Lee really loved all this shit.

'See you on the other side,' he said through his grin and settled into the plush leather.

'See you,' Sinclair said – not knowing what Lee Harvey Oswald was about to go and do.

# CHAPTER THIRTY EIGHT

Under a darkening gulf sky, over some of the most flavoursome food I've ever tasted, William Grosvenor told *The Washington Post*, and in turn the whole world, his greatest secret – and the truth of one of the most astonishing conspiracies of all time. Fiona touched nothing while he spoke in small chunks, pausing him so she could recount what he had just said into her Dictaphone. It wouldn't have his voice from which to retell the story, but it would have hers.

Rehearing the tale and our journey to this point serves to help me greatly, in terms of connecting the dots and grasping threads in my own mind. There is still so much to understand but one thing is certain. Someone wants this information, and someone has killed many times to get their hands on it.

Fiona, true to expectation, is no slouch. I can almost see the needle and thread pumping behind her eyes as she stitches this electrifying story together. How a young group of elite soldiers were sent to protect the president, but one of their number had orders to kill him. It's a storyteller's dream, and like the elite journalist her byline proclaims, it's plain to see that she will take this story and scream it from the print rooftops as loudly and as boldly as she can.

'May I see them again,' she asks, and Grosvenor duly slides the napkin over to her. The hard-bitten, bullshit-proof exterior is all but gone as she whispers, her head craned to the light, 'I'm not often speechless, but this...'

Once the story is almost caught up to the present and I've eaten my gator (not bad at all, and it made me feel extra-manly in a really most pathetic way), she pauses a moment and looks at Luca. 'My condolences, Luca. It seems, with your grandfather's passing, that any survivor of this day is gone.'

Luca nods, accepting her sympathies. 'Please... paint him in a good light. He was a fierce patriot. He'd never have been involved in something like this had he known.'

I speak. 'With his death, there's only one link to go. The lad on the frames. Sinclair.'

'When did you last hear anything of him, William?'

Grosvenor is back on the coffee. The guy guzzles it like it's his only viable source of nutrition. 'I never met him personally, just aware of who he is. If he was there, and these frames prove that he was, then Handshake can be proven – as can their involvement.'

Fiona's pen is flying across her pad, scrawling a shorthand that only she can read.

'What do you need to get the story to print?' asks Grosvenor. 'We've all thought about it, and we all want, not least for Luca's grandfather's memory, the story to be told and the truth to get out there.'

Fiona stops and sips, now onto her third Moscow Mule. I've nursed my first one, wanting to stay sharp. 'It's so out there. I mean, fucking miles away. There's only one thing that will separate it from *National Enquirer*, my dad was abducted by cross-dressing alien cowboys levels of out there. This really is one where the truth is so much stranger than fiction. You need to give me some kind of tangible proof I can share. Failing that, there's a chance the paper might not even run it.'

If I'd been on more of the hard stuff, this would have sobered me instantly.

'Think about it,' Fiona continues. 'This story comes at a time when the presidency is at its most fragile and scrutinised, and because the polls have Connors' popularity at an all-time low after royally fucking up the Covid-19 response, the White House is at its most defensive. So, without proof, it may get dismissed as just another fake news item designed to discredit the presidency.'

'What are you suggesting?'

'One of you goes on record,' she says, but then points at Luca. 'But not you.'

He looks hurt, like his place at the table has been invalidated. 'Luca, you've got motive. It makes sense that you'd want to attack those who arranged for your grandfather's death. That motive might mean that the public won't take you seriously. And for different reasons, you're out.'

It takes a second before I realise the finger is now pointing at me.

'You're a ghost. A nobody. Your name carries no weight. More than that, I believe you're discredited. Dishonourable discharge, right? They'd use that to make sure your testimony was the ravings of a madman. You're no more credible than the drunk sacked by the air force who wanted to get one back by telling stories about UFOs at Area 51. Come to think of it, I'm thinking you'd be seen as less valid than him.'

All eyes turn to Grosvenor.

'As a serving British cabinet minister – and a war hero, I might add – your words carry all kinds of weight. You have immediate credibility and no obvious axe to grind. If you do a full interview, with full transparency, about how you found out about all this, then this thing will stick.'

Silence. I know, a hundred per cent certain, Grosvenor will not go for that. Despite being an MP, he doesn't even like being in the paper. He's that rarest of things – a politician who shuns the press and seeks to stay out of the limelight.

'There is one more way...' Fiona says. 'You let me run these frames. Front page. Centre. Raise the question as to who the man in the pictures could be and let the public's imagination run wild. Aided by a few careful hints, of course.'

'Out of the question,' Grosvenor says, shutting the option down cold as soon as it had been breathed into life. An insect buzzes closer, and I dart my head to avoid any unwanted landings.

'Let me get them verified with an accompanying story from an unnamed source – which, I add, could be any one of you, and this thing will get traction whatever that interview says. The pictures, these lost pictures that show a part of American history that we have all got so wrong, they sell any story you chose to tell.' She's said her piece and settles back in her chair, hand played. But that insect is getting louder, the one I tried to avoid before. It's slowly getting closer.

Only it's not an insect.

It's a boat, it's navigation lights cruising down the blackened river towards us.

And it's only as I realise how fast it's going that it makes a sharp turn for the water's edge below our feet – and heads right for us.

# CHAPTER THIRTY NINE

A searchlight blasts on as the first gunshot rings out, but only the former came from the water. As I pull Fiona out of sight beneath the white table cloth, I see our other diners on the rear decking of the Rod and Gun Club rise as one and start spraying bullets at what I can now see is an airboat – a flatbed vessel with a huge fan on the back. One of the shooting patrons catches my eye, and I nod to him, his big, scabbed forehead punching north then south in response. Michael Brutoli, son and enforcer for Francesca Speroni.

He stands at his table and pulls out a large shotgun from beneath the linen, tinkling silverware and glass, and starts liberally peppering the incoming boat – fire, rerack, fire, rerack. Chunks of fly screen and white wood glitter the night and rain down on the grass and the jetty. Behind him, his brother Gus does the same, only with a more restrained 9mm pistol.

'Stay here,' I tell Fiona while pulling out the now-trusty Luger and risk a glance over the table.

Grosvenor is in perfect shooting stance, returning fire – but not for long. Brutoli and the Speronis, our hired help from New York who got in late afternoon, have completely fulfilled their remit of protection – and all it took was the suggestion of violence and the promise of drinks at a beach bar in Florida. Obviously, it meant more to Francesca, who I appealed to directly. What was it Francesca had said? Skin in the game? I like that. And with the murder of an Italian American ex-soldier in Luca Jones Sr, that skin increased.

The boat slowly drifts to the riverbank, and it's clear that our illegal protection service has done its job.

Five bodies, all clad in black, slump in the seats on the vessel. They are, as suspected, identical to the Secret Service goonies we fought off back in Maryland. The searchlight lowers and dumps into the water, casting a glow upwards until it hits the surface.

Shouts, suddenly, from behind us, inside the building.

'They're coming from the front too,' I say, as I haul Fiona up. We need her to tell the story, whatever happens to us. It has to reach the public. I grab her Dictaphone from the table and stick it in her hand. 'Don't lose this.'

I pass her into Grosvenor and Luca's care, as per our hastily arranged failsafe. We didn't know if we'd be found here but given the stakes and the nature of our pursuers, I wasn't going to risk it. They've tracked our every move without fail. No reason to think they wouldn't reach us here – and now I'm so glad we thought ahead.

'Come on, Fiona,' Luca says, before pushing her through the hole in the decking flyscreen. 'There's a boat, just along.'

They start to sprint. Grosvenor looks at me, unsure. His instinct is to stay and fight, like mine.

'Protect them. Get them to the airfield and I'll be right behind you,' I say. The airfield where Val is waiting with the jet. Phase three of the contingency failsafe.

I send him into the night then return to Brutoli's side. 'Coming through the lobby,' he says gruffly.

'Thanks, Michael, I owe you one.'

He points to the welt on his head, still there from when I smashed him into the pint glass just a couple of days ago, and breaks into a toothsome grin, lips wet with all the fun he's having. 'You owe me about five now, but who's counting.' It's amazing, the bonds forged under duress.

'At least two teams this time.'

'You popular motherfuckers. This proves one thing though.'

'What is that?'

'They were following that reporter tight.' Like a lunar dawn, his words are crisp, correct and epiphanic.

'You've got to be right.'

'And because of who it's brought out, you know who the bad guys are now.'

The Secret Service. The current presidency.

He's right again. This seals it.

'I bet two days ago you'd have been amazed to find it wasn't me.'

I can't help but smile because he's been right three times in a row. Brutoli directs two men either side of the French windows leading to the deck in a rough defensive cover formation – which is rendered immediately obsolete by the grenade that rolls right through the doorway.

These Secret Service fuckers don't mess about.

The room bursts in a white flash that doesn't sound deep but burns every sense open to it. By the table, Brutoli and I are merely cast aside like unwanted production line rags, bruises and disorientation our only injuries. At least two of the Speronis have been hurt badly, however, judging by the writhing. These are friends for Brutoli, I mustn't forget that, and his scream reflects that.

The first wave of the team of six agents bursts into the decking through descending silver smoke, the air carrying a charred taste alongside the heat, giving it somehow even more life.

I stand and, with a fully replenished eight-round magazine in the Luger, manage to double tap the first two intruders before there's return fire. The great thing is, I know there'll be no civilians. We rented the entire restaurant for the night, cancelled reservations, paid for the lot on the dime of the British government – all on the insistence that the famous journalist coming to town would mention the establishment rigorously and in glowing terms in the ensuing article. One waiter was permitted, with the instruction to lock themselves away if there was any hint of disturbance.

With four agents left just beyond the doorway, a hand to hand melee ensues, which I'm very happy to wade into, although the Speronis appear equally happy to let the fists fly. Immediately it's clear, however, that when it comes to the up-close stuff, the Secret Service is able to back up that tag of elite. They're taking our protection out with extreme prejudice. A stamped kneecap followed by a loud snap betrays a leg break.

I dive in, grab the first agent I can and clatter him on the ear with the butt of the Luger, while a carefully aimed knee to the lower back separates a couple of vertebrae as easy as fish bones.

But they are quick, this group. At hand to hand it's like fighting a fluid mass moving organically in and around each other. This new opponent goes for brute force and lifts me. He must have a stone on me, of nothing but brooding sinew, in order to lift me that easily, and he dumps me onto the table we'd just dined at. I land in the remnants of dinner, sticky yet cold, and feel cutlery dig into my spine. Rolling clear across and onto the floor alongside the debris, I try to find the gun I'd dropped – when my attacker suddenly yanks me to my feet again.

Wrong move, bucko. I didn't find the gun, but my other hand found something that would never have worked had he not picked me up. A gator rib. I jam it, pointy end first, into the soft flesh just below the ear, behind the jawbone. He lets me go and scrambles for it, spurting gouts of what looks like thick oil in the soft light. I drop again and find the Luger – and check the magazine. With my back to the action, I'm now facing the river, where I spot a third Secret Service team piling onto the drifting airboat, chucking bodies over the side as they go.

Brutoli sees them as I do. 'Go, go!' he bellows. 'We'll hold these off.'

I need no further invitation. I run for the gap Grosvenor, Luca and Fiona used moments ago and emerge onto the crisp blades of Bermuda grass. The agents on the boat are getting the fan going, taking their seats, angling down the river in the direction of my friends. I fire as I run, paying no real heed to aim, but my target gets bigger and bigger the quicker I go. The searchlights on the back of the property, now blazing, mask my approach. I'm just a black figure spraying them with lead. I know I catch two, and a third has taken evasive action overboard, by the time the magazine runs out and I'm hurling myself over the widening gap between vessel and land.

The airboat has three rows of seats – a two on the front, a three in the middle and a smaller double bench at the back for the driver. I land hard, dead centre, taking a seatback to the ribs.

The man closest to the front starts to bellow. 'Get going, get going! We can't afford another mistake!' I recognise the voice. This is the guy in charge from Maryland.

The fan, as if listening to orders itself, fires into life and we accelerate at real speed, my stomach adopting the sensation it was left behind at the Rod and Gun Club – which stands as a drifting bright blur, almost sadly proud and resolute, as we make hasty pursuit.

The driver's occupied, so I'll go for the two left over. I try to stand, but a rifle butt catches me from nowhere – it's suddenly fiercely dark, and I can only make out shapes in the distance. This, I learned from the research this afternoon when coming up with the plan, is the Ten Thousand Island Nature Reserve. A huge mass of mangrove communities, existing independent of and alongside each other in equal measure. It's vast, treacherous, and near unnavigable at night. Unless you have a GPS like the other boat was set up with. Forward planning equals future success.

I try to follow the direction of the rifle strike, but in the blackness, I can only feel another impact, this time to my shoulder and collarbone, as if a rifle has been swung like an axe into the tree that is me.

It really takes the wind out of my sails, and I feel loose all over the injured area. Like a worse pain is going to come, but my body is doing everything it can not to let me feel it just yet. I fall back to the seat when a right hand obliterates me, my nose taking the brunt of the blow. I know from feel that's my fifth career nose break. I slump into the seat.

'Do they have the envelope?' asks the leader, shouting over the fan.

I gasp blood that feels like it's churning gloomily around the u-bend of my airways. 'Yep,' I say, coughing up that sickly-sweet metal. 'But you ain't stopping them.' It's bravado, nothing more. Machismo. Defiance.

The boat slows, and in the haze of my pain, I think they might have listened to me. 'Tinker,' comes a voice behind me. 'Holy shit, sir.'

It's such a bizarre thing to say, and an even weirder way of saying it, that we all pause to look at him. He's younger, the driver, and his hands are off the throttle and on his helmet, which he buckles tight.

'What is it, Franks?' asks the leader, who I now know as Tinker.

Franks points the torch beams out ahead of him across the water and a galaxy of stars look back at us. But the stars sit in endless pairs, reflected immediately below by a waterline I can only just make out.

Gator eyes, glowing in the dark. Thousands of them.

All looking this way.

# CHAPTER FORTY

Despite the sudden death of the engine, we keep moving forwards. The silence is crushing and eerie as we slowly drift towards the reptilian mass. None of us dare move.

The here and now, the petty and the grave, is all sucked away. Whoever killed some fellow nearly sixty years ago, is a blip, a footnote, a skidmark on the cosmos. Our differences slip to nothingness, cast away by the silent omnipotence of the grand. We are specks in a bigger picture, bugs sucked into a giant machine that will vaporise us because deep down, brass tacks, we matter that little.

I hear a slight scraping on the bottom of the vessel as we slow into the garden of gators before suddenly coming to a stop. Not one of them has moved, their eyes constant in every direction as far as I can see and watching with silent animal judgement.

It's the strangest moment of my life. We daren't move.

I can't see another boat, so I pray to a God I don't necessarily believe in that my friends avoided this. That's what they are, I know now. My friends.

'Nobody move,' says Tinker.

I never did react that well to authority.

With as much weight as I can put behind it, I rise from the seat shoulder first and burst into the midsection of the boat driver angled just behind me. He screams pure terror from the pit of his guts as he sails into the myriad of stars, like an astronaut on a spacewalk abruptly cut from their tether with no hope but to drift to their doom and death.

He lands with a cacophonous splash, which sets off a startling chain reaction. The gators by the boat thrash, lunging across each other, the screams horrifying and ear-splitting before adopting a plaintive guttural moaning. I've never felt so small and insignificant. The gators churning below us kick off the gators behind them in an animal kingdom domino effect of euphoric bloodlust, and within seconds the entire section of river is a deafening sea of thrashing alligators.

Our boat starts to rock helplessly in the middle of it all, a sudden storm of my own making. The man who clubbed me with his rifle moments ago falls across the middle seat, but he's still holding that rifle. I grab the barrel and yank him towards me. If I can get something with bullets in it, I might get out of this alive.

He doesn't come without a fight though, so I grab and twist him to me, hauling him in, and I sit on the seat like a marlin angler and put my back into it. With the ever-shifting momentum and its unpredictability, he suddenly tumbles to me. I duck and, with my shoulder in his midriff, power through with my legs into a standing position and toss him over my head – onto the safety cage of the fan behind me, which gives way. It either got damaged during the firefight or it plain isn't supposed to have two hundred pounds of Secret Service agent crashing on top of it. He topples through and lands half-stuck in the paused fan blade.

'Hold it,' shouts Tinker, and as I look up, I see he's got a gun on me. 'You slippery fuck, you've been nothing but trouble.'

I bring my hands up.

'Where are they going?' he shouts over the churning.

'You'll never catch them. You're wasting time even talking.'

'Where are they going?'

'To take down your crooked boss.' I drop out of sight, the shots he loosens in anger piping over my falling body into the driver's seat behind me. I'm in the footwell – at the ignition and throttle. I hit the first, and as soon as I hear the engine take, I twist the throttle handle as far as it'll go.

The result is absolutely awful.

The man in the fan suddenly has giant steel blades through him, right across his middle, and everything else gets sucked in – spurting shredded humanity out the back of the fan enclosure, spraying the gators with the freshest chum they'll ever get to taste. He didn't even get a chance to scream. But I have the rifle now, as it drops onto the driver's seat. A bit of blood has sprayed forward – and by a bit, I mean a lot, but considering what's just happened, my standard unit of measurement for this kind of thing is proper skewed. The rifle is slick, and I realise I too am drenched in blood and bits of things I really don't want to put a name to.

I train the slippery weapon on Tinker – whose eyes are bugged at what just happened to his colleague. Coated in blood, surrounded by gators in the middle of the Everglades, I couldn't give a thimbleful of fuck at this point. Never mind him, I'm in shock at the sight of so much viscera. 'Toss your back-up pieces over the side – radio too. Now sit down and shut the fuck up. I'm no use to you… but you are to me.'

Mercifully, because I'm not sure how much energy or nerve I've got left, he does as he's told. And those thousands of eyes watch us move off slowly into the ink and mystery of the mangroves.

# CHAPTER FORTY ONE

The ride, once we're out of the gators and I start using the downed spot lamp to light the way, is smooth, and I only have to warn Tinker once to 'keep facing front or I'll blow your brains through your forehead'.

The mangrove community is magical – a forgotten, bewitching playground of things that feel prehistoric. It's like a boat jaunt through the Jurassic. At one point there's a very audible blast of air right by the boat, which I assume (and hope to be true) is a manatee signalling its discontent at being disturbed.

Having at some point been dragged away from the shoreline, which was our principal point of reference guiding us to our meeting point, I use the distant glow of light pollution on the shore to keep us on course and get us back to the planned route – and before long, we are cruising along waterfront properties that look like retirement dreams, even for me, a burnt-out vet.

Suddenly, flashes up ahead. A torch. Long, bright, then a flash. Repeated three times, then stays on. Anytime I see a light jump on and off again, for any lengths of time that appear to carry distinction, I start to translate. I'm looking at Morse code. Two letters, CK. Military abbreviation: Check. Grosvenor. It must be. And that's our rendezvous point.

I reply automatically, no memory recall required, it's just there, and the response is sent across the black surface. CFM. Confirm.

At least that means Grosvenor won't be waiting for us barrel raised but, as I angle the airboat to the jetty on which I see our small party, Grosvenor immediately aims his pistol at us. He's seen who I'm bringing along. I kill the engine and drift the last few yards in.

'If he moves in a way you don't like, put one in him,' I tell Grosvenor, but he's looking at me in shock. It takes me a second to remember I'm covered in blood. 'It's not mine.'

Grosvenor ties up the boat and immediately drags Tinker off. I root around in the storage bins of the boat and find some extra mooring rope, which I use to bind Tinker's wrists. He's very quiet and very calm, despite all he's been through himself these last few days – clearly a professional, clearly elite. His eyes betray no fear.

'I'm assuming you're a man following orders, Tinker,' I say. 'Me and this guy, we've been there. Ten years for me, thirty-five years for him. We don't do things we don't have to. Understand me.'

'I understand you,' he simply says.

We start walking into the darkness, away from the water, which once again, I'd got quite attached to. I feel its pull behind me. Maybe in twenty years one of those retirement homes would be the right thing. Who knows. Sit here with Jam as a ten-year-old, Jake and Gracie all grown up and Carolyn just… with me.

But could I ever be able to forget what I've just seen on this water? Could I ever be here and not immediately think of that?

Not likely.

'I'm sorry about what happened to your men,' I say without embellishment.

'They signed up for this,' he replies.

I don't think anyone signs up to be backdropped through a boat fan, but I'm not going to argue the point with him. 'Then I'm assuming you are patriotic.'

'Prepared to die for my country.'

'And its leader?'

'There'd be no greater honour.'

'We'll see about that.'

We emerge from the trees onto a dirt road which feels so close to the stars it's like they've crowded in for a look. Our rental car is sitting there, and I can see Luca and Fiona in the front, driver's side and passenger side respectively. Both look through the window back at us and I see Luca's expression change to fury. He jumps out of the car immediately.

'Luca, cool it,' I say. Grosvenor and I are on either side of Tinker, and we stop walking as Luca marches straight up to our captive.

'You bastard,' he spits as he launches a punch that catches us all off guard and lands flush dead centre of Tinker's face. I hear both crunch and crack. 'You killed an old man? Huh? You killed my fucking grandfather?'

'Easy, Luca,' I say. 'Take him.' Grosvenor directs the spluttering Tinker to the car and deposits him in the back, while I grab Luca. 'Mate, I know. I get it. But we don't know if it was him.'

Luca stops fighting and begins to sob again. I pull him into me and hold the grieving man. I notice that they're not stars pressing down on us, but glow-worms. Thousands of them. I can't help but smile, as Luca's sobbing eases.

I stand him straight by the shoulders. 'What I do know is that he's the best way we find out. And if we want justice for your grandfather, what he knows will probably be the key to getting it. All right?'

He nods and takes a few breaths for composure.

'Did you break a knuckle on his nose?'

'Yes,' he says, rubbing his hand. That's why the sound of the nose break carried an echo.

'Take a minute,' I say, and leave him. I go and wedge myself in the back of the Sedan, closing Tinker in the middle with Grosvenor on the other side. In front, Fiona sits goggle-eyed, her notepad on her knee, pen floating mid scratch, unable to look from Tinker.

'Good evening, ma'am,' he says, his voice thick with blood via a nose I can see is nice and off-centre.

'Keep quiet, please,' I say, which diverts Fiona's gaze from Tinker to me. I remember the blood. 'It's not mine.' Then I remember my nose is off as well, and I check it in the mirror. There's a kink in it, right in the bridge. I feel along the bone – and immediately find the ridge where it's dropped out of alignment. Right side nostril.

'Can I borrow your pen?' I ask Fiona, which she hands over mutely. 'Thanks.'

As I've done any number of times before, I stick it up my right nostril.

'You can keep it,' she says hurriedly.

With the pen up there to keep the airway open, I can reset it. A bit of play, one small crack, harder tug, serious bone on bone scrape that makes me actually shout, then a loud snap. I pull the pen out and look in the mirror again. I'm no Fabio, but I'm no Picasso either. It'll do.

Noting Tinker's slack-jawed expression, I place the pen in the breast pocket of his flack jacket. 'I'll do yours when we get where we're going.'

Without words, but hauling an obvious cloud of pure darkness, Luca jumps in the front, and we're out of there.

# CHAPTER FORTY TWO

Wings Park South is dark when we get there, slumbering with all those floodlights off. The gates are open, however, and I'm surprised to see Val manning them personally, as he waves us through before locking them. His jet is sat on the runaway, close to where I last saw it, except this time it's been angled back down the runway for our getaway. 'Park up and get in,' he says through the open window as we pass.

'We need to get airborne now,' I say as we park. 'Fiona, if you want the story, you'll have to come with us.'

'As long as you give me a ride home after,' she replies as she marches to the jet like she owns it. It makes me wonder about the lifestyle of a soon-to-be-very-literal high-flying reporter.

'Stand there,' I tell Tinker. 'And don't move. We're just going to discuss if we still need you, or if we should off you here.' That should keep him behaving, fighting talk and all that.

I quickly confer with Grosvenor in a low whisper. 'The destination you have in mind – you're sure?'

'Yes. If we want to expose them, this is where we go.'

'OK then, you tell Val, and I'll leave you to sort the, umm, economics of it all.'

Val walks past us to the plane steps. 'I knew you boys were all fun and games, but even this is a little bit bug nuts.' He looks at the state of me, top to toe. 'You missed a spot, son,' he says as he shakes his head and climbs into the plane – but he pauses at the top. 'Your extra passengers are all set too. Just waiting for you guys.'

Grosvenor nods to him and turns to Tinker. 'We're going to get on that plane, and we're going to find out what you know about what you've been working so hard to track down. And then, we might just tell you what it really is.'

I walk him up the steps, but the fight has bled clean out of him. He's in compliance mode. Still one of the opposition, but happy enough to play along for now – as any captured operative would. I follow and look instinctively for the seat I was in last time, but find it occupied. By none other than Francesca Speroni. She's settled in with a plastic glass of something fizzy and a little can of slimline tonic. She smiles knowingly.

'I sweet-talked him into a little waiter service,' she says, nodding at the cockpit door. 'Bet you're glad you called me, aren't you?'

I smile tightly and walk Tinker to the back of the plane, placing him in the spare seat opposite Brutoli and Gus, who have evidently caught up and come along. They stare at the Secret Service agent like he's a chicken drumstick.

'Who said you two were coming?' I ask, with more than a hint of playfulness.

'Are you gonna tell me I can't?' replies Brutoli, spreading his legs out, making sure every inch of his giant arse covers the entirety of the seat leather.

I hold my hands up. 'You two are muscle, all right? God knows we might need it.'

Thirty minutes later, I've cleaned myself up in the jet's bathroom, somewhere, I believe, over the Gulf of Mexico – and I'd suggest Val gets a proper valet from a crime scene cleaning service before he rents this jet out again. Fresh clothes from my Target backpack and I'm feeling a shade more normal.

Not returning to my seat, I grasp Grosvenor by the shoulder and gesture to the back. He comes with me, already keyed in to my intentions, and seconds later, we are swapping seats with Brutoli and his brother to face Tinker directly. He's quiet, stoic, reserved, holding it together.

'You be good cop, I'll be bad cop,' I say.

'I can do that. To a degree,' says Grosvenor.

Tinker gives no reaction as we settle.

'You're a man of honour, aren't you?' Grosvenor says. 'I can see that. I can see it because we smell our own. You're a man who, on any other given day of the week, I'd most likely agree with. I'd value any opinion you had, I'd listen to what you had to say and I'd tell other people what calibre of person you were. We're just on different sides at the moment, but only because of the separate information each side has at hand. You have different facts to me and until we have the same facts, we most likely won't see eye to eye. We can change this.'

Christ, he's good at this. I have to actually refrain from looking at him because I've forgotten to give Tinker the hard glare. But then Grosvenor brings out the envelope like David Copperfield, yet again, and speaks.

'You've been after this, haven't you? Did you know it would be so small?'

Nothing. No response, although Tinker looks at that little

white rectangle as if it contains an antidote to a poison that's killing him.

I'd like a go now. 'What were you told? What were your instructions? And please speak up because, between us, we've got a number of ways to get information out of you that I'm frankly bored with being so successful at. Fed up with all the screaming, sure you understand.'

He doesn't budge, so I lean closer. 'Or would a squeeze on the nose do it? Bet it stings like all hell.'

When he speaks it sounds like treacle lodged in a sieve. 'Information of a conspiracy that, if in the wrong hands, could bring down government.'

What do you know? The president told him the truth. 'Yes, but do you know why it would bring down government?' I ask.

'It's at the highest security clearance, but we know it proves a plot to attack the president.'

I almost laugh out loud. 'Yes, but did they say which president?'

'No.'

Grosvenor interjects. 'I give you credit, Tinker, and somehow I've got to credit your boss. You weren't lied to, and you *were* trying to stop a presidential assassination.'

'Bless him,' I add.

Grosvenor spills the frames onto his palm. 'Do you recognise these?'

Tinker is still proud, but cracks are emerging. 'No,' he says, after just the smallest begrudging glance, but it's clear to see that these frames have that beguiling effect on everybody we've met.

'I'm not surprised. Were you told what to expect?'

'Only that it was a small document. Letter size. In an envelope. Retrieve it and bring it home.'

I notice that Tinker has very expressive dark eyes. I'm only seeing it now they are cleared of the blankness of objective. He might well carry the honour and dutifulness Grosvenor was alluding to.

'There is a conspiracy, all right, Tinker – but its creation is nothing to do with us. We believe your boss, the president, wants to keep these three frames a secret.'

'Blow my mind,' says Tinker. There's still bluster, but it's open. You don't get to be top dog in the president's Secret Service for nothing, clearly.

Grosvenor tells him exactly what they are and, as he does, I catch Brutoli and his brother leaning over their seats to get a listen and a look-see.

'You can't be serious,' says Tinker when Grosvenor has finished.

'Shit me sideways,' says Brutoli.

'Your president misled you, Tinker,' says Grosvenor.

Tinker doesn't respond, though it looks more like he can't. He's physically unable, it seems – plus, he's still somewhat bound by protocols he's got ever less need of.

I can't be mentioned in despatches, but I want the truth to be known by hook or by crook. We've come too far, overcome too much, for it not to happen. 'We're going to the one other place that might have physical evidence to back this up and expose this story,' I say. There's another reason I want justice here, and it's for one man and one person's memory. 'Luca?' I call.

Luca joins us, having collected those elusive frames and now putting them back in the envelope, and sits on his haunches in the aisle.

'Tinker,' I say with slow deliberation, 'I want you to be specific and tell this man here exactly what happened to his grandfather.'

Tinker has softened to a significant degree, his faith in his objectives sufficiently dented. He can see our side, and like the age-old saying, everyone loves a story. 'It wasn't me, I'll make that very clear. We were on standby in Washington for New York.'

Luca isn't calmed by those words. 'If it wasn't you, who?'

Tinker breathes out, a sigh that reveals he knows the words coming will be painful to the listener, so much so that he already regrets saying them. 'The Secret Service has a number of different purposes and is commonly misunderstood. I mean, even just listening to you guys, you have no real clue at all. Most people think we're the guys who run alongside the president's car in suits talking into earpieces. You might think we're just a little box of toy soldiers for the president to play with, but it actually has over six thousand employees, over half of which are special agents like myself. A great number of those are trained in, or have been drawn from, counter-terrorist backgrounds and other similar organisations. Every now and then we farm out, and vice versa, to operations with the Joint Terrorism Task Force.'

'That's FBI,' Luca adds, for anyone not clued in – like me.

'Right. The Secret Service and the JTTF were engaged last week in response to a credible threat to national security.' Tinker nods at the frames, still resting in Grosvenor's palm. 'How that represents a present threat to national security, I don't know. But our instructions to reclaim them with extreme prejudice suggest they are suddenly of great importance to the current presidential administration.'

I'm fed up with the official speak. 'Can you talk like a normal bloke for one minute? Where does his grandfather fit in?'

'I'm getting to it. There was a briefing last week, high-security clearance, between a handful of special agents and the top brass of the JTTF. President's Chief of Staff chaired it. Your grandfather had been under surveillance for years, the files on him are huge. Middle of last week he made contact with a known entity in the UK. You.'

Tinker points at Grosvenor, who grimaces at the growing suggestion that contacting him had in some way sealed Luca Jones Senior's fate.

'He said he'd made arrangements for a package to be sent to the CIA regional offices in New York City. An operation was in place to intercept. However, there was an attempt to retrieve the package from Jones Senior's place before it had even been sent. It didn't go well, because when Jones Senior placed the call detailing his instruction, he'd already sent the item to New York. Crafty guy, already knew he was being listened to – he'd already sent it.'

'What do you mean, it didn't go well?'

'He didn't give anything up because there was nothing to give.'

It all suddenly makes sense to me. Jones Senior was left like that on purpose, to look as though he'd died unremarkably in his chair, and with the advanced warmth of the natural Naples climate and a little help from the heater, in only a few days, any physical evidence of injury would be lost to the terrible state of the body.

'I don't like being misled,' says Tinker. 'I was told I was going to protect our president, and it turns out we were lied to. All of us. What happened that day still gets people signing up to be in the Secret Service, and every one of them has also been lied to. I want to see this out now just as much as you do.'

I'm keenly aware how many of his men we've had to go through, in so many horrendous ways. 'We both know that the objective comes first. I had orders, we had orders. Anything that happened before that was on that mandate. I didn't enjoy killing your men, but it was life or death, based on our separate instructions. Can we meet in the middle on that?'

'Is the question really: am I going to kill you if you untie me for throwing one of my men through an airboat fan?'

'Yes. That's what I'm asking.'

'No.' He looks heavenward and crosses himself. 'We have an agreement.'

'Fine.' I untie him. 'I'm Ben,' I say, offering my open hand – which he takes. I thought he might refuse it, but combat and its pressures have created that warped brotherhood once again. He respects me for how hard it was to bring me to account (which, with a deep sense of pride I won't point out, he never did), and I respect him for being a tenacious adversary. I also find some admiration for him for admitting he was wrong.

'Where are we going?' he asks.

I take the pen from his front pocket and stand up over him. 'Back to where this all started. Now lean back. Let's fix this nose.'

# SINCLAIR

G-Man was where he was supposed to be, according to the shape of the new plan. Corner of Main and Elm.

Jinks was halfway up Main on the grass.

Luca on the grass beneath the pergola.

Lee up in the Book Depository, the eye in the sky.

And lastly, Sinclair – on the corner of Houston and Elm, on the far edge of the reflective pool.

No radios today, just eyesight, the feeling being that anyone roaming about with an earpiece could be seen as someone in the know. And since Handshake was the extra layer of protection, any suggestion they were there was to be avoided. It was all about line of sight. Every man could see the other, aside from Lee – they just had to trust he was there. And he was such a meticulous character, you'd stake your mortgage on it.

The atmosphere was akin to carnival. Standing on the edge of a road like this, waiting for something to go past that you could gawp at but not touch, made Sinclair think about his village back home in Great Britain. You could have all your skyscrapers, all your fancy flags and banners, but it still felt like a good old English summer fete. All that was missing, admittedly, was the beer tent, the home-made jams and the prize for the biggest marrow.

The thought occupied the young man's mind as he watched the crowds jostle slowly, more like seaweed in a soft current than anything. But he started to hear cheers down the street, east along Main to downtown, echoing off the higher office buildings and apartment blocks, creating a funnel effect.

The president would be here soon. He did a visual check on his team, once again, just to be sure.

The cheering lost its reverb and distance and was suddenly out in the open, the here and now, louder – and thanks to Sinclair's height, he could see over the crowd at the mouth of Main Street. The president was on his way to deliver a speech at Dallas Trade Mart, at the culmination of an eleven-mile route – but now, here he was.

Well, not quite.

There was a row of motorcycles in front. A wave of Dallas PD, stars and stripes adorning the handlebars.

Sinclair felt tension up his spine.

The intel was clear. Dealey Plaza. An attack on the president.

He could never erase that from his thoughts.

The first car. A white Ford. He could just make out the expected faces of the Chief of Police and the Sheriff, alongside Secret Service agents. Would they know Handshake was there? Sinclair had no idea. He had no clue what the intelligence networks shared. The Ford made the turn onto Elm, and there it was. There he was.

President John Kennedy, smiling and waving, oozing that easy-going charm that had made him a public darling. A convertible – which struck Sinclair right that very moment as a strange choice and made him conclude that the president's own Secret Service couldn't be aware of this threat. No way. They couldn't be. Nobody in their right mind would send a president into an area referenced in a threat without all manner of protection, even something as simple as a roof on his car.

Maybe the president had overridden the move. Maybe he had pulled the most executive of rank. Either way, Sinclair didn't like it.

The first lady dressed in pink. Smiling. Waving. Always regal and happy. The thought of pleasing her by keeping her husband safe made Sinclair himself smile. He liked doing things for good people, even though the world in which he existed rarely let him. This job was an exception, it felt, and for Jackie Kennedy, he had to admit his admiration carried the slightest whisper of a crush.

The dark blue Lincoln Continental started the turn and Kennedy grinned broadly, waving with brio. The cheers were now rabid – taking politics out of it, he was easy to get behind, in a personal sense. He carried a galvanism few did. Sinclair hoped that Alec Douglas-Home, who'd just been appointed prime minister back in Britain, would instil the same sentiment. He believed Home was a man of good morals and integrity, but whether he was cutthroat enough for modern parliamentary life was another thing entirely.

Sinclair found himself waving at the car as it passed him, followed by the third car in the motorcade, which had a secret service agent on each running board. Down the slight incline on to Elm.

They'd be speeding up soon.

If an attack was coming, it would be now.

He tried not to show how alert he felt. Tried to listen for

something. Anything.

But he could sense nothing he hadn't accounted for. The atmosphere was jovial. Hopeful. Happy.

The crowds began to quiet just a touch, when Sinclair heard the first thing that was wrong.

It was a pop. Not unlike a balloon. The average bystander would have thought that's exactly what it was, considering the occasion, but not a man like Sinclair.

In the car, the president wasn't waving anymore. Jackie was hunched up close to him. He was holding his neck, and she was trying to help him.

The agent from the car behind was suddenly running at the car, the crowds were quietening again when, oh dear God, Sinclair heard it that time.

Gunshot. The President's head burst in a spray of pink.

Charlie Foxtrot.

# CHAPTER FORTY THREE

It's just gone dawn. The grass looks tip-dipped in dew. It's dream-like, but not only because it feels softly focused by the haze that floats in the air. It's because I've seen it hundreds of times before, while never having actually been here. Each building feels carved into my mind. Each road curve indelible. The only thing that's different is the age of the cars. These are modern. Saloons and SUVs. No classic convertible Lincoln Continental in midnight blue anywhere to be seen.

This is Dealey Plaza. I'm at the corner of Elm and Houston. Behind me is the Texas School Book Depository. To my right is the Grassy Knoll. And in front of that, is the exact spot JFK was killed.

Talk about walking into history.

Grosvenor is on the opposite side of the street to me, lost in thought. As I look across, he's standing in roughly the spot depicted in those missing frames. It's as amazing a snapshot as I'll ever see, this moment. The occasion we talk about, that thing that happened here, is so seared into our histories – a real "where were you?" moment – and here we are, on the cusp of rewriting that very same story. Altering the truth of this matter forever. And in doing so, setting right so many wrongs.

The question looms. Why does the White House want this so much? Is it to keep it all in house? Not to stir up discontent about the jurisdictional bodies that police the country at an interstate level? Or is it for something more sinister, more insidious? Surely a plot to kill a president is one any president can rally against. So what is it that has the Secret Service snapping at our ankles?

I cross the street to join the MP, and it feels like stepping into those frames. For a moment, I've become Sinclair.

'Where were you? When it happened?' I ask. Grosvenor's eyes are fixed yet loose, as if pawing at a memory behind them.

'I was at Credenhill. Watching it in the mess room.'

'The SAS base?'

'Yes. It is… overwhelming, in a strange way, to be here.'

I follow his gaze, down to where Fiona is taking pictures of the Grassy Knoll with her camera. She looks nothing more than a tourist, but I know she's compiling images for the story that is going to break the nation's hearts. Brutoli and his brother flank Speroni as they walk along the pavement under the Book Depository. Tinker is sitting on the Grassy Knoll itself, as if he's about to break out the saddest picnic of all time, going off his morose expression. And he's joined by Val and Luca.

What a group we are.

'You can't go on the stand. You're covert military and an MP. There's so much stuff you can't talk about, and it'd be a tabloid circus from the minute your name was mentioned.' It's a statement I make to Grosvenor. I know he won't. There's no point framing my words in any form of question.

'I start looking back to my own actions through the years, exposing all the operations I've been on; the onion opens and we end up pulling apart all sorts. It gets messy. I'm a firm believer that the military should do things that the public doesn't know about, in order to keep them safe. That is per our remit. We both understand that. I notice you haven't put your hand up to come clean about what you know about this, either.'

'I'm still supposed to be in prison, mate. I don't think attaching myself to the biggest story of the last fifty years is going to help keep that quiet.'

'I nearly forgot about that... Nearly.' He almost smiles. 'But then there's this. We do things in the dark so that people can live safely in the light. Do you think the general public wants to know in exact terms what happens when you tackle a Taliban faction in a small village that has equal numbers of friends as enemies? No. But we do it so that faction doesn't blow up a tube stop back home. That's why we do it. We don't do it for the praise, we do it in the knowledge we did the right thing to keep our homes safe.'

'I do understand that in full.' I've only just got my head around the things I saw out in the Middle East. I've only just managed to start sleeping anything approaching properly, and it took having a family and settling down to get near it. 'So how are we going to prove it?'

'By coming to the source, we are applying pressure. Someone, round here, within a couple of miles of this location, will have seen something that day that can corroborate the detail in the story she's going to write.' He points a crooked trigger finger at Fiona, who is crouching to take pictures up at the Book Depository now. 'We just have to find them. Handshake's handlers acted with impunity that day by stoking fear – Zapruder himself being the prime example. I imagine a number of people were told to keep silent about things with the threat of violence to themselves or loved ones. We need to get these people to speak up.

'Have you got any idea where to start?'

'The warehouse. The HQ that day. Luca told me where it is, should such a day arrive. It's still there.'

My eyebrows flicker involuntarily. 'It is?'

He nods with a quiet conviction.

'It's a long shot,' I say. 'You really think someone there would remember?'

'Maybe. But that's not really what I'm thinking.'

'And what are you thinking?'

'That paperwork doesn't get old and die like the rest of us.'

I smile in full. The crafty bastard just might be onto something.

'Do you think you could get us there?'

And off we go.

# CHAPTER FORTY FOUR

It's no more than a seven-minute drive, but it seems Grosvenor has given this place some serious thought. As he tells me from the front seat, the perfection of this location is the sheer variety of ways you can get to it. You can go via the highway or through downtown or snake the back streets and follow the Trinity River. Whatever the occasion needs.

Into Rock Island Street pulls our ridiculous nine-seat SUV, which now includes me, Grosvenor, Luca, Val, Fiona, Francesca, Tinker, Brutoli and Gus, rented in haste from a dealership close to yet another sleepy airfield, this time in Dallas. As we'd travelled, the roads had grown sparser, the buildings less tall, and only two miles from where JFK went abruptly to heaven, we approach a riverside road in what suddenly feels like the arse end of nowhere.

'And this is another reason why this location is so perfect,' says Grosvenor, as he lowers the speed and leans closer to the windscreen to peer through the glass. 'Nobody in their right mind would expect a secret military unit to be occupying one of these places.'

He's right. Out there, the buildings just couldn't be more derelict and tired. Warehouses that still carry the ghost of occupation, that also look like licks of paint wouldn't get near making them look hospitable. Battered wood, junk-strangled yards, grimed windows. We trawl along them until we get to the very end, where the road stops abruptly with grass, no barrier – the green simply slopes down into the rapid flow of the Trinity. Grosvenor pulls over and turns to our misfit band.

'This calls for softly-softly, but we need to work together. Every one of us.' I struggle to imagine Michael Brutoli doing anything softly, wedged in the back there next to his poor mother who looks like a granny dragged along on the family holiday. 'These are all still family businesses, from the looks of things. That's exactly what I was hoping for. This building on the end here is the one we need to find out about – and to do that we are going to need to find someone who was working here in the '60s. They'll be my age now, possibly older. Knock these doors and see what we can turn up. Meet back here in thirty.'

Everyone piles out like a mad group on a day trip, and as Tinker exits, I pause him. 'Stick with me, mate.' My trust in him is growing, but I don't want to leave him on his own just yet.

Gus, Luca, Brutoli, Fiona, Val and Francesca start walking down the street, and I get ready to follow with Tinker when Grosvenor grabs my arm. 'Come with me. Let's knock on the building itself.'

I need no further invitation.

The warehouse is red brick with a black garage door on the right-hand side. A high-pitched roof, a rusted fuel pump out the front. A crumbling Jeep Sahara parked next to it in a bleak pea green.

'Hope someone's home,' says Grosvenor as he approaches the recessed door next to the garage, which is shaded in that exact same chipped black. The sun beats down, the heat of the morning swelling, and the thumps echo loudly somewhere inside as Grosvenor pounds the wood three times.

I really hope we find something here.

Two metal clunks herald the door swinging inwards to show a young woman, early thirties, flannel shirt and jeans.

'Good morning,' says Grosvenor. Immediately the accent and statesman-like demeanour seem to catch the woman off guard, because her eyebrows shoot upwards and her head pulls back, revealing a dark tattoo snaking up from her torso onto her neck.

'Good morning,' she replies.

'I'm looking for someone who may have worked here back in the '60s.'

'The '60s?'

'Yes.'

'Are we another JFK nut?'

With those words, it hits me again just how big the issue we're dealing with is – and just how much these people, living in the direct shadow of the incident and its local impact, must have been stigmatised ever since. Dallas and its suburbs are forever rendered footnotes by what happened.

Grosvenor passes it off with a smile and glances up at the exterior of the building. 'Just trying to follow in the footsteps of an old friend, ma'am.'

'Well, I bought this place back in 2010, from a guy that had it for years before that. His name was Tilletson, is that the guy you're looking for?'

'Possibly. Did he leave anything behind?'

'Oh yeah, boxes and boxes of paperwork, receipts and all sorts of stuff. A real hoarder.' I feel Grosvenor suddenly tense next to me. 'We had to burn it all up, only way to get rid of it.' I can almost hear William's excitement deflate with that same suddenness with which it appeared.

'Nothing left from that time?'

'Nothing left from that time, or the times either side of it. Clean slate from twenty-ten.'

'Bugger.'

'Bugger indeed.'

'Could we take a little look around?' I ask, and put on my most charming, shit-eating grin. 'We've come a long way.'

'Umm… OK, I guess. Sure. I'm Daphne.' She moves to the side to let us in.

I pass my hand in the direction of myself and Grosvenor. 'Ben, William and…' My hand hovers in front of Tinker, both of us with our wayward noses.

'Geoff.' He smiles, although in his cargo pants and scuffed black t-shirt, it doesn't quite work. Nevertheless, Daphne lets us inside. The door opens into a small passageway before opening into a high-roofed workshop with a couple of skylights at the apex, facing each other on either side. Below that is what looks like a mountain of pure crap, albeit carefully curated.

'What is it you folks do, Daphne?' I ask, stepping into the space, trying on new words like I've got in my dad's wardrobe.

'Antiques. On eBay, for the most part.'

There's a cello, a King Kong bust, a gramophone, a stuffed warthog, a framed watercolour, a set of old skis and a vase made of mud – and that's just in the square yard next to me. The rest of the space, reaching up to the roof, is composed similarly. Junk of the widest composition.

I hear the door go again behind us and Luca suddenly tumbles into the warehouse.

'We've got something,' he says breathlessly.

# CHAPTER FORTY FIVE

When we troop back outside the red brick warehouse, there's a man waiting for us, looking nervously over his shoulder at Brutoli, as if one false move might set him into psycho mode. Luca can't stop himself from speaking, so eager is he to share what he's found. The guy looks to be in his sixties. I'm not sure if he's old enough for the era we need.

'This is Marty,' says Luca. 'His family have had that auto parts place since the '50s.' Luca points down the street to a white structure made of corrugated iron which has an exhaust pipe hanging over its door like a thin awning. 'He looks after it day to day, his grandfather still owns it.'

Marty is nodding, a thatch of ragged black-ash hair bobbing up and down. He brings his hands from behind his back, and it's clear he's holding something for us to see.

'He had some pictures on the wall behind the front desk. One of them was of this street.'

Marty hands it over warily with fingers thickened by hard labour. 'I'm five in this picture, one of the greatest days of my life. That is, until what happened later,' he says in a soft, tentative voice. 'It was like being one of the big boys.'

Grosvenor takes it. 'My God… The baseball game,' he says with unconcealed wonder.

I look at it myself. It's a black and white, eight by ten snap, depicting this end of the street on a similarly sunny day. Against the backdrop of the red brick warehouse, in the middle of the road, a group of young men are playing baseball in their shirtsleeves. A couple of kids are joining in, and it's a scene of undeniable happy laughter and joy.

'I'm there,' says Marty, pointing at a little boy running between bases, his arms over his head, his face split wide with glee.

'Luca told me all about it. Said it was the craziest memory from the day, given how it all ended up,' says Grosvenor, pulling the picture slowly closer.

'Yes, sir.'

'It's amazing to think what happened mere hours later.'

There are pieces falling into place here. It's not a hunch, it's more than that, aided by this blast from the past.

There are a number of adult faces visible, all smiling, as if they weren't involved in the murder that was to come. I suppose it's accurate to assume that some here will have known about it, while others wouldn't. But there's one on first base, his eyes light with respite, adrenaline burning sideways just for a time before the main thrust. I can spot it a mile off, having been there myself. These are boys on a break.

'Do you recognise any of them?' I ask.

'Well, yes,' Grosvenor replies. He's holding the photo alone now, and we all crane in to listen like he's a medium about to offer a message from the dead. 'There's Luca Jones. The original. Senior, God rest his soul.'

If my understanding of baseball is right, he's occupying second base, which has been offered shape via a pile of jumpers. I can only see the back angle of his face, but it's clear where Luca Jr gets his jawline from. The young Italian American looks at me with pride, nodding.

'I've never seen him at that age,' he says. The corners of his eyes suddenly glint.

'Where's Sinclair?' asks Fiona.

'I believe that would be him,' says Grosvenor, pointing at the tall man poised on second base. His back is to us, but his rangy frame and blond hair are all too obvious in guaranteeing that it is him.

'Where's Lee?' I ask.

'Can't see him,' Grosvenor says. 'This could be when he was receiving his final alternative briefing.'

He doesn't need to add the words "to kill the president", but we know what he's saying.

'Any idea who of this lot playing ball is Handshake, and who are those in charge?'

Grosvenor looks across the assembled faces and half faces. 'I'd say comfortably that the youngest ones are the Handshake boys – oh my God.'

'What?' I say, looking at the photo over his shoulder. His fingertip is hovering over a man in what could be the outfield but who was, in reality, down on the grass separating the road and the river.

'That's why the president wants those frames so badly.'

'Who is that?'

'He must be in charge – he has to be.'

Before I can follow up with the deluge of questions that burst to mind, it seems I hear it before anybody else. A rumble. From up the street. I look to the bend of the entrance road, and a canvas-sided military truck suddenly booms into view, followed immediately by another.

'Everybody inside!' I shout, then, 'Excuse me' to Francesca Speroni as I lift her bodily and start to run to the warehouse. By now, the rest of the group have seen where I'm looking, have seen the trucks racing down the road to us, and are running for the warehouse door themselves. Marty and Daphne follow suit, more out of confusion than anything else.

'Get out of sight,' I tell them. 'We'll deal with this.'

Grosvenor and I watch from the office window as the trucks pull to a stop outside and a military detachment spills out. They are not playing around, not one bit.

An old man in a suit steps down from the cab of the first truck. He's small, his grey hair perfectly quaffed, combed and pristine. I don't recognise him, but it's obvious that Grosvenor does.

'I can't believe this. That's Harold Connors.'

'Connors?'

'As in President Connors' father.'

Grosvenor, in an act seemingly beyond his control, opens the warehouse door and steps onto the drive, and I hear the immediate clink of metal as rifles are raised in his direction.

# SINCLAIR

Pandemonium had split in the harshest of ways. There was screaming, clamouring, an outpouring, all immediate, all too close. As the Lincoln sped away, it dragged coherence away with it, leaving a vacuum choked by confusion. Everyone knew something major had happened, but it was too raw and visceral, too fundamentally improbable to accept or process. But because what had actually happened – gunshots fired at the president with at least one of them hitting its target, before the entire drama sped out of sight – was impossible to come to terms with, there could be no acceptance or closure. One could only ask "Did I really see that?" without having the answer confirmed.

But Sinclair knew. Rooted to the spot, the soles of his feet glued and bonded in place, he knew. He'd seen it before. Knew from the meeting of that second bullet and the president's skull, that the president was dead. From the reaction of the immediate crowd that the violence, while without warning, was soul-shaking. Knew from the way the first lady crawled back across the boot – trunk – of the Lincoln, to try to retrieve a displaced piece of her husband's head, that JFK was dead before they even reached the underpass, just yards away.

And that brought into immediate focus the undeniable. The burning, sickening, incontrovertible truth, that they – Sinclair, Luca, G-man and Jinks – had failed their mission this time. He looked up across the street at the window of the Book Depository, exactly where Lee was supposed to have been, and looked away. He knew that's where the shots had come from. Thanks to time in all kinds of different combat hellscapes, all over the world, he could tell where a bullet had come from just by hearing it. Lee. Lee Oswald had been entrusted to protect the president, and instead of doing so, gunned him down.

This operation had gone wrong in the kind of way Sinclair had never experienced before – with one of their own ignoring orders and going rogue, who then not just opposed orders, but full on switched sides and subverted all objectives.

Sirens began firing all around, compounding Sinclair's failure – and Handshake's monumental error. The people around him either scattered or fell about, babies in pushchairs suddenly shoved away, as shouts rang out.

The map of Dealey Plaza erupted in his mind, the lines of streets and dots of where Handshake was supposed to be, and it all started to blur. He frantically clawed at the memory of his instructions and found the only one that mattered at a time like this. If it all goes Charlie Foxtrot, get out of there and back to HQ for immediate debrief and post-mortem. What a chat that would be…

Dallas PD was swarming the area, and it wouldn't be long until potential suspects would be rounded up. Not one of them had looked at the building opposite yet, or approached any of its doorways, but they would soon enough – and Sinclair didn't want to be in the street when they did. Lee was on his own now.

He looked around for anyone he knew. The grass-covered hill opposite was choked with people mid-scatter, mid-crisis, but with relief he saw Luca, striding up the bank to the pergola. Getting out of there sharpish, Sinclair thought, although his direction was aimed square at one person in particular.

A man. Holding a camera.

Sinclair broke into a sprint.

Over the road and up the other side, one eye on the window he knew Lee had fired from, maintaining he was just another confused bystander.

Luca had reached the man and had taken the camera from him. By the time Sinclair had made it to the pergola, Luca was pointing at the film strip itself, evidently pulled from the camera, while the man snipped the film with a small pair of scissors.

'And don't you fuckin' forget that,' Luca was saying as Sinclair arrived. His voice had gone heavy on the Italian-New York vibes that he usually suppressed.

'What happened?' Sinclair asked.

'It's gone to shit, that's what. You have an envelope or something?'

'What do you mean?'

'We have to take these.' He held out his palm, and there were three small film frames nestled in the meaty folds.

Sinclair checked his suit pocket, found an envelope that he'd kept a movie ticket in. The 8.30 pm screening of *The Great Escape* with Steve McQueen for that night, at the famed Texas Theatre. That was going to be his treat, but he'd never make it now. He ripped up the ticket and dropped the little frames in to take its place.

'Now for the last time,' Luca said, turning to the stricken man, who was busily trying to reassemble the pieces left behind, 'If a word of this gets breathed to anyone, I'll fucking come back and kill you myself. Understood?'

The man nodded, and in confusion and to his eternal shame, Sinclair did nothing.

'We gotta go,' said Luca, before starting to run. He tucked the envelope into his own jacket pocket as he ran.

'What was on there?' asked Sinclair between breaths and strides.

'The whole damn thing. All of it. But in the background was you. I'd recognise your blond mop anywhere.'

Sinclair nearly stopped, felt overwhelmed with a sickly gratitude.

'Thanks,' was all he could say.

They didn't speak but knew exactly where they were going. Didn't run anymore, but didn't dawdle either. They reached the Trinity River, just like their instructions dictated, and followed it south. After a couple of miles, both silent as they came to terms with a world fundamentally altered, the warehouses loomed in the distance. Sinclair felt sanctuary bloom in his chest, but it stopped short before it reached full radiance. They were in for a career-ending bollocking.

The Handshake handlers would want answers. And Sinclair didn't have them.

But Sinclair himself wanted answers.

The street was empty as they left the river, passed across the grass onto the street and headed for HQ. Luca opened the door first and they both entered. Sinclair breathed out so hard it felt like a purge – an expulsion of every split second of all the shit he'd just witnessed.

'Fuck.' It was Luca. 'Fuck, FUCK!'

Stepping into the main body of the building, under the high roof, it was laid bare – the emptiness. Nothing was left, not a scrap, no evidence at all that Handshake had ever existed, let alone been there. The operation, their involvement, all gone. This was not how it was supposed to go. They were on their own.

The two men stood, dust settling on their toes and shoulders, and silently accepted their fate and what had to be done next. They opened the front door, shook hands, looked each other in the eye – then ran in opposite directions.

And it was only hours later, when he was travelling the back road of Franklin somewhere in Tennessee, and he was able to think even half-clearly, that Sinclair remembered the envelope in Luca Jones' pocket.

# CHAPTER FORTY SIX

'You,' Grosvenor says as he steps out into the glow and the heat from the resting trucks.

'You,' Harold Connors says as he emerges from the front truck cab and lowers himself down the steps.

I remain in the shadows of the door, watching from the recess of the dark entryway. I don't keep up with US politics as much as I should, on the basis that it's even more barmy than our own, but even I can work out that the little bloke outside in the navy suit, who's nimbly dropping to the tarmac, could pass for the current president's father. I can only hear snippets of the conversation thanks to Connors' faltering voice and the noise of the engines.

Rumour, supposition and idea gel together to form something solid at last – the current Republican president's father was part of a Cold War conspiracy to murder the then Democrat president, the final trigger-pull having come from a Russian-sympathiser under his direct instruction.

I'm amazed to see the man himself here but recognise the urgency. You wouldn't want this out. Bad for all kinds of business. Not least the family one.

I can make out chunks of conversation. '...what with the... never imagine... fall down...'

It's doing my head in not being able to tell what Connors is saying, but I catch the next bit loud and clear, just as the engines of the trucks cut out, one after the other in quick succession.

'There'll be a massacre here, Grosvenor,' says Connors calmly. 'Everyone here will have to go. Fires in all these units, and you can bet your last nickel that nobody will ever hear about it. Not a word... unless. Unless you give me the envelope and the nine of you who arrived here today come out from hiding and go for a ride.'

'Why in God's name would we do that?'

'The president is willing to give you a pardon. A personal pardon, a commendation – the first ever granted to a serving UK politician – and an Oval Office reception to thank you for uncovering the truth of one of our nation's greatest secrets.'

'Only it won't be the truth, will it?'

'It'll be *a* truth, applied with just enough force to make it stick. What the public doesn't need to know, it gets over very quickly.'

'And if I don't?'

'These boys won't fuck around.'

Grosvenor goes quiet. Whatever it is he decides, I'll back him – tooth, nail, claw and all.

'A pardon?' Grosvenor asks.

'My boy, he lent me the plane. It's going back to Washington at my say-so.'

'Let me go in and get them.'

'I want this to go down with civility – but don't dally.'

Grosvenor takes a second to eye up the man. The little guy is elderly now, far removed from the taut, vital officer I saw in the baseball game photograph, so the threat here isn't physical – but some threats are much more potent.

As soon as Grosvenor's back in the building, I'm there to meet him.

'We've got no choice, have we?' I say.

'Not if we want all these people to live.'

We walk into the warehouse, which appears empty. 'You can come out,' I say with a raised voice, and out they come.

'We've been offered a pardon and a ride to Washington,' says Grosvenor.

'Bullshit,' says Francesca Speroni, emerging from behind a battered grandfather clock.

'I'm with the crime lord,' says Fiona, arms folded.

Grosvenor replies flatly. 'It's what we've been offered.'

'You know they'll never follow through on it,' Fiona adds. Her eyes crest upwards in the middle in pure disbelief. 'They'll bury this.'

'They're offering to tell a version of it.'

A booming chuckle emits from the back of the room, as Brutoli emerges. 'Fuck that. I'm thinking we take 'em.'

'There's a fuckin' platoon out there,' replies Francesca, whacking him on the arm in admonishment, as if he'd just contemplated nicking a packet of gum.

'Ben, can you come here a sec?' I turn to the voice edging forward from beneath the stairs that lead up to a small room over the office. Luca.

'Can it wait?' I ask as I get to him.

'No.'

I give Grosvenor the two seconds hand signal and join the younger man.

'You have to see this,' he says, as he ducks under the stairs. Following him, I see it's a dark space lined with boxes, no doors, and zero order to the array of stuff stacked there, except for the thing in the middle, which rests on a couple of crates. It's an outdated school projector.

Essentially a metal box containing a large bulb, with an opaque glass top, which beams light up through a projector slide onto a mirror on an adjustable arm, which reflects the light through a lens, out onto a given surface, illuminating and enlarging the image. In the gloom, I can make out what's on the glass top, ready for projection.

The three frames of Zapruder film.

'I couldn't believe it when I saw it,' says Luca, almost apologetically. 'And, well… I couldn't resist.'

'You've looked?'

'Yeah.'

My interest is piqued. 'Go on, join the others and I'll be right with you.'

'OK,' he says and hands me the empty envelope. 'I'm not sure if it changes things, but it might.'

He leaves me to it, and I pause, looking at the machine.

All this trouble for these little squares of film.

Best see what so many have died for.

I find the orange lamp button on the side of the unit and, with a suddenly trembling finger, I hit it. I'm about to see a lost piece of history, and the weight of that suddenly feels crushing.

A soft hum accompanies the sudden brightness, and there, against the bare wood of even more stacked crates, flashes up three squares. Three images that are so close in composition to instantly recognisable pictures, but only now discovered.

This is the biggest I've seen them, and to suddenly have this new detail is revelatory and intoxicating.

'You coming?' shouts a voice.

'Be there in a sec,' I shout back.

My eyes scan each one in turn, roving through this new information. The colours, the shapes.

And, like a sudden nuclear impact, it hits me and changes everything in one bright, scarring flash of revelation.

I scoop them up, returning them to the envelope, and run to catch up with the rest of the group, who are being loaded into the backs of the trucks with the encouragement of rifles.

'So, this one has the envelope?' asks Connors when he sees me emerge. His eyes have such a slickster quality, I feel he may blink sideways.

'Yes,' I say, holding it. It's too late in the game now to make a scene about looking after them, the stakes way too high – even though, to my relief, Marty and Daphne have been separated from the rest and stand on the edge of the drive, confused, bewildered and wondering what the hell is going on.

I approach Connors and hand it to him, and he immediately looks inside. 'Jesus Mary and Joseph. I still get chills.' I feel sick to my stomach. 'Put him in the front cab, man either side. He's the troublemaker.' I don't know whether to be flattered or want to hit him as hard as possible, so I settle for both.

Just as two sets of hands take my arms, Connors speaks louder. 'Now, where's that traitor?'

'Connors, you don't need this.' I can't see him, but I know that's Grosvenor.

'Traitor, where are you?'

'Here, sir.' The voice is strong and resolute, and I see Tinker put his hand up as he moves through the soldiers to get to the front.

'Special Agent Tinker, isn't it?'

Tinker walks purposefully in front of Connors and salutes. 'Yes, sir.'

'Thank you.' Connors brings his right hand up, and from nowhere, there's a gun in it, and it pops once in Tinker's surprised face. The special agent crumples onto his ruined nose, which is abruptly the least of his problems.

I shout, there's screaming from somewhere, and I buck until two gut punches shut me up sharply, air suddenly more of a priority.

As I'm bundled up into the cab, I look down to see Grosvenor shaking his head, stood over the body of the Secret Service agent who, no matter how many times he'd tried to kill me, I'd really grown to respect.

# CHAPTER FORTY SEVEN

The trucks are ushered through a perimeter fence on the edge of Dallas/Fort Worth airport, the cheery disposition and instant recognisability of Harold Connors greasing more wheels than IDs or palms of hidden fifties could ever do. Out onto the tarmac, it exists at such a different speed to all the other airports I've been to in the last few days. This actually has baggage handlers and, well, people. The trucks weave effortlessly between baggage carts, transit buses and those golf carts with big stairs attached to the front of them, and head towards a series of dark hangars at the far end of one of the runways. Jets pull off the ground at speed as we cruise by, their power and noise rattling my guts each time.

The afternoon has clouded over, but the dull light can't dampen the impact of the sight that greets us as we round the last hangar. A massive jet sits on the runway, lights on in the cockpit and along the portholes of the cabin, but the majestic blue stripe which wraps around the entire aircraft, nose to tail while fattening to fully encase the front, sets it apart from any others in the world.

Air Force One.

'When your son said he'd lend you the plane, he really meant it,' Grosvenor says to Connors, both of them in the front with the driver. I'm on the bench seat behind, flanked by a soldier on each arm, having been pointed out as 'the troublesome one I keep hearing about' back at the warehouse. The rest of our group are in the back under literal armed guard – most of whose guns are aimed at Michael Brutoli.

'Air Force One is actually the call sign for any aircraft transporting the president of the United States,' Connors explains with no small hint of pride. 'And that there is the second of two Boeing VC-25s. Both identical, both fuelled, staffed and ready to go. The real Air Force One is actually in Pennsylvania this afternoon, with the boy. We've only got a skeleton crew here, sorry, but you understand.'

I'd like a word with this guy some time in the near future. He's put everything into getting to this point to claim moments like these, using millions of taxpayer dollars at his disposal for playtime and power. All the sacrifices, including one of his son's presidential predecessors, on the way up the ultimate greasy pole. I'm used to a lack of accountability from those in positions of influence, as well as that politico habit of using their mouths to get where they want to be, then failing to follow through on any of it – a popular move back home in the UK. This guy, however, got his hands dirty – and bloody – for everything he now has. He's a different breed of politician. And I don't doubt that he can make us disappear with the click of a finger if he so chooses to.

The trucks pull up close, the size of the jet ever more impressive, especially when you consider that it usually carries but one man and his requirements. We get out and, under armed gazes, approach the plane steps. One by one, a singular selection of animals boarding a very different ark, we board, directed by the cool instruction of our military handlers.

'What about my plane?' Val says as he enters the cabin, to anybody who will listen. 'I can go home and say nothing, nothing to a soul. I don't need this, I don't need this shit, I've got retirement coming up…'

His pleas fall on deafer ears than I think even he was expecting. I'm directed left on entering, but I see that William and Fiona have been taken right. I start to remonstrate, but a rifle barrel under my nose helps me see sense. Pissed off and trying to choke it down, I follow the rest of our group – who are ushered into a conference room. It's as plush as any executive setting I've ever been in, although that's not really saying anything. The presidential crest is emblazoned centrally on a walnut wall, overlooking a similarly composed table, surrounded by plush cream leather chairs. At the head of the table, a bigger, plusher chair sits empty.

'Take your seats,' the commanding officer instructs us. 'Buckle up, be good. No trouble – especially you, big man.' He points square at Brutoli. 'You fuck around and the door's on an emergency release catch. You can fly back to Queens.'

Brutoli puts his hands up in mock outrage. 'I was only wondering what the in-flight movie was.'

'What about the others?' I ask, with little time for any machismo or posturing. We land in Washington, and there's a strong chance none of us will ever be seen again.

'Never mind the others. There'll be four of us out here at any given point. And our open-door exit policy extends to you all.'

The door is shut and locked.

'What do we do?' asks Gus now that, as a group, we are alone. When I turn, I'm again faced with a sight I can't quite get my head around. Our heights range from sub-five feet to over six and a half, and we've all spent the last couple of days jetting about the country shooting each other and trying not to die in equal measure – yet each one of them looks to me for an answer.

'What do you want to happen?' I ask them all with my arms outstretched. 'You've all risked everything to get here, to fight for... whatever this is. What do you all want?'

'The truth,' says Francesca. She's taken a seat, buckled herself in and has even put her handbag on the conference table in front of her.

'We all want the truth, but it'll come at a cost – are you sure you all want that?' As I ask that last question, the plane starts to move under our feet. We obviously aren't waiting around.

'Yes. These bastards have hidden this for too long.' Luca looks at me with a weary determination. 'It needs to come out, all else be damned. If not... what was all this for? More secrets and numbers swept under an old man's carpet? No. Not for me, and not today.'

He's near enough me that I can put a hand on his shoulder. 'OK, mate. I'm with you.' I turn to the rest of them, standing around the president's about-to-be-airborne conference table. 'Everyone?'

'Yup,' says Brutoli. 'We all get shit on from on high. All the time. This time we don't.'

I nod and find myself smiling at him.

'What he said,' says Francesca, whose mouth is pursed around a boiled sweet she's conjured from nowhere.

I move my gaze along to Gus. 'I've followed the big guy into every situation he's asked me to, and you know that more than most. I'm in.'

Lastly, I look at Val – who is striding around the room admiring the fixtures and fittings. He seems unaware of what I asked. 'Val, what do you say?'

He pulls back into the present absently. 'Oh yeah, sure. Whatever gets my plane back.'

I nod slowly. 'And for Tinker too. Poor bloke was just doing his job, to the best of his ability.'

Everyone nods at that.

'We'll wait till we're at cruising altitude. How long will that take, Val?'

He doesn't turn around from examining the screws holding walnut fascia panels to wall. 'About ten minutes.'

'Ten minutes, then,' I say, taking the president's empty chair while placing my hands on the conference table in front, knuckles down, leaning forward at such an angle they crack. 'How can we take this bird and bring it down safely?'

# CHAPTER FORTY EIGHT

Ten minutes later, I knock on the door of the conference room.

A muffled voice answers. 'Yes?' I can't tell if it's the soldier who put us in here.

'Can a couple of us take a toilet break?' I ask, as casually as I can.

'The toilet?' comes the response in a mocking British accent. 'He wants the bloody toilet.'

'The bathroom, dickhead.'

He huffs with am-dram exasperation. 'Didn't you go before we left?'

'Wasn't much chance while you were bundling us into those trucks, was there?'

'There's a trash can under the desk, use that,' says the soldier.

'You're not going to reduce us to that, are you?'

'I bloody am.'

I fake a grand sigh. 'Come on. Look, wherever it is you took our friends, they're hashing out the details of a story to the press about why we're here and what our experiences are. And you don't want us telling them that you made us relieve ourselves in a rubbish bin in the president's conference room on one of the president's planes, do you?'

When this gets out, I don't think any of us not being allowed to take a piss will be anything more than a footnote at best, but you have to play on what you think will hit home. Bottom line, no US soldier wants to be responsible for a non-toileted bowel movement anywhere near the president's belongings.

They're talking beyond the door in quiet voices, and while I angle my ear to try to hear them better, I look at my friends in the room. My friends.

The door unlocks, and indeed it is the same soldier who put us here I'm met with when it swings open. 'Who needs to go?' he asks.

'There's me, and Francesca here.'

Ms Speroni stands next to me, having volunteered for the role. 'I look like an old woman,' she had said. 'And nine times out of ten, we're needing a piss.'

'The lady goes. You're definitely holding it.'

'You can't do that,' I remonstrate, but that's fine. All we need to do is get Francesca beyond the soldiers.

'Oh, dry your eyes,' she says as she walks past me and into the corridor. Our captor wasn't lying. There are four soldiers out there.

I try to follow her into the corridor, and that's all I really need. A hand on my chest stops me, and as soon as I see that Francesca is beyond the last man, who's turned to escort her, I shout, 'GO!'

I start to go for throats, necks, bollocks, anything sensitive – because even though they're armed, each with a full military rifle about the same length as the width of the corridor, it's a bugger

265

to pull up and aim, especially if I've tanned you in the knackers or bruised your windpipe. Behind me, in the room, our plan is thrown into action, and even though I can't see it, I know what they're doing.

Val, the old cowboy of the skies, had wondered how those lovely walnut panels had been secured to the walls – and it turned out, they're merely vinyl stickers. Thin fascia pieces, nothing like actual wood at all, and held in place with the same fixtures and fitments as any aeroplane – the kind of thing that Val works with daily. And the kind of thing he knows how to remove.

The far one he displaced enough to ascertain there was nothing beyond it, so using nothing more than a bit of leverage from a disassembled seat-belt buckle, he lifted it up out of its bracket. It's just hanging in place now – or at least it was, because when I shouted the signal, Michael Brutoli ploughed through it, throwing every atom of his enormous frame with it. Through that new opening, right behind Brutoli, fly Gus and Luca. And confusion breaks out in real earnest.

I'm fighting relentlessly against these guys, but it was only ever a stalling tactic. I just have to hold on for reinforcement because the idea was, if the guys could get through the wall, which they just have, then they were free to double back and get behind the soldiers I'm fighting with. It was a risky plan – guns, planes and hand to hand combat never go well together – but it was the only thing we could think of.

God knows what Connors is doing to Grosvenor and Fiona to make sure the story stays a secret.

Just as I'm beginning to feel overwhelmed, I can feel the attention of my combatants is drawn elsewhere – and sure enough,

Brutoli and Gus have appeared behind them and are pulling them off me, trying to yank rifles clear. It's a melee, fists and feet everywhere, before a woman's voice bellows, 'Hold it right there!'

It's with enough volume and command to give us all sufficient pause to look to where it came from – and there at the end of the corridor, walking back to us, is Francesca Speroni, a small handgun in her hand, aimed and levelled at every one of us.

'Nobody ever bothers to check the little old lady's purse.'

I smile, knowing I'll never doubt her again – and neither will these boys.

# CHAPTER FORTY NINE

To make it even more difficult for these hard soldiers to swallow, the gun that saw them beaten is a snub-nosed Smith and Wesson .38 Special with a candy-pink grip. Francesca hands it to me, and it's used to coerce the rifles into the hands of Gus, Michael and Luca. The men are rounded up and placed in the conference room, with Gus on armed guard, overseen by Francesca, who takes the president's conference chair.

'I'll have no issue in spraying that crest with your traitorous blood, believe me,' Gus tells them. I don't doubt it either.

Brutoli gives me a nod and disappears with Val, while Luca, fully loaded and heart on fire, follows me.

We stalk the main body of the aircraft, hoping that when Connors said "skeleton crew" he really meant skeleton crew and that there'd be barely anybody else. There're at least two armed soldiers unaccounted for, and I'm looking out for them.

At the end of the corridor, it breaks into a service area for air stewards to prepare food and drinks, and beyond that, two aisles either side of banks of executive seating. Luca takes the one on the left, and I take the right.

Nothing in this section of the cabin, every seat empty.

Another empty service area, followed by another empty cabin. But this time, the end of the aisles stop on a door each.

Now we're getting somewhere.

'There're two soldiers, remember that,' I say. 'Don't fire unless absolutely necessary.'

He nods, without looking at me, but I see his fingers flex on the rifle barrel. He's bursting to look down those sights at Connors and pull that trigger till both his face and his own pain disintegrates. It's plain to see.

'I'll go first,' I say. 'Wait three seconds, then come in.'

Let's confuse whoever is beyond this door.

I take the handle and push it open into a comfortable reception area with a wraparound beige sofa and a coffee table. It's like a doctor's waiting room – and it's empty.

'Luca,' I hiss, and he enters through his side.

Opposite us, in the back wall, is the grandest door I've ever seen on an aeroplane, and it features a carved wooden plaque which reads: "The Oval Office".

That's where they've taken them.

I motion to Luca to come up close and say, 'One up, one down,' in his ear. Still demonstrating what a quick learner he is, he gets into a crouch, with the rifle aimed low, eyes straight along the iron sights. With myself standing over him, the pink-gripped revolver at the ready, we take position at the door.

'As soon as the door is open, we go in hard, got it?' I whisper.

'You fuckin' bet.'

Five shots in the revolver, and I see the back of four bullet casings, the last in the chamber.

I knock twice.

I feel movement on the other side of the door, see the handle go, and as soon as I see light at the edge of the frame, I kick it hard and follow it, moving in and left, Luca moving in low and right.

The Oval Office usually represents something stately, reverential and deeply historic. What has been happening here is anything but.

Grosvenor has been tied to a chair in the middle of the room, facing the president's desk – but the man behind the desk is no world leader. With his feet up on the desk, his jacket off and shirt-sleeves rolled up, he sits opposite a beaten, bruised and bleeding William Grosvenor. Next to him, with tears running trails down her cheeks, is Fiona, typing on her laptop. Over them both stands a soldier. A big one.

They've been hashing out a story all right. Connors has been telling them what to write, using Grosvenor as leverage.

On the desk, in front of Grosvenor, just beyond where his fore-head sags, sits the envelope and those three frames, now splashed in William's blood – which also, I notice, coats Connors' hands.

I have to act. I know I told Luca not to shoot, only in emergencies. But the shot is clear, close, and I'm convinced I can drop the big soldier right between the eyes. I just hope his skull is thick enough to hold the bullet.

Just as he reaches for his own rifle, I aim over his nose and fire. The Smith and Wesson is perfect at this range, little did Francesca know, and she smuggled in the perfect gun for an airborne firefight. The man drops, and I wait for the hiss of cabin pressure seepage like I've come to expect from the movies, but nothing happens.

Luca is behind me, spinning to try to get a bead on the one who opened the door, but he's up and at us, and they both scuffle for their lives on the floor by the door. If I go to help him, that leaves Connors in reach of a rifle. I can't let that happen.

I run to the president's father, vaulting the Oval Office desk, but my God, he's quick, and he's round it in a flash, holding something gold at Grosvenor's throat.

'Stop there,' he says, digging what I now see is a letter opener, gold with the handle of a bald eagle, into William's throat. William doesn't say anything, but as his head is pulled back by Connors' gnarled fingers, our eyes meet. He's trying to convey a message, but I don't know what it is.

'You on the floor, stop,' says Connors, as Luca and the soldier separate. 'Of course, Luca Jones. Junior. Grandson.'

'The third, you bent prick,' Luca spits.

'You know, when Luca ended up in the CIA he was viewed as untouchable. They looked after him for years, kept him and the truth safe. A nice golden handshake deal. It was only when he retired and exhibited a change of heart, with the Brit here, did we have to get things sorted. And by things, I mean him of course.'

Luca breathes harshly, fire and fury swelling.

'So killing you as well will really settle the Jones balance. Might not be able to do it quietly though. Not like I did your grandfather.'

I need to shoot this guy and end this now, but if I do, the sudden movement might propel that letter opener deep into Grosvenor's neck and give the soldier behind us the chance to kill us all. Think, Ben, think...

The decision is made by movement but it's not my own – it's Fiona. She jumps up with the laptop and arcs it upwards in a swinging motion, right through the air and into Connors' shoulder, forcing him to lose balance. He talks the talk, and for the most part, walks the walk – but at the end of the day, you cannot argue with Father Time. This man is in his eighties and his feet betray him.

As he stumbles, I turn and shoot the soldier behind Luca, double tap, centre mass, close range, that's him taken out. Then I swing back around to Connors – who starts laughing.

'What are you going to do? Arrest me? I've got the weight of this country behind me; my son is the fucking president. You lay a finger on me, and you'll be put to death. Capital punishment is one of the great things our country still has.'

I lower the revolver and walk around the desk. 'And you think you're equally capable of administering that, don't you. His grandfather? The other members of Handshake?'

He tracks back the other way and moves round to sit at the desk. 'You're damn fucking right I do. You could see what low-life victims we were going to become under that idiot Kennedy. Anyone could see it. But we couldn't be like that, no, this is America. Good job there were a few of us in useful positions who felt the same way.'

'And you used a bunch of kids to get it done. Then left them high and dry. The boys in Handshake.'

I see Grosvenor raise his head, but only to shake it. The MP spits blood out onto the desk in defiance and disgust.

'Casualties of war. Numbers on a spreadsheet. The good of a country always outweighs both those things.'

'Was JFK a number?'

'Oh no, not him. Organising that shit was fun.'

I pause and turn to Fiona. 'Tell me your tape is still running.'

She smiles at me. As I ran out of the warehouse to join them back in Dallas, I caught her in the entranceway to the building jamming that little Dictaphone in her sock. 'Since we heard their trucks pull up,' she replies, a wily smile playing across her lips as she bends to pull the very device up into view. The red record button is visible for all to see.

I look at Connors, whose face has gone stone still, his mouth drooping.

'Speaking of the death penalty for murder… you just admitted to one, didn't you?'

'Statute of limitations would never allow it,' he spits. 'That was sixty years ago, you'd never get it through, besides, I'm the president's father, I'm a national fucking treasure!'

I shake my head. 'I'm not talking about that murder. I'm sure they'd tie a court in knots over that one. No, I'm talking about the one you admitted to in Florida a couple of days ago. His grandfather.'

His eyes widen as he switches gaze from me to Luca, who returns it with pure hate.

'And if I remember rightly,' I say, 'Florida definitely still has the death penalty, doesn't it?'

His eyes go blank before his defiance kickstarts again. 'This plane is going to Washington, where you'll be met by my son himself and the entire weight of the Secret Service. They'll offer me immediate protection and you'll never get away with this, not now, not ever.'

'Oh yes, I nearly forgot.' I pick up the phone on the desk. 'Is that the captain speaking?' I lay the handset down and press the large speaker button on the unit.

'This is Captain Val with co-pilot Mikey, over.' Connors' face drops.

I'm so glad they actually managed to take over the cockpit, or else I could've looked a proper dick. 'What's our ETA, please, Captain?'

'About an hour or so. Sun shining in Florida – we'll be touching down at Miami International in time for happy hour on South Beach.'

'And it's all going to plan?'

'These guys up here have been real helpful. Turns out nobody likes a traitor. We've got a landing party of Miami PD's finest waiting for us.'

'Thank you, Captain, keep up the good work.' I bet the original captain and co-pilot were helpful – Michael Brutoli with a rifle would make anyone do their level best to please.

I put the phone down. 'So, after sixty years, the game is up. Luca, keep that rifle on him while I get Grosvenor here more comfortable.'

'Grosvenor?' says Connors in a last flash of indignation. 'Who the fuck is Grosvenor? That man's Sinclair.'

Luca and I swap glances before I nod with a sigh. 'We know.'

# EPILOGUE

## SINCLAIR

It's late but he's not ready for bed, so he has a cold beer instead. He felt so battered only a couple of hours ago, but telling the truth, or nearly all of it, for the first time in years, had been transformative and revelatory. He feels, for the first time in well over half a decade, despite the massive reinvention of himself he has already undertaken more than once, a new man.

He nurses the beer, the beach-front bar lively yet still quiet enough to hear each other talk.

After the first tranche of questioning, the police put them up in a hotel, and the three of them had taken a taxi out to find somewhere for a drink and something to eat. It had felt like days since they'd had either. So now William Grosvenor, Sinclair, sits with his bruised face at a low-lit Miami Beach bar table with the young Luca Jones, who appears to have aged years in days, and the soldier he knew he could trust, Ben Bracken.

'Fiona is filing the story as we speak. The fact that she was already a known White House reporter really helped,' Bracken says, holding his beer in one hand while absentmindedly rotating his phone in the other.

'Will she be all right?' asks Luca.

'She's seen worse, she'll be fine. Plus, she'll get a Pulitzer for this. Biggest story of the century, fits you up for the big awards.'

'What did you tell them?' asks Sinclair. It's the question he's been itching to ask but has only just brought himself around to doing so.

Bracken goes first. 'Told them everything as I understood it before we were taken in Dallas. Sinclair and a bunch of guys, including Luca Jones Senior, were unwittingly involved in a plot to kill JFK and there was sudden evidence to support that, which could prove Harold Hector Connors' guilt and complicity in the plot.'

Luca clears his throat. 'The same. No detail, just the fact that we managed to stay ahead because we thought nobody would believe us.'

Sinclair nods, but Bracken speaks again. 'What about you?'

'I told them everything I knew from the perspective of William Grosvenor.'

'So they still don't know you're the man in the frames?'

'No. You two are the only ones who do.'

'Why didn't you tell us? Bracken asks.

'It was the worst day of my life. I went on to do what lots of people would say were great things, in the SAS, in the army and all over the world, but only once I'd adopted the guise of William Grosvenor. And every last thing I did, even now working in Her Majesty's government, is to make up for that one day.'

'It was never your fault though, William or Sinclair, or whatever we call you now.'

'Try telling yourself that.' Sinclair finds himself smiling, knowing that even though these two men know his real name, he still can never use it. 'I'm William Grosvenor now, grey-haired Minister Without Portfolio. I'm not that straw blond kid Sinclair, the watchman from Dealey Plaza, anymore. Maybe finally I can cast that off.'

'Then we won't need these,' Bracken says as he pulls out the decrepit, blood-spattered envelope that caused all this. They agreed on the spot in the airborne Oval Office that, because they showed William Grosvenor explicitly and could cause serious prolonged embarrassment and strain to the British government, they would tell the authorities that Connors destroyed them on the plane to get rid of the evidence of his role in JFK's murder. Either way, the confession is on the Dictaphone, clear and bright as day. And now, Ben Bracken holds the frames aloft in his hand.

He's a fascinating specimen, Bracken. Deeply melancholy and tortured in a number of ways, and capable of doing awful things. Yet he's so resolute and so hell-bent on the notion of responsibility and duty. Grosvenor had been right to call on him, and again he had proven his unique worth. And now… he's finding light again.

'Let's consign this to history, once and for all,' Ben says, before tossing the frames one by one into the tea light candle that sits in the middle of the table, while the cool air from the dark sea licks the flame up the frames.

Grosvenor watches in suppressed shock as those lost pieces of history bend and buckle in the heat, before crumpling in on themselves. In no time at all they are ash, and thanks to that same salty breeze, the remnants are carried into the night.

'The conspiracy is over,' Bracken says, before standing. 'Now, if you don't mind, it's just about to go seven in the morning at home, and I'd really like to talk to my partner and kids before the school run. I've got a jungle gym I need to plan building.'

Luca smiles and waves him off, while Grosvenor simply nods, watching the last of the celluloid burn up. As Ben Bracken walks out of the bar terrace and onto the quiet of the beach, he thinks, good on him. He's finding his peace.

And now, as the man once known as Sinclair sips his beer, watching the candle finally go out, he realises maybe he can, at last, find his.

# Acknowledgements

To everyone at Lume Books, most notably James Faktor, Rebecca Souster, Rufus Cuthbert and Imogen Streeter. Working with you is always a joy.

To my brilliant editor Alice Rees, who keeps making me a better writer. These books would be nothing without you! And a big thank you to Hannah Groves.

To the Northern Crime Syndicate - Trevor Wood, Judith O'Reilly, Fiona Erskine, Chris McGeorge, Adam Peacock, Robert Scragg and Dan Stubbings - and my Blood Brothers - Sean Coleman and Chris McDonald. Collectively, you have helped keep me sane these last eighteen months, and it's been so much fun collaborating and learning from you.

To my family and friends. Simply, I love you all.

To the writing community - bloggers, readers, authors, everybody. Thank you for everything you do. It's a fabulous place to be, and I feel so lucky and grateful to be a part of it.